This Song Is For You

Jessica Madden

For those who struggle, you aren't alone

Chapter 1
Tessa

A phone call in the middle of the night is never a good thing.

I groan at the sound of the landline ringing from downstairs. I wanted to curse whoever was calling. Seriously, but who on earth calls at this hour of the night? I hide my head under the pillow, but it does nothing to block out the sound. I give up, lying on my back as I stare up at the ceiling in the dark, hoping I will be able to get back to sleep after whoever called and interrupted my sleep. I have an assessment tomorrow I don't want to mess up because I couldn't sleep well.

It stops ringing. I wonder if Dad had maybe answered it or if he had missed the call.

A few minutes passed, and I figured whoever called must have realised no one was going to pick up. It was nearly midnight anyway. I roll onto my side and closed my eyes. Within seconds the door creaks open, and I groan. It's not even morning and my eight-year-old twin brothers think it's okay to sneak into my room to wake me, just like they do every morning.

"Kaiden, Jackson, get out of my room right now," I scold, sitting upright.

But it wasn't my brothers standing at the door. With the hall light shining behind the tall dark figure, I see it is Dad. When I see him there, my body goes cold, and it wasn't because it was winter. The last time he came into my room at this time of the night was when I was eleven; informing me that Mum was killed by a drunk driver on her way home from her shift at the restaurant.

Whoever was on the phone, it can't be good, I tell myself.

"It's just me, sweetie." He switches on the light. I shield my eyes from the brightness. "I didn't mean to wake you. I wanted to see if you were up."

"Who was on the phone?"

Dad doesn't say anything as he strolls into my room. There's something unusual as the way he walked. He always held his head high. Instead, he has his head down, and it instantly takes me back to the night he woke me up to tell me what happened with Mum. Was he coming in here to tell me that someone has died? Or was he coming in to break some other bad news to me? He sits down beside me. For a moment he just sits there, not making any eye contact as he thought about his words carefully. "Corey Roland was on the phone. Tessa... something happened to Casey this evening."

When he mentions my ex-best friend's name, I wanted to laugh. I'm sure whatever happened to Casey, she only did it for attention. But by the tone of my father's voice, it was no laughing matter.

"Tessa, Casey took her own life."

I feel the blood drain from my face. I wanted to believe it was all a joke, that somehow Casey was pulling a prank on everyone and had gotten her older brother to make the phone call. It was something I was sure she would do to get attention. That's all she has been doing for the last six months since our friendship drifted apart. She has always been jealous of me for having a boyfriend and of my band M TripleT. She would do about anything for me to notice her.

But of course this wasn't a joke. I recalled the message she had sent me earlier today. ***If our friendship is truly and definitely over, then I just want to say goodbye.***

I laughed at her message and replied ***Of course it's truly n definitely over. R U stupid or something? Our friendship has been over since U began getting jealous when I started dating Mark, n when I started hanging out with the band.***

She never replied back. Now I wonder why I even wrote that. As soon as she sent that message, I should have taken it seriously. Casey and I have been best friends since kindergarten. I was being bullied by some older boys in another grade and they had taken my lunch. Casey came and sat with me, offering me a vegemite sandwich. I wasn't a huge fan of vegemite, but I took it because I didn't want to wait for school to be over to eat. Since then we have been inseparable. She has been there for me too when my mother had died, and I was there for her when her parents would argue until they finally divorced last year right before our friendship drifted apart. We were more like sisters than friends, especially when we both didn't have sisters.

"H-How did she die?" I ask when I find my voice after the shock of the news. *Could I have stopped her if our friendship wasn't over? If I had listened to her rather than pushed her away, could I have saved her?*

"Corey didn't say." Dad wraps an arm around my shoulders and pulls me into a hug. I didn't want the hug. I didn't deserve it. I made Casey end her life. I know I did. She is dead because of me. "I'm so sorry, Tessa."

Dad hugs me for what seems like a long time before getting up, telling me to get some sleep as I have school in the morning. He promises to tell my brothers not to come into my room in the morning to wake me like they annoyingly do every day.

I lie back down once Dad had turned off the light. I should be crying, but I'm too shaken by the news to allow my emotions to takeover. I imagine Casey for a moment, wondering what her last thoughts were before she had taken her life.

Did she hate me for what I did to her?

Chapter 2
Casey

A year ago

The fighting was starting again. Mum and Dad had fought in the past, but lately it seemed they were arguing even more. I lay in bed with my earbuds on, hoping my music would drown out their argument, but it doesn't help.

Usually when my parents start fighting, I would hide out with my brother Corey in his room, where he would comfort me until the yelling stopped. When I was younger, I was always afraid they were going to get divorced. Corey told me it was normal for grown-ups to fight like they do, and they weren't getting a divorced. But tonight my brother wasn't at home. He was in his first year of university, and on weekdays he stayed with one of his friends who lived near the university he attended, saving him from travelling long distance back and forward to campus each day. He only came home on weekends and holidays.

The argument has been going on for half an hour now, and I couldn't take the yelling anymore. I thought about calling my brother to tell him what is going on, but it's a Friday night. He is probably out with friends or at a party. I couldn't wait until I was eighteen so I could get out of here and don't have to worry about putting up with my parents' fighting. Unfortunately, I wasn't eighteen until next year in November. Only a year and five months to go. Corey probably wouldn't want to be bothered. Besides, I couldn't always call on my brother every time my parents fought. Corey wasn't always going to be around to comfort me.

Another person I knew who could really help me keep my mind off my parents was Tessa Ross. It was almost eight o'clock, but I'm sure she wouldn't mind if I came over to get out of the house. Her Dad, though, was a different story. Being strict, I doubt he would even allow me to come over this late, even if it is a Friday night.

My parents are fighting, I typed into my phone. *Can I come over for a little while and get out of the house?*

It doesn't take long for her to answer back. *I don't think coming over is a very good idea right now. Dad n I got into an argument over my grades after reviewing my report card. Let me sneak out n I will come get U. We can hang out somewhere.*

I smiled at her message. Tessa has never been in a great relationship with her father since her mother passed away. Her twin brothers don't help, always finding a way to annoy her. The loss of her mother is what has driven her grades down over the years, mostly maths. She hated school and much rather grab a record deal for her future music career. But no matter how many times her brothers annoyed her or when she fought with her father; she always made sure to be there for me when I needed her.

Sounds great, I texted back. *Any idea where we should go?*

Gianni's Gelato? She added a strawberry ice cream sundae emoji. ***I'm in some great need 4 ice cream. Meet U out at front in 10 minutes.***

I took out the earbuds, and set them down on my bedside table. Putting on my shoes, I switched off the light in my room to make it look like I have gone to bed, and snuck out the window to meet Tessa at the front.

The June air is freezing cold as I stepped outside, tip-toeing alongside of the house so my parents' argument doesn't turn to me on why I'm sneaking out in the middle of the night. The yelling can be heard outside, and I can't imagine what our neighbours must think. With all of the arguing that has been going on lately, I really hope none of the neighbours call the police. I wouldn't be able to walk out of the house without my neighbours or even going to school without anyone whispering about the domestic disturbance happening in my own home.

Carefully I opened the side gate, praying silently that my parents won't hear the click when I closed it. Luckily it didn't make too much noise when I closed it behind me, clicking lightly that wasn't loud enough to hear. I walked down the driveway, and stood at the kerb. I glanced back at the house. The blinds in the lounge room are closed so there was no way of seeing what my parents were doing through the window. The yelling can still be heard, and all I wanted was for it to stop. Half of me wanted to walk through the door and tell them to shut up already.

Ten minutes passed and I soon see a pair of headlights driving down the street. Tessa's blue sedan pulled up beside me. I opened the passenger door and hopped into the front seat where it was nice and warm with the heater on full blast.

"Thanks for coming to get me," I said to Tessa, putting on my seat belt.

She smiled at me. "Anything for my best friend." She nodded towards the house. "Do you have any idea what they are arguing about?"

I shrugged. "I don't know anymore. I think it was something about my mum moping around the house. Mum lost her job last week because she kept missing too many days; only because she is depressed about the miscarriage she had, even if it was almost a year ago. She blames herself for losing the baby even if it wasn't her fault."

Mum had been trying years to fall pregnant again after having me, but had no such luck. After doing a majority of tests, the doctor told her fertility count was low and she had little chance of ever conceiving. But after five years of being told she might not be able to have any more kids, she somehow fell pregnant last year in September. But sadly, after thirteen weeks she lost the baby. Although all of that happened seven months ago, she drinks her sorrows away. Some days she was okay, other days she wasn't. Sometimes I wonder if my baby brother or sister is the cause of my parents' constant fighting lately. Or if there are other things that I don't quite know about happening within their marriage.

"I think they are arguing about money as well," I added.

Tessa pulled away from the kerb. "I'm sure whatever they're fighting about, they will work it out. Don't think anything negative. Let's get some ice cream, and I'm sure by the time you get back home, the arguing will be over."

I nodded slowly, not sure if I wanted to believe Tessa, but I'm sure whatever happens, she will be there for me to get by. Changing the topic of my parents, I asked Tessa about what her father had said about her grades.

"I'm mostly failing Maths," she replied, concentrating on the road, making her way to Mansfield's town centre. "I got straight Ds for it while my other subjects have a mixture of Bs and Cs. I don't see what the big deal about failing Maths is. It's not like I'm going to be using most of it once I finish school, especially algebra. Who uses algebra anyway? I most definitely won't need algebra in my music career."

"So what's happening? Is he going to make you study harder?"

Tessa laughed. "He said he will be getting me a tutor to help my maths grade to improve. Yeah, like that would ever help. I have never been any good at maths. Equations and I don't click together. But I know he is trying to impress Hazel, and he most definitely wouldn't want the media to know that his oldest child is failing school."

Tessa's father, Kale Ross, was a television presenter for the morning news that featured from 9am until 11am on weekdays. Hazel Franklin was his co-host who started working on the show at the start of the year. Mr Ross had started dating her two months ago, which really pissed Tessa off.

"How about you, Casey? What did your parents say about your report card?"

I shrugged. "I left it on the coffee table for them to look at, but none of them looked at it yet." I'm sure my parents wouldn't mind what I have gotten. I wasn't the perfect straight A's student, but I do get a few As, Bs and Cs. I haven't gotten any Ds for my report card.

We reach Gianni's Gelato, our favourite place to hang out, and where you can find the best gelato in Mansfield, maybe even the whole of Sydney. I went to pay for the raspberry sundae with strawberry topping and chocolate chips, but Tessa offered to pay as she was the one who wanted to come here. She said it was her special treat to keep my mind off my parents.

Seconds later we were sitting in a booth eating our sundaes.

Tessa moaned once she placed a scoop of chocolate ice cream in her mouth. "This is what I definitely needed after tonight."

I nodded with agreement, letting the raspberry ice cream melt in my mouth. Being here with Tessa has really made my night after the disagreements my parents have been having. Not just tonight, but the other nights throughout this week.

The bell above the store's door rang. Tessa looked over my shoulder to see who had entered. I turned in my seat to get a look as well when Tessa had been staring at the people who had entered for more than a second. It doesn't take me long to see what she is staring at. Three boys from our grade had entered, walking over to the counter display of the twenty flavours of gelato. Tim Young and Travis Mitchell I have seen around the school, but I didn't know them personally or have them in any of my classes.

But the one person standing amongst his friends, who Tessa had her eyes on, was Mark Brady. He was tall with dark hair and eyes, and had a killer smile that could make any girl go weak at their knees. He was incredibly handsome that I could see why my best friend had a crush on him. She had been crushing on him since the start of the year where they have Music together.

Mark saw us and made his way over while his friends decided on what dessert they wanted.

He smiled brightly at Tessa as he stood beside our table. "Hi, Tessa. Fancy seeing you here."

Tessa blushed. "Hey, Mark. I could say the same to you."

Mark glanced my way, giving me a nod. "Hey, Casey."

I give him a smile. "Hi."

He turned his attention back to Tessa. "You did a really good job on your performance in class today."

Tessa smiled nervously at him. "Thanks Mark. You did well in your performance too."

"I will see you in class on Monday."

"Yeah, I will see you too."

Mark headed back over to his friends.

We sat there in silence, eating our sundaes while the boys made their order. Tessa looked like she was about to burst with happiness after the small talk with Mark.

"Oh gosh, I wasn't expecting to see him outside of school," Tessa said once the boys had left with their gelatos in waffle cones.

"At least you didn't get all tongue-tied the last time he said hi to you at lunch."

"Oh, please don't remind me of that. It was so embarrassing when I forgotten my words. Do you think Mark likes me?"

I smiled. "Of course he does. He wouldn't have come over here otherwise. Maybe you should ask him out."

"Yeah, my dad will definitely disapprove with me going out with someone."

"I'm sure when your dad meets Mark, he will be happy for you."

"Let's hope that happens, but knowing my dad, he wouldn't."

I pull out my phone from my pocket to check the time. It was now nine o'clock. "We should get going, Tessa. I don't want to be gone for too long in case my parents come check up on me."

We finished the sundaes and headed back to my place. When Tessa pulled up outside my house, my stomach twisted into knots. The lights were off and my dad's car wasn't parked in the driveway. Most likely he had gone to stay at a motel for tonight. Hopefully whatever they argued about they will make up in the morning.

Tessa placed her hand on my shoulder. "Let me know if you need anything, and I will be here."

I smiled; glad I had her as a friend to make me feel better. I hugged her goodbye and climbed out of the car, bracing myself for whatever awaited me inside the dark house.

Chapter 3

Tessa

I didn't get a wink of sleep after what Dad told me about Casey. I woke up crying a few times, calling out to Casey, telling her I'm sorry.

But why am I'm feeling sorry about the way I had treated her now that she is gone? Why didn't I just apologise right from the start with the way I have treated her? We acted like babies, fighting over a rattle. What did we even start fighting over anyway? Whatever it was, we could have worked things out rather than letting our relationship go sour.

Maybe then Casey and I would still be friends, and she wouldn't have taken her own life.

When my alarm goes off for school, I just lie there, wondering if it was worth getting out of bed. Is this how Casey felt every morning when I used to treat her like she was garbage?

I expected my brothers to come in and wake me; instead there was a gentle knock on the door, followed by my father's voice asking me if I was awake.

I sit up. "I'm awake."

Dad opens the door ajar. He gives me a small smile. "How are you this morning? Did you get any sleep?"

"Tired."

"Why don't you stay home today?"

If it was any other day, I would jump to the chance of skipping school, anything to get out of it, but that was before I began dating Mark. He is the one who makes it worthwhile to be at school. Plus, today our Music teacher Mrs Grover is getting us to perform in class, which our marks will go to our reports at the end of June in a few weeks. Mark and I are performing a song together. I couldn't skip out on the assessment because my former best friend died.

I shake my head, pulling the covers off me and stood up. "No. I need to get to school today. I have an assessment due for Music."

"Are you sure, sweetie? I'm sure Mrs Grover will understand if you don't come in today. I can speak to her if you like."

I sigh with frustration. "No. I'm fine."

Deep down inside I wasn't fine. It's eating me to know if I'm the one who is responsible for Casey's death. For the past six months I have been horrible to her. I ditched her to be with Mark, and I have bullied her so much that it drove her to take her own life. Not unless it wasn't because of that reason and there was something else going on in her life I didn't know about.

I shut the door, wanting to be left alone with my thoughts for a while. I was afraid too that if Dad was to stay in my room any longer, he would somehow see through me and know what I had done to Casey. He doesn't know that our friendship ended or what I had put her through.

I lean my back up against the door. I hear Dad's footsteps walking away. It was less than a second that I was alone when I hear tiny feet patting along the floor. I roll my eyes, wondering why my brothers have to choose this moment to annoy me.

"Not now, Kaiden, Jackson."

I open the door to see my brothers standing at my door in their blue school uniform. Kaiden or maybe it was Jackson, had their arm in mid-air, ready to knock on my door.

As soon as he puts his arm down at his side, I figured which brother it was when he speaks. Kaiden. He is the loudest twin while Jackson is quiet and didn't speak unless his brother spoke first. "Dad told us about your friend."

"We're sorry about Casey," they say together.

The anger begins to build up inside of me when they said they're sorry about Casey. Sure, they're sorry about her. Is everyone really sorry that she is gone? Is this what Casey wanted? To die and have everyone feel some sympathy towards her for the pain she has gone through? Yeah, that definitely sounded like Casey. Killing herself was the only way she could get attention she'd wanted.

Maybe I shouldn't feel any sympathy towards her, or for any guilt that I may have caused her to end her life. After everything that happened between our friendship in the last six months, I'm glad our friendship ended. I'm glad she is dead. She is nothing but a loser.

Rather than thanking my brothers for their sympathy, I slam my door shut and lock it. I grab my maroon skirt and jumper with the school logo on the left-hand side, as well as for the white shirt from my desk chair, changing into it. I'm going to school and act like nothing has happened. I'm not going to let my day be ruined just because Casey is gone.

Besides, I still think this was some kind of prank she is pulling on me to get me back for all of the crap I have put her through. Nice try, Casey. You can't fool me.

***

The front door opens as I walk down the hall from my room to the kitchen. Hazel. The one person I did not want to see first thing this morning. In two days I will be seeing her every day when she marries my dad.

She smiles when she sees me, giving me a small wave. "Good morning, Tessa."

I frown at her. Its obvious Dad hasn't told her about Casey, as I don't think she would be all smiles if she knew. She would be showing sympathy towards me. I didn't want her sympathy. I didn't want it from anyone. Casey isn't dead. It's all a joke.

"What's so good about this morning?" I say.

Hazel is startled by my response. She should be used to my bad moods around her by now. "Oh. Well, I feel like it is a good morning."

"Well, it's not."

I walk past her, heading to the kitchen. Dad passes me, greeting Hazel. Even though he says it in a low voice, I'm still able to hear him tell Hazel the news about Casey. I escape to the kitchen before I could hear her response.

My brothers were sitting at the table eating the scramble eggs and bacon Dad had cooked. The smell of the food made my mouth water, but I wasn't hungry. I head over to the coffee maker and made myself a cup, sitting down at the table as Dad and Hazel walked in. Hazel sits down beside me while Dad walks over to the coffee maker to pour himself one and for her.

My phone beeps and I pull it out from my skirt pocket. I smile when I see Mark's name pop up on the screen.

"Tessa, you know the rules," Dad says. "No phones at the table."

I unlock the phone anyway to read my boyfriend's message.

Have you heard about Casey?

I shove my phone in my pocket and stand quickly, my chair almost toppling over. I tell dad I'm leaving for school.

"Tessa, sit down and eat something," he says, setting Hazel's coffee on the table.

"I'm not hungry."

"Well, if you're going to leave now then your brothers can come with you, and they haven't finished eating yet. Besides, it's only six thirty. You will be too early if you go now. Wait for another hour before you leave. Hazel and I will be leaving very soon to get to the station."

I glance at my brothers and their half-eaten food. I hated it when Dad makes me do the school drop offs every morning. Since he and Hazel has to be in front of the camera by nine, he is out of the house just before seven, which leaves me with the responsibility to make sure my brothers get to school on time. Ever since I got my licence last year I had to take them to school, where they kick at my seat or do annoying things to distract me while I'm driving. When I used to take the bus with them, they would do what they could to annoy me. Of course, when I mention all of this to Dad, he lets my brothers get away with it.

Without saying another word to my dad and not caring how my brothers get to school, I leave the kitchen with Dad yelling at me not to leave. I roll my eyes. Just minutes ago he was showing how much he felt sorry for me for losing my best friend. Now he was yelling at me for wanting to get away to head to school early, all because I refused to take my brothers to school. Dad follows me out the front door, yelling at me that just because my best friend is dead it doesn't give me the right to not listen to him.

Yeah, what do you know about not listening? I say silently to myself, hopping into my car. *You never listen to me when I need you to hear me out.*

Dad knocks on the window, telling me to wind it down. I don't. I turn on the ignition and start backing down the driveway, where Dad steps away from the car. I just wanted to get out of here. Maybe I will sit at a coffee shop before heading to school.

And school was the last place I wanted to be, but I had to go.

***

There was something different about Mansfield High when I pulled up outside the school. It had a different atmosphere in the air, something I couldn't quite explain. It had that feeling of like the school was suddenly turned into a cemetery overnight. The atmosphere felt dead, cold and haunted. No one seemed alive.

I locked the car and headed to the front entrance of the school. Students from my grade were hanging out at the front, huddling and sobbing quietly as they mourn the death of a schoolmate. When I see them, it's then I knew none of this was some sick prank Casey was playing on me. She really was gone. The uneasy atmosphere around me proved she was dead.

And I may have been the one who killed her. I'm the one who made her end her life.

"Tessa."

I turn around to see Mark heading over to me. As soon as I see him, I run to him and embrace him. He pulls me into a tight hug. We stand there for what feels like forever.

"I wasn't sure if you were coming or not," he says. "You didn't apply to my text."

Mark pulls away from me and my body suddenly felt empty without his arms around me. "Sorry. I didn't feel like replying."

He nods with understanding. "Can you believe what happened to Casey? I would never have guessed she was depressed to want to end her life. When her brother posted what happened on Facebook, I didn't want to believe it at first."

I don't want to believe it either, but I should because I'm the one who drove her to do this.

"If you want to, we can skip band practice this afternoon," Mark suggests. "I'm sure Travis and Tim will understand."

I shake my head. "No. I'm not going to let Casey's death stop me from doing practice. We need to make sure our song is perfect for the contest tomorrow. It's our only chance to score a record deal."

Mark nods. "You're right, but I care more about your mental health more than scoring a record deal. The guys and I will be alright with practice if you need to have some time to yourself."

I smile at him and peck his lips. "Thanks Mark."

Mark then takes my hand and together we walk into the school grounds to wait for our other friends. As we walked, I wonder to myself if I have only paid any attention to Casey's mental health, would she still be here?

Chapter 4
Casey

I lay awake, listening out for the engine of my father's car to indicate he was home, and that he will make up with mum from whatever they were arguing about. But the house was silent, with no sound of movement. I wasn't sure if Mum was awake or if she had gone to bed. I was afraid to leave my room in case I find something I don't want to see.

In the morning, the first thing I do was looked out the lounge room window to see if dad's car is parked in the driveway. My heart sank in my stomach when I saw it empty. Dad doesn't work Saturdays, so where was he? A million thoughts ran through my head, wondering if dad is okay, and when will he come home. Sometimes when he chooses to stay in a motel for the night, he usually came home by eleven, so I just have to wait until then.

Mum was passed out on the kitchen table, a half full bottle of vodka in front of her while she held onto an empty glass. Careful not to wake her, I took the glass and bottle over to the sink. I washed out the glass, placing it on the drying rack and then poured the rest of the vodka down the sink. Mum doesn't even stir from the noise I am making.

What was Corey going to say when he comes home?

I popped some bread into the toaster then filled a glass with water. I leave the kitchen to grab some pain killers from the bathroom. Mum was going to have a huge hangover when she wakes up. I set everything on the table and shook Mum gently.

Mum opened her eyes, sitting up too quickly and groans in pain as she crutches her head. "Casey, can you close the blinds, please?"

I listened to her and closed the kitchen blinds to shut out the light. I then move the glass of water and two pain killers towards her.

"Take these, Mum."

Mum listened to me and swallowed the tablets with the water.

"Make sure you eat, too." I moved the plate with two slices of toast with vegemite closer to her. I then make my own breakfast, popping two slices of bread into the toaster.

"What time is it, honey?" Mum wanted to know. She hasn't touched her food yet.

"It's almost seven thirty."

"Have you seen your father? Is he home?"

I don't look at my mother. I can't bear to see the pain in her eyes when I tell her that Dad hasn't come home. "No. He isn't."

Mum pushed her chair back, which makes a loud scrapping noise across the floor. "Thank you, honey, for breakfast."

She left the kitchen and disappeared either to her room or to the bathroom, her food untouched.

***

Dad doesn't return home until the next day. As soon as he walks through the door, Mum goes off at him for disappearing for a couple of days. This causes Dad to lose his temper, not wanting to be told what to do. Corey and I sat in the kitchen, listening to everything. I was thankful my brother was here with me. I couldn't bear to listen to the argument on my own again.

And then the heartbreaking words slipped out of Dad's mouth. "I want a divorce."

Everything goes quiet and it feels like time had stopped. I think my heart even stopped beating.

This wasn't the news I wanted to hear from my parents.

"You don't mean that, John," Mum cried. "You love me, don't you, sweetheart?"

"I once loved you, Grace, but I don't think I can love you anymore."

My heart crumbled to pieces that very moment. I wanted to believe everything I had just heard was a misunderstanding. My parents had fought in the past, always working out their differences or whatever they would fight about. So why can't they work out whatever they're fighting about now? Why is divorced the answer?

Mum lets out a high pitch wail, begging my father not to do this. At the sound of her cries, Corey and I leap off our chairs and hurry to the lounge room. Mum was on her knees, sobbing so hard that her body shook. Dad stood in front of her, not giving a care in the world that he had just ruined my mother, making her own depression worst.

Corey stepped forward, clenching his fist as he stood up against our father. My brother stood at my father's neck in height, and I watched in fear, wondering if my brother was going to take a swing at Dad. He isn't a violent person so I can't imagine him punching Dad.

"How can you say that to her?" Corey demanded.

"Stay out of this, Corey. This is between your mother and I."

I stood there, unsure if I should be at my mother's side as she continued to wail, or if I should stay out of it all together.

"No, Dad. This isn't between you and Mum. Your decision will affect the whole family," Corey pointed out.

"Corey, stand aside. You and Casey can both go to your rooms."

"No. Whatever you discuss with Mum, you might as well discuss with Casey and I too."

That's when I flew through the room and out of the front door. I couldn't be here any longer. I don't want to watch my parents fight. I don't want to know the reasons why they're ending their marriage.

Both my father and Corey called out to me to come back, but I ignore them, hurrying across the grass to the footpath. The tears are falling down my face as I walked down the street. I don't even glance back once to see if anyone is chasing me. I kept walking as fast as I could until I ended up at the front door of Tessa's house.

Inside I hear her screaming at her brothers to sit down at the table to eat. She must be baby-sitting her brothers because her house is never this chaotic when her father is around. Kaiden and Jackson are always on their best behaviour around him, acting innocent when they do something to annoy Tessa.

Tessa answered the door. As soon as she sees me, her expression turned from frustration to concern when she sees how red and puffy my eyes are. "Casey, what happened? Is everything alright?"

I shook my head. "No," my voice croaked.

Tessa pushed me inside and closed the door. "Come in, Case. Would you like a glass of water or anything to eat?"

"A glass of water would be great, please."

She promised to get me one in a second. She then stomped over to her brothers who are on the couch, engrossed with their iPads. She grabbed at the iPad, but her brothers had a firm grip on them.

"I told you two to put these away and eat your lunch," she scolded at them.

"No!" the boys cried.

"Yes! Eat first, and then play with these stupid things."

I wiped my eyes and strolled over to help my friend. "You know, Kaiden, Jackson, if you get off these iPads and eat your lunch, Tessa and I will take you out for ice cream later."

The boys' faces lid up with delight. "I want ice cream!"

"And you can have it once you eat the food Tessa has prepared for you."

Both Kaiden and Jackson handed their iPads to their sister, got off the couch and head to the kitchen.

"Thanks, Casey," Tessa groaned. "Now we have to take them for ice cream, and sugar is the last thing I want them to have."

I suddenly felt bad for what I had said to help out Tessa. Maybe I shouldn't have shown up here. "Sorry, Tessa. It was the first thing I could think of to get them to listen. I can leave if you are busy."

Tessa shook her head, resting a hand on my shoulder. "No, stay. Sorry. It's not you. My brothers are giving me hell. Dad decided to leave me with them while he went out on a lunch date with Hazel. I have no idea when he will be back. Take a seat, and I will be back in a sec."

Tessa left the lounge room. I sat down on the couch, waiting for her to return. She came back a few minutes later with a glass of water.

"Well, the ice cream bribe did the trick." She handed me the glass. I thanked her and she sat down next to me. "The boys are eating quickly. So thank you for showing up at the right time."

I let a small smile cross my face. "Thanks." I took a sip of my drink.

"You know, when I was my brothers' age, I was never allowed to have an iPad. In fact, I don't think we even had iPads when we were eight."

I shook my head. "No, we didn't."

"Exactly, and the unfair part is that my brothers were allowed to have their own when they were six! I'm almost seventeen and I'm not allowed to own one. I'm only allowed to own a phone and a computer, but no iPad." She let out a frustrating groan as she leaned back on the couch. "I swear my dad likes my brothers more than me."

"I am sure he does care about you, Tessa."

She sat up straight. "He has a funny way of showing it." She turned to face me. "Anyway, tell me what is going with you, Casey. Is everything okay?"

I leaned forward, setting the glass on the table, feared of dropping it once I break down. "Dad didn't come home on Friday night."

Tessa let out a small gasp, and rest a hand on my shoulder. "Casey, I'm so sorry."

"He came home this morning to announce to Mum that he..." A lump formed in my throat as I recalled Dad's words earlier.

Tessa pulled me into her arms, patting my back as she told me everything was going to be alright. The feel of her arms around me made me choked out sobs. I shook my head. None of this was going to be alright.

I pulled away from her, wiping my eyes. "They are getting divorced, Tessa."

She gave me a sympathetic look and pulled me in for another hug. "I don't know what to say, Casey. I'm so sorry."

We stayed in each other's arms for a long time, Tessa rubbing her hand on my back as I sobbed. We were so caught up in it that we completely forgot about Kaiden and Jackson until they were standing in front of us.

"Is Casey okay?" Kaiden (I think) asked.

"Casey is fine," Tessa answered for me. "She is just going through something at home."

I pulled away from Tessa. "It's alright. You can tell them. They will find out eventually." I turned to the twins. "My parents are getting a divorced."

"Oh," the boys said softly.

"You can come out to get ice cream with us," Jackson said. "Ice cream makes everything better."

Smiling at him was all I could do. If only he knew that ice cream was not going to make everything better, and wouldn't stop my parents from splitting up. But I gladly tell him that I will tag along with them.

Chapter 5
Tessa

Our principal Mr Kelman gathered our grade into the assembly hall for first period. He breaks the news about Casey if we haven't already heard about it. He doesn't go into full detail on how she ended her life, but he offers counselling services for anyone who may need it.

Glancing around the hall I see some of the girls in my grade sobbing quietly while the guys remain silent. I had to resist to hold back the anger that's building up inside me to stop from blurting out what I thought of everyone here. *No one* here cared that she is dead. They never cared about her when she was alive. Casey was shy and the only friend she ever made was me. It took her a lot of courage to approach me that day in kindergarten after those older boys took my lunch, thinking it was alright to tease a kindergartener because they were like, I don't know, a year or two above me? Casey didn't have to approached me that day, but she did.

Before our friendship ended, Casey was never bullied. She was too shy to really be noticed by anyone. And if she was notice, it was because of her friendly and welcoming nature. It wasn't until our friendship went sour that she began to get notice by others. But it was for all of the wrong reasons. She was teased by rumours *I* had started. Like at the time I tricked her into thinking Max Downing liked her, which I only did so she would get off my back for being with Mark. She made a fool out of herself, and then the rest of our grade began teasing her about her crush on Max, a crush she had on him for a long time until I started a rumour that he liked her back. Max's girlfriend at the time, Amelia Smith, was furious when she found out Casey had tried to ask Max out. Little does she know I was the one who told Casey to do it.

And when I think about it now, why did I tease her over that? Why did I make up those rumours? Casey had never done one single bad thing to me or to anyone, and looked how I repaid her for befriending me. All of this started because of my selfishness being with Mark and with the band. What kind of person am I?

I spot Katie-Lynn and Beth Adams from across the hall. Katie-Lynn hugs her twin sister, sobbing on her shoulder. Of course the twins were one of the people faking their sadness over Casey. After all, I drew them both to hurt Casey, especially when their friend Amelia found out about her asking Max out. How I ever became friends with them, I don't understand anymore. All I did was hurt Casey for being with them. I'm glad that for the past few months I have been doing more band practice and I didn't have to hang around with them anymore.

I leave the hall, not wanting to be surrounded by these fake people. I stroll over to the shelter area and sit down on a silver seat beside the toilet block. I don't care if I get into trouble for being out here and not in the hall with the others.

"Are you alright, Tessa?" Mark asks as he comes to sit down beside me. He puts his arm around my shoulders. Travis and Tim follow behind him and sit down across from us.

"I'm fine," I answer. "I just didn't want to be in the hall surrounded by our grade, pretending to grieve over Casey when half of them didn't know who she was, or they bullied her."

"I'm sure they are sorry about what happened to her," Tim says. "Not everyone bullied her."

I want to tell him he is wrong, but I don't. An argument is the last thing I wanted.

"Tessa Ross?"

Mr Carlton, one of our school counsellors, approaches us. What could he possibly want? Is he going to somehow convinced me I need counselling to mourn my ex-friend's death? If he is, I don't need it. I'm fine.

"Boys, would you mind going back to the hall until the bell rings for second period?" Mr Carlton says. "Tessa, I would like a chat with you."

"No," I groan. "I'm fine. I don't need counselling just because Casey Roland is dead. *She* was the one who needed counselling."

Mr Carlton nods to my bandmates, silently asking them one last time to leave so we could be alone. The three of them move off the seat and headed back inside the hall.

When they're out of earshot, he turns back to me. "Tessa, I think it's a good idea for you to come to my office so we can talk."

"I don't want to talk. I'm fine."

"You may seem fine, but are you? You and Casey have been best friends."

"*Were*," I correct him. "We stopped being friends when she became jealous of me for having a boyfriend. Anyway, how would you know if we were best friends? You have never spoken to me before."

"Right, I haven't. But your dad—"

"My dad? Of course. He always acts like he is concerned about me, but really, he doesn't give a damn about me."

He narrows his eyes at me. "Language, Tessa. Your father left a message on my answering machine this morning, asking me to speak to you sometime today. He told me you two have been best friends and believe Casey's death has taken a toll on you this morning. Now I'm offering counselling sessions all of this week for all Year Twelve students to come talk to me. You can talk to me about whatever is on your mind. It can be about Casey, or maybe you have some troubles going on within your life and you need to speak to someone about it."

I roll my eyes, standing up from the seat. "Thank you for your concern, Mr Carlton, but I really do not need your help. I don't know what my dad spoke to you about, but he really does not have a clue with what is going on in my life. He is only contacting you to make himself look good for his reputation. But really, he would not care if I drop dead tomorrow. He would be happy to have me out of his life. Just like I'm happy to have Casey out of my life."

Without another word, I storm back to the hall where I sit in a corner away from everyone, pulling out my lyric book. I write in it to get things off my chest, to express my anger towards Casey. Mark and my other bandmates don't come over to me. They know never to interrupt me while I'm writing a song. I keep writing until the bell for second period rings.

***

I was thankful when it was finally fourth period. Music class will be the only class I had today that could help distract me from everything. The atmosphere still felt like we were at a cemetery, where teachers and Year Twelve students moped around like they were attending a funeral. This place just didn't feel like a high school at all. I honestly couldn't wait for the day to be over. I couldn't stand to be in school any longer.

My mind drifts off a little, not paying attention to my classmates' performances. Mark and I were the last to perform. He sits on a chair and then rests an acoustic guitar on his lap. I stand beside him, ready to sing. Mrs Grove had gotten our class to write an acoustic version of a song, either existing or we could write our own. As songwriters, Mark and I chose to write our own song. I wrote the lyrics while Mark put together the tune.

Mark begins to strum the chords. I glimpse over at him, smiling. He returns the smile. I turn to my classmates, opening my mouth to sing but no words come. Why aren't these words coming out? I know the lyrics. I have practiced with Mark many times before. Mark gives me a blank look, raising a brow before restarting the song. I clear my throat. I can do this. But as I open my mouth again, the same thing happens. I can't sing this song.

The song was about Casey and me, how our friendship ended. Everyone in this classroom will know it's about her. Everyone knows our friendship went sour, but no one knew the truth. And as I stare back at my classmates and my teacher, I couldn't perform. I see the sadness in my teacher's eyes from the loss of a student. Casey didn't study music, but she had Mrs Grove for two years in Year Seven and Eight. My classmates don't show that same emotion as Mrs Grove is, but I couldn't tell what any of them were thinking. It would be a terrible idea to sing this. Not on the day news broke out that she ended her life.

Why did I even write this song about Casey in the first place? All because I was mad at her? No wonder she ended her life. I'm a terrible friend. Maybe not just as a friend, but as a person too.

"I'm sorry, Mrs Grove, but I really can't perform today," I tell my teacher, tears threatening to fall.

Mark stops strumming the chords. I couldn't see his face, but I knew his expression will be full of concern. He knows today is not a great day for me.

Mrs Grove nods. "I understand, Tessa. Today is a difficult day for all of us. I will give you tomorrow and the weekend to have some headspace. You and Mark can do your performance on Monday, but no later than that day."

"Thank you, Mrs Grove."

"That's so unfair!" Sun Nguyen cries out, speaking for the rest of the class. "Why do we have to do our assessment, but Tessa and Mark don't have to do it only because her best friend committed suicide?"

I can't help but feel a stabbed in my chest at his words. Like having him say it made it feel more reality that Casey was gone.

Mrs Grove gives him a stern look, but doesn't yell at him for his inappropriate remark. She then turns to the rest of the class. "I want you all to talk quietly amongst yourselves." She turns to me. "Tessa, could you wait for me outside, please?"

I listen and exit the room, resting my back against the wall outside. Alone for a few seconds I can hear Mr Chester in the other music room teaching his class with the door open.

Mrs Grove joins me out in the corridor, closing the door behind her. She stands in front of me. "Are you alright, Tessa?"

I sniff, wiping my eyes. "I'm fine. I'm sorry. Everything is just too much today. My dad did suggest for me to stay home, but I didn't want to because of the assessment."

"I understand, Tessa. This sudden news about what happened to Casey is hard on all of us. I'm glad to give you some time to yourself, and on Monday you can perform." She gives me a friendly smile, showing me she was someone I could trust. "I'm here if you want to talk, Tessa."

I give her a small smile, but I really wasn't in the mood to talk to anyone about my feelings. No one will understand how I feel. "Thanks, Mrs Grove, but right now I just want to be alone."

She nods. "Well, I can't dismiss you so you can go somewhere to be alone. You have fifteen minutes until the bell rings for lunch. If you need some time to yourself, I can let you sit in the band room."

I thank her once more and enter the band room next to the classroom, which can only be opened by one of the teachers in the Performing Arts department. I closed the door behind me, feeling relax and not feeling the guilt about my ex-friend's death.

There isn't much in the room. There was just a drum kit in the left-hand corner of the room, and a keyboard on a stand on the other side of the room. An acoustic guitar was beside the keyboard, resting up against the wall. There's also a tall cupboard that has smaller instruments inside like sleigh bells and the triangle.

I pick up the guitar and sit down on a chair that's in the room. I strum a few chords, the tune instantly making me feel better.

The bell rings, but I don't move. I don't care for lunch or even for my last two periods. I just wanted the day to end and move on from all of this mess that Casey had caused.

A knock comes from the door and then opens. Mark pokes his head in.

"Hey, are you okay?" he asks. "Would you like some company?"

I smile at him. "I would love some."

Mark walks in and closes the door behind him. "Mrs Grove said we can stay in here for lunch, but we must leave ten minutes before the bell."

He comes to sit beside me, moving the guitar from my lap and pulls me into a hug. I close my eyes as I nuzzle against his neck. The warmth of his body closed to me instantly makes me calm. If we weren't in school, this feeling he was giving me made me want to be even closer to him where I could feel his skin and the flex of his muscles beneath my touch.

Mark rubs his hand along my back. "Is there anything you want to talk about?"

I pull away. "I'm fine. I just want today to be over."

"Tessa, if you weren't feeling up to doing the assessment today because of Casey, you should have told me."

"I know. I thought I could do it, but I was wrong."

"That's okay."

He kisses my neck, his lips over my sweet spot. A soft moan escape my lips. He then slips one of his hands underneath the hem of my jumper and school shirt. His hand moves up my side, underneath my bra, and cups his hand around my left breast.

I suddenly knew what I needed to feel better and to forget about Casey for a moment. And Mark was the only one who could make me feel good.

We get out of the room fast, not wanting to be caught by Mrs Grove or by someone else. We sneak out of the school, running to my car, to go some place private to finish what we have started.

Driving down the street to the nearest park, which we hoped will be deserted. Mark had his hand on my thigh, moving it slowly up under my skirt. I hated how it was winter and the stockings I had on under my skirt prevented him from going further.

I come to a park that's near our school, and pull into the parking lot. It's deserted, just the way we wanted. As soon as the engine is cut off, and the parking brake was up, Mark pounces on me, his hands cup around my face and kisses me.

We move into the backseat to where there was room. I saddle Mark, taking off my jumper while he unbuttons my shirt. I capture his mouth. Mark's hands move around my back to unclip my bra. His lips move down to my neck.

This is what I needed to get Casey off my mind.

***

Mark and I didn't bother to head back to school. Instead we headed to Mansfield Shopping Centre for lunch, trying out this new Chinese restaurant that had just opened there.

After lunch we stroll around the mall. My mind was at ease until we walk pass Freddy's Bookshop. Casey comes flooding back to my mind. I remember after her parents announced they were splitting, she applied for a job at the independent bookstore that had opened up here at the shopping centre two months before.

Letting go of my boyfriend's hand, I wander into the store. Freddy's Bookshop always had that welcoming feeling when you entered, even if you weren't a reader. I hated books, but Casey loved them. When I used to visit her at the store, she would always show me the new stock that had come in, hoping I would somehow become interested in reading. When we were kids, she would ask me to come to the public library with her. Corey would often come with us.

I walk over to the new release shelf, which was three bookshelves near the entry way. I stand there and stare at the books. I imagine Casey standing beside me, explaining excitedly about new titles and which ones she is planning to read, or the ones she had heard are so great. She would even point out books she thought I would like. I would only just laugh when she suggested books to me like that. I'm sure I will like them once they're adapted into a movie or TV show.

Mark puts his arm around me and pulls me closed, kissing the top of my head. "Are you sure you don't want to talk about anything?"

I shake my head. What was there to talk about besides being the horrible friend I am, killing my best friend? I thought I could get Casey off my mind, but it's like she was haunting me, reminding me of what I made her do.

I realise then what I needed to do. I tell Mark I had to go, promising to see him and the rest of the band at my place, hurrying out of the store to my car.

Chapter 6
Casey

My entire world felt like it was crumbling around me. Coming home after returning from Tessa's didn't feel like I lived there. It may have only been a couple of hours since I left after Dad's bombshell, but the house was lifeless. Mum was in her room crying and Dad was nowhere to be seen. How long ago did he leave? Has he taken all of his belongings or will he come back for some of it later?

I find Corey sitting at the kitchen table, his arms folded and his head resting on them.

I pulled out a chair and sat down beside my brother.

"Dad is gone," he told me without glancing up. "He is never coming back."

I had no idea what to say. There was nothing to say, really. I wanted to believe I was trapped inside a nightmare, but it wasn't one. Our family was broken and there was no way to fix it.

I leave my brother and go to see how my mother was doing. She lay on her side of the bed. She seemed to have stopped sobbing. I stepped inside the room and crawled into bed with her, wrapping an arm around her. Mum moved placing her hand on my arm.

"I'm sorry, Mum," I said.

Mum turned around to face me. She looked like a mess, unrecognisable with blood-shot eyes from last night, along with red and puffy eyes from today. She looked older than her forty-year-old self.

She stroked my hair. "You know I love you, don't you, Casey?"

"Of course I do, Mum."

She forced a smile, kissing my forehead and held me close to her.

***

I don't go to school the next day. I couldn't find a reason worth going for. I can't even find the energy to get out of bed.

By ten o'clock I could no longer stay in bed, my stomach grumbling loudly. I didn't worry about getting changed as I went to bed with the clothes I had on yesterday. The house was silent as I walked out, unsure if Mum or my brother were still asleep or if they would be around.

I walked into the kitchen to find Corey in there, cleaning up. On the kitchen table sat a plate full of pikelets with two small bowls of cream and strawberry jam. It surprised me he was home. He had class today where he was studying a science degree in something to do with the environment.

"I'm surprised you are here," I said. "I thought you would be in class."

Corey turned to me where he was cleaning the sink. "I told my teacher I needed the week off because of a family emergency. Of course there is no emergency, but I know this house will be turn upside down with Mum being depressed. So he is sending my work through email, which I need to make sure to have completed by the end of the week, as well as to have my assessments complete by the time we break up for the holidays next week. I'm not even sure how I am going to be able to do my assignments, attend work and make sure Mum doesn't go off the rails all at the same time." He rinsed the cloth. "Sit down, Casey. Have something to eat. I doubt Mum will eat anything."

I listened to my brother and sat down at the table. I picked up a pikelet, spreading the jam on it and some cream. I take a bite, but my hunger wasn't there, even when my stomach grumbled.

Corey folded the cloth and rest it over the tap. "Would you like a hot chocolate?"

"Yes, please."

Corey strolled over to the jug, switching it on to boil. He then got two clean mugs from the cupboard, scooping the hot chocolate powder into them.

"Have you checked on Mum yet?" I asked, grabbing another pikelet, forcing myself to eat.

"She is a mess, Casey." He pulled out the milk from the fridge, setting it down beside the mugs. "I'm really worried about her. I'm not even sure if I should contact her doctor to let him know what is going on. And since she has been out of work for almost two weeks, she is not going to want to look for any. We are going to be short on money until Mum can get herself cleaned up and back into the work force. My part time job is not going to be enough to cover the bills."

I couldn't imagine getting by with little money. We may not have been wealthy, but we had enough to get by where my parents had a stable income. But now Dad has walked out with the only source of income we had. Who knew when Mum would be able to get herself a job?

Maybe there was a way I could help out. I couldn't put all of this pressure on my brother.

"Are you going to school tomorrow?" Corey asked me. The jug stopped boiling and he poured the water into the mugs.

I shrugged. "I will see how I am tomorrow."

"Don't miss out on too much school, alright?" He poured the milk in next.

I nodded. "I know. I will ask Tessa to give me any homework for English and then tomorrow I will ask my teachers for the work I missed today."

Corey comes over, setting the mugs down and sat down across from me. I thanked him and reached for mine. He had placed two marshmallows in both of our mugs. I blow on it gently and take a sip of it. I then set it aside to let it cool a bit.

"Listen, Corey, I don't want you to take the responsibility of everything so I'm going to search around for a job. I will help you with money."

Corey smiled at me. "Thank you, Casey. I really appreciate it. I really do."

***

Job searching wasn't easy. For the next few days, I went around the shopping centre with Tessa to pass out my resume to shop keepers. A lot of them rejected it, saying they don't take resumes or I had to go online to apply or they weren't hiring. I applied for a few jobs online as well, but no one got back to me.

By Friday Mum was slowly moving around the house, doing things rather than lying around and feeling sorry for herself. For four days she didn't eat until Corey demanded her to do so.

Tessa was doing her best getting me through the week without thinking about my parents. It wasn't easy. Dad hadn't even bothered to contact Corey or me to see how we were coping. It's like he didn't care that for the past nineteen years he had raised two children. When I wasn't hanging with Tessa, I tried to concentrate on my school work so I wouldn't fall behind or I kept my mind open with finding work, anything to forget about last weekend.

On Friday night Tessa invited me over to her place. Her brothers were at a friend's place for a sleepover, and her father was on another date with Hazel.

We sat on the couch with a bowl of popcorn in between us, but we were hardly watching the movie.

"Any luck with any jobs?" Tessa asked me.

"So far nothing."

"Keep trying. You will find something."

"It feels like I won't."

"You have only been looking for a week. Give it time."

I smile at Tessa's words, taking a handful of popcorn from the bowl. Her positivity is what I needed to ensure I will find a job. Earlier today when I had returned home from school, there was a pile of bills sitting on the table in the kitchen. If I didn't find a job soon to help Corey, the bills will get higher. I don't want to think what will happen if we couldn't pay our bills on time.

"So guess what happen this afternoon when I arrived home?" Tessa said with a giant smile.

There was only one reason to why my best friend's smile was huge.

"Mark asked you out?"

Tessa nodded. "He followed me home from school and then showed up on the doorstep, asking me if I was doing anything on Saturday."

I squealed with delight, hugging her, knocking the bowl of popcorn in the process. We didn't worry about it at first.

"I'm so happy for you, Tessa."

She pulled away. "It's about time he came asking. I wasn't sure if I should have waited for him to ask me out or if I should have done it."

"I think it's good that you waited or it might sound like you were desperate."

Tessa nodded. "You're right." She looked at the spilled popcorn on the floor. Thankfully, the bowl was plastic and not glass or ceramic. It was faced down on the floor under our feet. She cursed softly, getting onto the carpet to start cleaning up our mess. I get onto the floor to help her, scooping up the pieces of popcorn and kernels into the bowl.

"Casey, if you aren't doing anything tomorrow, could you please come over to help me get ready for the date?" Tessa sat the bowl on the table. "I'm really nervous about Mark. I have butterflies just thinking about him."

"Sure, I will come over and help you. I don't know anything about dates, but I will gladly help you. I'm happy you have this date with Mark. At least it will keep your mind off that guy you met years back when we went camping."

Tessa goes quiet when I mentioned him. I never learnt the boy's name. She never told me. My parents took my brother and I camping when I was fourteen. Tessa came with us. She met a guy near our campsite. She told me it was no use knowing his name when his family left the camp before us. I wanted to meet him, but never got to. Tessa got to meet him on a night walk near the lake when she couldn't sleep. She kept in contact with him for a while, but then something happened between them and they stopped talking. From time to time Tessa thinks about him, would often wonder what he was up to. But I told her to move on. The boy from the lake was not worth thinking about.

"Yeah," Tessa answered. She smiled, looking at me. "I'm happy to be given this chance to be with Mark. I have a good feeling about him."

"So do I."

Tessa got off the floor, grabbing the bowl. "I should get you a date and then we can go on a double date. You still like Max Downing, don't you?"

I nodded. Max Downing was in my Travel and Tourism class. I have had a crush on him for so long that I never really had an opportunity to talk to him. He doesn't know I'm alive. I have had a few classes with him over the years, but the idea of talking to a guy just terrified me.

"I will see if I can set you up with a date with him."

I smiled, my heart skipping for joy. I hope that happens, and if it does, I hope I don't get all tongue-tied around him.

***

When I get home later, I checked my email. My face lights up when I see the first message in the inbox was from Freddy's Bookshop. I click on it to find that the manager Freddy wanted me to come in for an interview Monday afternoon. I replied back to say that I will be there.

Hopefully this job will be enough to help my brother pay our bills.

Chapter 7
Tessa

I pull up outside the Rolands' home. I try to think of the last time I was here, but it was such a blur memory. The front lawn was in the need of a mow, and the whole house had this uneasy feeling now that Casey wasn't here. I had so many opportunities to come by here and tell Casey to forget about the stupid fight, but I had chosen not to. Now being here after she is gone felt wrong, and I was tempted to drive off.

But then my eyes divert to the silver hatchback in the driveway. Corey. The thought of him made the butterflies I was sure I was over, dance around my stomach.

I lost my virginity when I was fourteen. But I never told Casey who I did it with. If I did, most likely our friendship would have ended.

It's not a rule that is discussed between friends, and it's something Casey and I definitely didn't discuss. It was a rule that was just common sense not to cross, unless you had permission to do so. Definitely Corey was off limits. Casey never said I could date him, but it didn't seem right that I did.

Losing my virginity and the boy I lost it with has been something I was too shameful to tell Casey, afraid of what she will say. Like maybe she would look at me in a totally different way.

Casey had invited me along for the camping trip her parents were taking her and Corey on. We were there for the week, enjoying summer before school started the week later. Corey was sixteen, and I will admit that I have always found him attractive when I started to take an interest in the opposite sex at the age of twelve. Of course, I never told Casey that I found her brother attractive.

I wasn't sure if Corey knew about my crush on him when he caught me staring at him when Casey and I sat beside the river. It was hot and all I wanted was to go swimming, but I stayed on shore with her because she can't swim. Well, she can, she just isn't a confident swimmer and prefers not to go in the water. Being the good friend I am, I sat with her so she wouldn't feel lonely or anything if I am in the water, or feel ashamed for not being able to swim. While sitting on the shore I was able to watch Corey who was shirtless. Just watching him made butterflies dance around my stomach, wondering what it was like to be kiss by him or to run my hands over his body. I made sure Casey didn't know I was watching him. I pretend my eyes were looking at something else when really, they were on Corey. He caught me staring at one time, gave me a winked and a small smirk.

As it was my first time camping, I had trouble sleeping for a few nights on the ground. The Rolands had gone camping a few times and was used to sleeping on the ground. Casey and I shared a tent. Corey was lucky to have his own tent. Once Casey was fast asleep, I would sneak out and take a walk around the campsite, hoping to exhaust myself enough so I could fall asleep. On my third night I found Corey sitting by the river. I joined him and we talked until he kissed me. He was my first kiss, and I wanted to so badly tell Casey everything. But I couldn't in case she didn't want me being with her brother. So when I woke up in the morning with a dreamily look on my face, I had to come up with some kind of lie to tell Casey. I told her I had met this guy at a nearby campsite, who I met while being out here at night when I couldn't sleep. She wanted to meet him, but I said she couldn't because his family had packed up and was gone that day. I then said we had swapped numbers and I might be able to see him. And of course I will be.

On the night before we left, Corey invited me to his tent once everyone had gone to sleep. There my virginity was lost. We promised ourselves that we would keep our hook up a secret from Casey. It was best she didn't know anything.

Corey and I continued seeing each other in secret. It was hard to sneak around as we couldn't be at the house when we did want to hook up. Corey also had his learners permit so we could not go in his car to drive somewhere. We were also minors so booking a motel room was out of the question. We agreed that once I was sure my father was in bed, he would sneak over and climbed through my bedroom window so we could make love.

I was definitely sure Corey was in love with me. Maybe we would even tell Casey what has been going on between us when the time was right. But by the time it was his seventeenth birthday four months later after hooking up for the first time, he proved to me that our love was nothing. He used me for his own pressure, and it was something I couldn't tell Casey. Corey began dating some girl from his grade. For the past few weeks I felt empty without him. It was hard going over to Casey's. I couldn't tell Dad anything because he would have killed me for having sex at just fourteen years of age, and then there would be that long lecture about what would happened if I fell pregnant. So I made up a lie and told Casey I was no longer in contact with the boy I had met at the campsite.

We never mentioned him again. Two years later is when I met Mark. He helped take away the emptiness Corey left me feeling. He told me he was happy for me, never mentioning the mistake he made. We left what we had in the past, and perhaps it was all for the best.

Now that I sit here staring at the house, I wonder if I could face Corey. I can't remember the last time I have seen him now that he is hardly ever home since starting university. What would Corey think of me if he knew I had killed his sister?

I wander up the front lawn and knock on the door. I hear the footsteps and the door opens. Corey stands there, his eyes red and puffy.

"Hey," I say softly.

"Hey. I'm surprised to see you here. Come on in, Tessa."

Corey moves aside so I could enter and closes the door behind me.

"How come you aren't in school?" he asks.

"I thought I could get through school, but I couldn't. So I skip out at lunch." I leave out the reason why. He doesn't need to know what Mark and I got up to.

"I have to take the next two weeks from uni off so I can organise Casey's funeral, and to care for my mum. If I can make it to the last week before school ends, it will be great. And then over the holidays I have to balance my school work and job. Anyway, would you like anything to eat or drink, Tessa?"

I shake my head. "I'm fine thanks, Corey."

Corey gestures to the couch, and we sit down together.

"Where's your Mum?" I ask.

"In bed," he answers. "She hasn't been able to get out of bed this morning."

"Have you told your dad about Casey yet?"

He shakes his head. "No. We lost all contact with him when he left last year. We have no idea where he is. I did contact his side of the family to pass on the message, but I have no idea if any of them did. If they did, Dad hasn't contacted us or checked in to see how we are coping."

My heart sinks with sadness. I may not have a great relationship with my dad, but I wouldn't want him to not care if I had died. I would want him to pay his respects and to show my brothers that he supports them with their own grieving, the same way he did when Mum died. Kaiden and Jackson were too young to remember her.

"I'm sorry about Casey," I say. "I just wished I could have been there when she was going through a hard time. But she never said she was feeling depressed or showing any signs that she was." *That's because you weren't there to help her! You pushed her away like she didn't matter!*

"Don't blame yourself, Tessa. It wasn't your fault. It wasn't anyone's fault. No one knew what she was going through. She could have told someone what was bothering her, but sadly she kept everything bottled up inside. It got all too much for her to handle and she ended her life to stop whatever was bothering her."

But it was my fault! I wanted to tell him.

"How did she die?" I ask instead.

Corey sits there in silence for a few minutes. "Casey told me she was going over to your place."

I shake my head. "No. She never came over."

"I know. She went for a walk somewhere. About an hour later the police called me, telling me that Casey had been in a tragic accident. She ran onto the highway and was hit by a car. She was killed on impact."

A few tears fell down his cheek. I was tempted to wipe them away, but I don't. A chill runs down my spine at the thought of what Casey had done. She never seemed like the kind of person who would do this to herself. Casey was always unsure about trying something dangerous. Running onto a busy highway was something she would never do. But something triggered her mind to not listen to her fear and to do it. She caused the pain she has been going through to stop by ending her life.

And I wished I could have stopped it or didn't cause the pain she had felt.

All because I was the selfish one who didn't give a damn how she felt.

I put my hand on his thigh. "I'm here, Corey, if you ever want to talk."

He glances down at my hand and then places his over mine. He looks up at me, letting a small smile cross his lips. "I know you will, Tessa. You were always there for Casey, and I know I can count on you for anything."

If only you knew what a lousy friend I have been in the past six months.

I remove my hand from Corey's grip, resting it in my lap. What would he think of me if he knew what I have done to his sister? Especially if I am the one who caused her to end her life?

We sit there in silence for a long time. I remember the days when I had so much to say to Corey, but since the incident between us, it was like we were strangers.

"I'm entering this band contest tomorrow," I say, breaking the silence. "It's going to be held over at Martin Place. My dad and soon to be step mum is hosting it on air of their morning news."

He looks up at me with a smile. "That's awesome, Tessa. I hope you go well with it. I can't get to Martin Place as I have made arrangements to meet up with a funeral planner, but I will definitely watch you on TV."

I return the smile, but I then let it fade, turning away and stare at my feet so Corey couldn't see my face. "The song my band and I are performing is about you." I force myself to look at Corey. He is staring back, curious of what kind of song I had written. "It's about how much you had hurt me when you started dating that girl in your grade. I don't know if I should even have considered you as my boyfriend as we never really went on a date. We just snuck around behind Casey's back and hooked up. I wanted to believe we had something, but you ended up using me for your own pressure."

Corey looks away in shame. He doesn't try to deny anything with what went on between us. "I'm sorry I hurt you. I didn't mean to. I should have been honest with you. I was immature at the time and I didn't think about your own feelings. All I could think about is what if Casey found out and what she would say. I didn't even know how to tell her I was sleeping with her best friend. I didn't want her to think I took advantage of you."

"But you did take advantage of me. You knew I was a virgin. You knew I had a crush on you. Did you even like me?"

Corey nods. "I did. I just didn't have the guts to stand up to tell my sister how I felt about you. When we started sneaking around for four months, I knew I had to tell her and that we couldn't sneak around forever. I was too busy thinking about myself then thinking how you would feel. And I'm truly sorry, Tessa. I wished I could make it up for being the jerk I am. I should have told you how I felt. We could have worked something out together."

"We could have, Corey. I thought I did something wrong when you stopped talking to me."

He nods, but doesn't say anything.

"Did you ever wonder what could have happened between us if Casey didn't mind us being together?" I ask him before we sat here in awkward silence.

"I thought about it all the time. But I don't think she would have approved. I mean, it's just an unspoken rule between siblings that you don't go around sleeping with their friends unless they give you that permission."

I nod. "Well, I guess it doesn't matter anymore."

"Do you hate me, Tessa?"

I glance up at him, surprised to hear him say it. "Why would I hate you?"

"You know, for sleeping with you, and then dating another girl, like what happened between us didn't matter."

I shake my head, twisting my body around on the couch so I was facing him fully. I rest my hand on his shoulder. "No, Corey. I don't hate you. I was just hurt. At first I didn't understand why you treated me like you did, but I now know it was so Casey wouldn't find out. You probably saved our friendship as well because it would have ended if she had known and didn't approve."

He nods. "Do you forgive me, Tessa for the way I have treated you?" His blue eyes search for mine, pleading with me to say yes.

I scoot closer to Corey. "I forgive you."

Without thinking of the consequences, I kiss his cheek, the butterflies dancing around my stomach like they always do when I'm around Corey. My cheeks grew hot and I wondered to myself if I did the right thing to kiss his cheek. Will he even have feelings for me still?

Before I had the chance to move away, reminding myself that I had a boyfriend, Corey reaches out to me, placing his hand on my cheek. His thumb rubs the corner of my mouth. He searches for my eyes to allow him to kiss me. For a moment, I forget about Mark as the old feelings I had for Corey return and I wanted him close to me. I move closer to him so he knew he had my permission. He smashes his lips against mine, kissing me with such force, energy from the last three years that we had missed. I didn't think we had any feelings left for each other.

I saddle him, moving my arms around this neck. Corey rests his hands on my waist, hesitating to whether or not if he should slip his hands under my clothes.

He breaks the kiss. "Wait. Don't you have a boyfriend, Tessa? We don't have to do this."

I did think about this, and I shouldn't go behind Mark's back to have sex with someone else.

But right now, I didn't want to think about hurting Mark. This was a one-off thing.

I pull my jumper over my head, tossing it on the floor. Corey watches me as I unbuttoned my shirt. His Adam's apple bobbing as he swallows. His eyes travelled from my face to my body as I drop my shirt on the floor with my jumper. A smile spreads across his face.

"I want this, Corey. I need this. We both need this. It can be your way to make it up to me. Mark doesn't have to know." *And he won't know.*

His eyes travel back up to meet mine before crushing his lips against mine, flipping me onto my back so he was on top of me.

As we made love right there on the couch in the lounge room, I didn't regret anything.

***

Mark and the rest of my bandmates were waiting for me outside of my home. As soon as I lay my eyes on my boyfriend, my stomach clenches knowing what I have done minutes ago with Corey. I have never once cheated on Mark, but for some reason I just needed this one time with Corey, to have that closure we never had. Besides, I'm sure once this funeral is over, I most likely wouldn't need to have anything to do with Casey's brother or her mother. Definitely I won't be seeing them once our band hits it big.

And Mark will never have to know I have slept with someone else.

I pull into the driveway and get out of the car.

"Hey, Tessa, next time you and Mark decide to skip school, don't forget Travis and I," Tim says.

"I'm sorry, guys. Mark and I just needed some private time."

"Yes, I bet you guys did. Come on, Tessa. Open the garage door. I'm freezing to death out here," Travis complains, shivering.

I open the garage door for them so they can get the band equipment ready for practice. Tim helps Travis to get out the drum kit from his van that's parked on the street, taking it into the garage.

Before I had a chance to help my bandmates set up or to unlock the front door, Mark approaches me with a concern look on his face.

"Are you alright, Tessa?" he asks. "I was worried when you left me at the shopping centre. Where did you go?"

"I'm fine, Mark. I just had to visit Casey's house to see how her mother and brother were doing."

He nods. "How are they?"

"Her mother can't get out of bed, and Corey is organising the funeral."

I search his eyes, looking for anything in them to tell me he was suspicious of me, but there was nothing to indicate that there was. My secret was safe from my boyfriend.

He pulls me into a hug. "I'm glad you're alright. It really worried me when you ran off like that without telling me where you were going. But I knew it had something to do with Casey."

"Sorry. I just felt like it was the right thing to do to see her family. Corey told me how she died. It was something I would never expect her to do." I feel the tears prickling my eyes as I think of how she had chosen to end her life. *She had run into the highway and was hit by a car. She was killed on impact.*

Mark pulls away. He wipes the tears from my eyes. "Tell me later, okay? Maybe after band practice we can go some place private, and you can tell me everything."

I smile, nodding. "Okay."

He returns the smile, pushing back some loose strand of my hair, tucking it behind my ear. He then kisses me softly.

"Hey, lovebirds!" Tim calls from the van. "Do you think you can give us a hand?"

Mark takes my hand and we stroll down the driveway to Travis's white van on the street. On the side doors Travis had written our band name on it, as well as music notes around the car. If Travis wasn't going to be a musician, he would be an artist.

Tim hands me Mark's guitar case from the back. I started walking up the driveway when Dad's Mercedes-Benz pulls in. I roll my eyes. Does Dad really have to come home with my brothers right now?

My brothers leap out of the car, running pass me and almost knocking me over. They don't apologise for it either, running to the front door. I place the guitar down by the drum kit. I hear my brothers yelling out to Dad that the door is lock. Dad tells them to go through the garage. They listen and run pass me. I head out to join my friends to get more equipment out of Travis's van. He and Tim walks up the driveway carrying a speaker while Mark guarded the van.

"Tessa, can I have a word with you?" Dad says, making his way over to him.

"Not now, Dad. I'm getting ready for band practice."

"Tessa." The tone of his voice tells me not to push him.

So I stand there, resting my back up against my car and cross my arms across my chest. "What?"

"Why didn't you talk to the counsellor today? Mr Carlton called me back to say he had tried to talk to you, but you weren't interested. Instead you were acting rude towards him."

I roll my eyes. "Seriously, Dad? Is this what it is all about?"

He points his finger at me. "Don't roll your eyes at me, young lady."

"Dad, if I want to see a counsellor and talk to him about Casey, I would. But I don't need to talk about her. I'm fine! How many times do I need to tell people that?"

"I'm concerned about you, Tessa. I don't want you to end up like Casey. I want you to see Mr Carlton tomorrow. You only need to see him once. I want to make sure you're fine."

I shake my head at Dad. Did he really think I will end up doing what she did? I clench my teeth together as I speak. "I'm not going to end up like Casey. I'm nothing like her."

I turn and head over to the van where Mark was watching us.

"Even if you won't Tessa, I want you to see the school counsellor tomorrow. I want to make sure you're coping okay with Casey's death."

I chuckle softly to myself. If only he knew that I wasn't planning to show up to school tomorrow. I'm not worried what he is planning to do to me when he finds out I have entered the contest. And I most definitely wasn't going to let Casey's death stop me from performing well, not like how it was today. Tomorrow I am going to make sure my friends and I can make it big. All of the work we have been doing in the last year when we first got this band together will be worth it once we win the contest.

And when we do, I can get out of this place.

Chapter 8
Casey

Friday afternoon I went over to Tessa's like I had promised to help her select an outfit to wear for her date tonight with Mark. Tessa wasn't a dress kind of girl, so there weren't many dresses in her wardrobe. I'm not even sure if she would wear a dress on a date.

I sat down on the edge of Tessa's bed while she stood in front of her wardrobe.

"I don't know what to wear for the date, Case," Tessa said. "What do you even wear on the first date? I really wish my mum was here. She would be able to help me."

I let a small smile cross my face even though she wouldn't see it with her back to me. "I'm sure wearing anything is fine. I don't think Mark will be so worried about what you wear."

"I want to wear something that will impress him. I want to wear something and have him look at me saying. 'Wow. This girl is incredible.'"

I get up from the bed and join at her side, glancing at her clothes. She had a few dresses in there that I thought looked alright to wear on a date. "Hey, Hazel is downstairs, isn't she? Why not ask her for some tips? I'm sure she would –"

Tessa spun around swiftly, her hair whipping around her face. She frowned at the mention of her dad's girlfriend. "Are you kidding me? There is no way I'm allowing my dad's girlfriend come into my room or allow her to give me advice on anything. I don't want her to think I accept her."

"Why don't you want to accept her? She seems so nice."

"Because she isn't my mum, Casey." She left the wardrobe doors opened and strolled over to her bed, sitting down on the edge of it. "She isn't my mum. With my dad dating her, it feels like he is replacing her. For seven years since she had been gone, it has just been my brothers, me and him. No one else. And then Hazel walks into the picture. My brothers have no memory of my mother since they were barely one years old when she passed away. They look up at Hazel as a mother figure. But I don't see her as a mother figure."

"You see her more as a threat, right?"

"Well, maybe not as much as a threat, but a stranger. She's a stranger walking into my life, thinking it's okay to replace my mother."

I try my best to understand Tessa so I could comfort her better, but I had no idea what it must be like to be in her position. To lose your mother at a young age, and then later to have a stranger to walk into your life that could take over the replacement of your mother. I have no idea what I would do if Dad was to do that. I still wonder what else could be behind the reasons why Dad made the decision to split up with Mum. Was it something more than just my mother's drinking addiction? Did he meet another woman? Whatever is the real reason for my parents to go separate ways had to be more to the story that my brother and I will never know about.

And I'm sure for whatever reason for Tessa to be against Hazel, I'm sure she is a lovely person. It's just taking Tessa a long time to see it. I notice how Mr Ross has been happier since dating Hazel, but I won't ever mention it to Tessa how I think.

I sat down beside her and swing my arm around her shoulders. "No one is going to replace your mother. Never think that."

"It feels like Hazel has."

I get up and held my hand out to Tessa. "Well, don't think it. Come on, let's pick an outfit for your date with Mark."

Tessa smiled, taking my hand. I pulled her up, embracing her.

"I'm glad to have you here with me even if I couldn't have my mother," Tessa said as she pulled away.

I smiled at her. "It's no problem, Tessa. I'm happy to help. Now let's find you an outfit before you're late for your date."

***

I stayed with Tessa until Mark came to pick her up. She thought if I was there, it was less likely that she and her father would have an argument. It turned out she had never informed her father that she was going on a date. She knew her father would disapprove.

After about ten minutes of deciding what to wear, Tessa chose to wear a knee-length midnight blue dress with a denim jacket. Since it was cold out, she wore stockings underneath. I helped with her hair, straightening it.

I watched as my friend's face lid up when Mark showed up at the door. She promised me she would call me later to tell me everything on how to tell me how the date went.

When she does ring me up later that night, she told me about the restaurant she had gone to, the movie she had seen, and then sharing a kiss with Mark. As she tells me this, I was glad she couldn't see me through the phone. I make an effort to keep my choice cheery. Don't get me wrong, I really am happy for Tessa. I just couldn't help but feel the loneliness in my heart as Tessa told me everything. The loneliness was mixed with disappointment. It was something I have never felt before. Was it jealously? Maybe. But I didn't want to be jealous of my best friend.

From the happiness in her voice, I knew Tessa would be seeing Mark again. And when I realised that, the loneliness and disappointment grew. I wanted to cry. From now on, everything will be different between us as Tessa enters the dating world. It would be stupid to let a boy come in between our friendship. We have been friends for almost seventeen years. It has never really occurred to me until now how much our lives will change once we graduate from high school next year. Tessa was the first to start dating. Boys hardly take any notice of me, and I wondered to myself if I would be able to get a boyfriend. Mum always tells me there is no rush and I had my entire life to meet someone.

But I only hoped that this awful feeling I had didn't mean I was going to lose my best friend. I often dreamed of us being the bridesmaid at each other's weddings, and growing up our kids together so they too can become great friends.

And I hoped that once we do start going off our separate ways that we will remain friends forever.

***

I attended the job interview on Monday afternoon. By Thursday afternoon I was working at the bookstore. All day I just wanted school to be over so I could start my first day. Tessa promised to stop by later to see how I was doing and also to give me a ride home once I finished.

Freddy showed me everything I needed to run the store, and how to serve the customers. For the first few hours of my shift, he trained me on the cash register. The whole thing was confusing at first as it was my first time using a cash register that wasn't one of those self-serve checkouts. By the end of my shift, I pretty much got the hang of it. Just a couple of days at working it I should be alright.

I knew my way around the store since I have come in here a few times. I helped customers as much as I could with anything they might need in finding a book. Keeping myself occupied here actually helped me to keep my mind off my parents. It's almost two weeks since they announced their divorced, and I hadn't heard anything from Dad. He never called to check up on Corey and I. It was like we were no longer apart of his life.

I was busy fixing up the shelves in the children's section where many young kids liked to mess everything up, when someone walks up behind me, asking me if I could help them look for a book they wanted.

I spun around when I recognised Tessa's voice. I gave her a hug. "It's good to see you, Tessa. Especially in a bookstore."

"Oh please. This will be the only time I will ever step foot inside a bookstore. I really don't see how anyone can enjoy reading. If it has pictures it's fine, but reading a whole bunch of words on a page is just not my thing. I hate it when we are in English and we are forced to read a book."

I laughed, making sure the books on the display shelf were neat so they don't tumble over and the title of the book was facing the right way when parents pass by with their kids. "Reading isn't that bad. It lets your mind escape reality for a short time."

"I rather escape reality by actually getting away, and not through a book. So how is your first day so far?"

I turned to walk down the aisle to see if there were any other shelves that need to be fixed up or if there were customers who needed assistant. "I'm loving it."

"That's great to hear."

"Keeping myself occupied here has been helping me to keep my mind off my parents' divorced."

"Have you heard anything from your dad?"

I shook my head. "No. He has not bothered to check in on us to see how we are."

"That's ridiculous."

I led Tessa over to the new release shelf, pointing to the young adult shelf. "Can I attempt you into buying a book?"

Tessa chuckled. "Nice try, Casey. You may be working in a bookstore now, but it will still not make me read anything."

"You never know that someday you will be interested in reading. There's always that one book that can hook someone and change their lives forever."

"I don't think there will be a book out there that will be for me. Unless of course the author of the book was written by you, then I may consider reading it. I will make sure I will be first in line at the store to buy the copy."

I couldn't help but laugh. Writing has never been something I have been good at. I may read a lot, but words and I don't go well together.

Tessa leaves me to finish my shift while she said she will meet me in the food court.

***

On the way home from work I filled Tessa in everything that happened on the first day of my job. It was great to be working that I couldn't wait to be able to work tomorrow afternoon and for Saturday. I wished I could do more than just three days, but I had to also make sure I had time for my studies. But for the money I earned, I hoped it was enough for my family so we didn't lose everything and live on the street. Or we would have to move somewhere for cheaper rent, which was hard these days. Sydney was an expensive place to live. I can't imagine moving away. I hated the idea of moving away and being far from Tessa. I needed her in my life.

Hugging Tessa goodbye, I head inside the house, ready to tell my mother about my first day. She didn't show a lot of excitement as Corey or Tessa did when I told them about the job, but I knew deep down inside she was very happy for me. It was just right now with everything Dad had done, it was like the life had been drained out of my mother, worsening her depression.

I call out to her letting her know I was home. The television was on, an episode of *NCIS* playing, but Mum was not sitting down in front of it. I call out to her again, but there wasn't a response. The kitchen light was on so I wander in there.

Passed out on the kitchen table with an empty bottle of red wine, along with an empty glass beside it, was my mother. Like her depression, her drinking problem had worsened since Dad walked out last week. I was worried Mum might drink herself to death. I really need to discuss with Corey on how we can get her help. He will come home maybe tomorrow if he isn't doing anything with his friends, or maybe Saturday. I will discuss it with him then.

I cleaned up the glass and threw out the bottle. I gently shook my mother awake, helping her to her room so she was sleeping in a warm bed and not the kitchen table. By the time I get her into bed, she is fast asleep again. I tuck her in and then turned everything off before heading to bed myself.

Chapter 9
Tessa

Casey haunted my dreams that night. I couldn't close my eyes without seeing her face. I tossed and turned all through the night as I dreamed about her. Corey and Mark even wandered into my dreams as I thought about yesterday afternoon, wondering what Mark would say if he ever found out about Corey and I. It wasn't like I went behind his back on purpose and slept with someone else. It wasn't my intention to do so. Old feelings got to me and it just happened. With anxiety keeping me up, I almost overslept when my alarm went off. Today I had no time to sleep in or think about my ex-friend. Today was about my band and I. There was no way I was letting Casey ruin my music career.

I get up an hour before Dad wakes up. I was half asleep, but I figured I will grab a coffee later to wake me up. Right now I had to get dressed and get out of the house, or I will never be allowed to leave. Dad will throw a fit if he knew I was skipping school to enter a band contest where M Triple T could make it or break it. My bandmate's parents were okay with them entering. But with Dad, he will lecture me on how school is far more important than my music career. If only he knew how school and I just don't mix.

Still half asleep, I get ready and then snuck out of the house to head to Mark's where Tim and Travis were meeting us. I leave a note for Dad to let him know I was heading over to Mark's, but I leave out the part of me skipping school. I already knew how much trouble I will be in later.

As soon I reach Mark's place, my phone rings. I didn't even have to check the caller ID to know who it was.

"Hey, Dad," I say, causally.

"What are you doing at Mark's, Tessa?" he demands. "Especially at six in the morning. What about your brothers? Who is taking them to school?"

"Relax, Dad. I have to help Mark with something before school. And I'm sure Jackson and Kaiden will be able to get to school the same way they got there yesterday."

"Tessa, I want you to come home. Today is a very important day for me, and I need to get to the station early."

"Sorry, Dad. I have to go."

I hang up the phone, slipping it into my jeans pocket.

I'm definitely going to be dead later on today.

Mark comes out of the house to greet me as I step onto the veranda. He embraces me before pecking me softly on the lips. "All set for today?"

"I'm all set. Listen, my dad is pissed at me for coming here early, and I feel like he could easily come here to drag me home. So maybe we should meet Tim and Travis at the train station rather than here."

He nods. "I will let my parents know we are leaving, and I will text the guys to let them know there has been a change of plans."

He heads back inside, calling out to his parents to let them know we are going. Mrs Brady comes to the door, surprised we were going off early. She wishes us good luck on our performance, promising to watch us on the television.

On the way to the train station, Mark asks me, "What are you going to do when your dad finds out you have entered the contest? I mean, you can run away right now, but later your dad will confront you when we are at Martin Place."

I nod, not looking at my boyfriend as I kept my eyes on the road. "I know, Mark. I will figure it out later. Right now I want to keep focus on the competition."

And I hope Casey wouldn't cross my mind when I sing. Especially when the song is about her brother.

***

Martin Place was crowded as people either came by to watch the contest, or they were off to work or they were tourist. The stage was set up outside the TV station and near the stairs of the train station. Seeing the crowd made me feel nausea. It was the first time our band was performing in front of a live audience. But at the same time the nausea feeling was mixed with excitement. I couldn't wait to expose our music to everyone other than my garage.

We registered ourselves in, and while we waited for our turn to be on the stage, we stood on the sidelines to watch the other bands performed. My bandmates and I stayed cleared of the back of the crowd where the set for the morning news was going to be filmed with the audience and stage as the backdrop. So far Hazel or Dad hasn't seen me or know I was here.

About thirty bands had entered the contest. Waiting for our turn to be called made me feel anxious and the nauseous feeling in my stomach grew. We were the fifteenth band to play. So when the thirteenth band was playing on the stage, my bandmates and I went backstage to get ready.

Our band was on right after the commercial break of the morning news. My bandmates and I position ourselves on the stage, ready to give the performance of a lifetime. I stood centre stage with a microphone, with Mark and Tim at my sides with their guitars. Travis is behind us on the drums.

On either side of the stage is two TV screens for everyone to see the stage no matter what position you were standing at. It also showed Dad and Hazel as they hosted their show. The screens currently showed an image of Dad and Hazel as their show came back from the commercial.

"Welcome back to this special edition of the morning news," Dad says into the camera. "Today Hazel and I have the honour of hosting the Battle of the Bands contest right here in Martin Place."

"It has been an incredible morning watching these amazing bands performing on stage, and live on TV for us today," Hazel says. "The band who is selected as the winner will receive a record deal with Mad Star Records."

"Please welcome the next band to take the stage. M Triple T."

The attention is turned to us. I'm glad where I am I couldn't see my father's face, knowing he will be furious when he reads out the name of my band. But right now there was no time to worry about Dad. Our time has come to perform. It was now or never.

I take my position on centre stage, with Tim and Mark standing either side of me. My stomach does a flip as I stare back at the crowd, waiting for my bandmates to start playing. I search the front row, hoping to see Casey, like maybe everything was just a bad dream and she wasn't really dead, standing in the front row ready to cheer me on. But I don't see her. I don't see her.

Focus, Tessa, I say to myself. *Now is not the time to worry about Casey.*

Travis starts off with a beat of the drums. Tim and Mark bring the guitar in next. I bob to the beat of the music, smiling at the crowd as they also bobbed to the tune, ready to see what our band can do.

"Remembering you the first day I saw you
Sharing our first kiss together
What a magical feeling that was
But when I look back at it now,
I realise that what we had
Was a waste of time

Forget it
You aren't worth it
How could you be so selfish?
After all the things we went through together?
It was nice to know how much you care
Even though it was fake
Now I feel like a fool
A fool who believes in love
Well guess what,
Love sucks
So just forget it."

The crowd dances along to our music. I catch a glimpse of my bandmates, seeing the smiles on their faces, and it builds up the energy inside me. The stage fright I had earlier disappeared. I engaged the audience as I continued to sing.

"Didn't you think I will ever find out to what you were doing to me?
Didn't those kisses mean anything?
Didn't it mean anything when you were holding me in your arms?
When you said you loved me, did that mean anything to you?
Or maybe love doesn't mean anything
The lies you told,
The secrets we shared between us
The promises you made when it was just you and I,
Was our love a lie from the start when you left me for her?"

As I sing the chorus, I hear some people in the crowd sing along with me. It made me feel like a true rock star, and whether or not we win this contest, I couldn't wait until the band could do more of this.

When the song ends, the crowd breaks into a loud cheer that could probably be heard all over Sydney. My cheeks hurt as I smile brightly. I blow a kiss into the audience, thanking them one last time before I wander off stage with the rest of the band.

My phone beeps in my pocket, but I pay no attention to it as I hug my bandmates, praising each other for how well the performance went.

We then joined the crowd on the sideline to watch the next band perform. Meanwhile this all-boy band played, I checked my phone to see who had messaged me. I was almost afraid to answer it, thinking it could be dad. But my heart skips a beat when I see it was a message from Corey.

You did a great job on the stage, Tessa. I enjoyed the song as well. I'm so sorry for the way I had treated you. If Casey was here, she would have loved the song. She would have been proud of you.

I stare at his words for a long time as seeing Casey's name brought tears to my eyes. So much for hoping I didn't have to think about Casey. But somehow, everywhere I went since yesterday she has been haunting me. Was it because of guilt? Some kind of karma for the way I had treated her?

I reply back to Corey's text, thanking him. I don't mention anything about Casey.

I glance up at the band on stage, but I don't pay any attention to their song. All I could think about was what Corey had said about his sister. If Casey was here or if we hadn't ended our friendship, would she be here with me today, standing in the front row cheering me on? The thought brings a smile to my face. Casey had always supported my music, and deep down inside I knew Corey was right. If Casey was here, she would be proud of me living my dream of being a musician. She believed in me more than anyone ever had.

And when I think about it, my heart breaks how I wished my former best friend could be here to celebrate this special moment with me.

Chapter 10
Casey

Tessa's singing was so good that I almost didn't want to interrupt her by walking into her room. When she was lost in writing a song, she will be the kind of person who will bite your head off if you wreck her concentration. Tessa began writing songs and learning how to play the guitar after her mother passed away. She said music was a way of distracting her from her death.

Instead of knocking, I turned the knob and entered the room. She looked up from where she was sitting on her bed with the guitar. She smiled at me, and kept playing until she finished the chorus.

"Great song," I said, sitting down beside her.

"Thanks." Tessa put the guitar down beside her bedside table.

"What is it called?"

"*Forget It.*"

"Can I hear more of it?"

Tessa got up from the bed and walked over to her desk. "Maybe another time. I'm still working on it." She grabbed her English book along with her copy of *To Kill a Mockingbird* that we are currently reading in class.

"What is the song about?"

Tessa doesn't answer me straight away. She sits down on the bed crossing her legs. "It's about the boy who I met at the lake when we went camping."

"Oh." I turned to face her, crossing my legs as well. "I thought you were over him by now."

"I am, but sometimes I do think about him. I wrote this song on how I felt about him when I started dating Mark."

"Are you going to perform it at the talent quest next term?"

Tessa shrugged. "I don't know yet."

I pulled out my English book as well as my own copy of *To Kill a Mockingbird* from my bag. "You should, Tessa. You have never performed any of your music in front of anyone, except for me. If you're going to have a career in music, you need to start performing in front of others."

Tessa nodded, saying she will think about it. She had always enjoyed performing more than I ever did. In primary school when we would be asked to do performances for special days our school held like the Christmas concert, she always begged teachers for the lead singing role, while I shy away hoping I will get a small role and hide in the background. Since we got to high school, she hasn't performed in anything, especially not the school musicals. The music department teachers had occasionally asked her to perform for school assemblies, which she has, but never once has she ever performed her own music in front of an audience.

"And I promise to be in the front row cheering you on when you do," I go on. "I will also be there when you have your first big break."

Tessa smiled. "Thanks, Casey. You're a great friend. At least someone appreciates my music and my future career."

"Never say I'm the only one. I'm sure others will appreciate your music too."

I flipped open my English book to the last page I had written in class. Our teacher had gotten the class to write out a set of questions from chapter six of the book, which we had to complete over the weekend. Whenever Tessa and I had to study a book in English, we did it together. Tessa could work on the questions herself, but because she hated the idea of reading, and had trouble comprehending what the questions mean, we work on it together. Also, studying and doing my homework at her house helped me not to worry about what was going on at home. Especially right now when all I could think about is my mum, and constantly making sure she was okay.

"Oh, you will never guess what happened yesterday," Tessa said before I could say anything about working on our homework, her face lighting up with a smile. "Mark came over after school. When I said I write songs, he wanted to read some. So I showed him my lyric book. He then asked me if I would be interested being a part of this band he and his friends were starting up. They have two guitarists and a drummer. They just needed someone to sing. I told them I would be glad to be a part of it."

I smiled brightly at my friend. "Tessa, that is great. I'm so happy for you."

"I'm meeting up with them tomorrow after school for the audition."

I set my books aside and hugged Tessa. "I'm sure you don't need to audition. You're already great."

"I know." Tessa pulled away. "Mark said they have auditioned a few guys, but none of them seemed to have the right voice. I'm the only girl who is auditioning so far."

"That's great. What's the name of their band?"

"They have no name yet. Once they cast the singer they will come up with one."

I continued to smile. "I bet your dad is proud."

Tessa snorted. "He knows nothing about the audition. He wouldn't approve me being a part of a band anyway."

"You never know, Tessa."

Sometimes I really wonder if Mr Ross is really this uncaring father Tessa made him out to be. He has always been supportive towards her talents when we were younger. He proudly paid for her guitar lessons too. I feel Tessa puts him to the test to see how far he will go. I understand their relationship has gone downhill ever since her mother's death, but maybe it was the attention he had given Kaiden and Jackson. There has been an enormous pressure put on him after his wife passed away, raising Tessa, caring for two babies who were barely one year old, and balancing his job. When Tessa's grades began to slip in school, the two would argue. Her father wanted her to try hard, but Tessa lost all interest in school once her mother died. As she improved her guitar skills, all she wanted to do was play music.

I grab my book and flipped it back to the page I had it on after it closed on me. "Right, let's start getting this homework done."

Tessa groaned, lying down on her bed. "Do we have to? It's such a boring book, and I really don't know why we need to study it in class."

"It's part of the curriculum."

Tessa sat up, grabbing her books that she had on her lap, setting the paperback beside her, and flipped opened to the last page she had written the teacher's questions down in her notebook. "Well, the curriculum sucks. I don't see what this is teaching us."

"I'm sure there is a reason why this book is part of the curriculum. But let's not worry about that right now. Let's just get this homework done."

***

Tessa invited me along to her audition after school. I wasn't sure how nervous Tessa was about singing in front of Mark's friends, wondering what they will think about her voice. If she was nervous, she was great at hiding it.

We met at Mark's place. Travis and Tim were sitting on a three seated couch in the living room where the audition was being held. The coffee table was full of snacks in bowls and drinks. Mark invited us in.

I sat down in an arm chair, ready to give the support my friend needed. The guys sat together on the couch while Tessa stood on the other side of the coffee table with the television behind her.

"Apologises for not having enough space in here," Mark says. "We don't really have a bigger enough space to practice. Travis lives in a flat so there's no room for a band to practice there. Tim's house is way too small. When my parents aren't home, we will practice in the garage. At the moment I'm trying to convince my parents to convert our garage into a studio. But anyway, that's not important right now. We can sort it all out where we will practice once we have our fourth member."

Tim took a sip of his drink. "So, Tessa. Mark tells us you're a singer and a songwriter."

Tessa nodded. "I am. I can also play the guitar."

"Before we get you to sing, tell us why you want to join this band or be a musician?" Travis said.

"I love music," Tessa explained. "It's a way I can express myself. After my mother died, I turned to music for comfort. I want to join this band because I want to be a part of something to inspire people with, and to be able to have my music make an impact on someone the same way music made it for me."

The guys nodded at what she had said, glancing at each other, impressed with her answer.

"Are you able to sing something you have written?" Travis asked.

Tessa nodded, and then began to sing the first verse and the chorus of the song she was playing yesterday. I watch the guys' faces lid up with interest as she sings.

When she finishes, the guys leap up from the couch, clapping and cheering.

"I don't know what you guys reckon, but I say Tessa is the lead singer of our band," Travis said.

Tim and Mark agreed. Tessa squealed, jumping up and down. She hugged all three of them, thanking them for this opportunity. She then hugged me.

Chapter 11
Tessa

The last band plays. In the next five minutes we will find out the winner. When the final band walks off the stage, Dad and Hazel walked up onto the stage, thanking everyone who had participated in the contest. They then go to a commercial break while the judges made their decision.

The nausea feeling returns. It wasn't because I was nervous or anything about winning. Okay, maybe I was a little, but I was mainly worried what Dad was going to say to me once all of this is over. I haven't been able to see him from the stage when I was performing, and I knew he will give a poker face in front of the cameras.

My bandmates and I head to the backstage so we could be ready to walk out onto the stage, joining the other musicians. Mark holds onto my hand, which instantly calms me and helps me to not to worry about Dad. This moment shouldn't be about him. This moment was mine and the rest of the band's. In the next few minutes, we will know the fate of our band.

Dad holds onto the envelope that contained the winner of the contest where he and Hazel were now standing on the stage. Once the camera is rolling and they're back on the air, congratulating everyone for coming out here, and for all the bands who have particulate in the contest, wishing us luck.

"The winner of the Battle of the Bands contest is…" He waits for a few seconds before revealing the band, making everyone hold their breath. "M Triple T."

As soon as the name of our band slipped off his tongue, I jump for joy, hugging Mark and then gave him a quick kiss before the four of us walk out onto the stage. The crowd breaks into a deafening applause. I keep the excited smile on my face as we approach Dad and Hazel. Hazel's smile wasn't fake, but with Dad I could see he was only putting on a smile for the camera. He makes eye contact with me when we shook hands, and I see a vein pulsing on his neck that told me he will be speaking to me later when all of this was over.

But away from prying eyes. He wouldn't want anyone to see the real him around me.

When the crowd's cheers die down, Hazel speaks. "Congratulations on your win."

"Thank you to everyone involve with this contest that gave us this opportunity to perform here today," Travis speaks for the band. "We formed this band a year ago, and this is the first time we have performed our music in front of anyone."

"You did an amazing job out there for your first performance," Dad says.

Mark swings his arm around my waist. "And of course this band wouldn't be what it is today without our amazing lead singer Tessa Ross."

I feel dad's eyes burning into me as he tries to keep his anger hidden from the camera, and I knew once they were off, he will turn on me. Of course he will wait until we are alone before he starts giving me a long lecture about how I should have told him my band was entering the contest, or why I wasn't attending school. Definitely he will yell at me for leaving the house early this morning.

Once the cameras stop rolling, Hazel turns to me with a smile. "Congratulations on your win, Tessa. I'm so proud of you. I wasn't aware that you entered. You did amazing out there."

I give her a small smile, but don't thank her for her comment. I turn to walk off the stage with my bandmates when Dad put a hand on my shoulder.

"Once I finish up here, you and I are going to have a long talk," he tells me.

I don't reply back and walk off the stage. Other bands approach us and congratulate us on our win. When the excitement dies down for us, a man dressed in a suit approaches our band.

"Congratulations on your win, M Triple T," he says. "Please let me introduce myself. My name is Zane Maddox. I'm a producer at Mad Star Records. You did quite a performance out there today."

We thank him. My stomach twisted into knots as I stare at the music producer in front of us. Never have I thought this day would become a reality.

Zane reaches into his suit and pulls out a card with a logo of the record company in the right-hand corner, along with his name and contact details. He hands it to us.

"This is my card," he goes on. Mark takes the card from him. "I look forward to working with you and putting together a record. I have arranged to set up your first sound recording this Sunday. I have also managed a limo to come pick up from your home to our recording studio."

I wasn't expecting for us to start recording straight away. I wasn't even sure if I could do it on Sunday as this weekend is already hectic for me. It was bad enough that tonight was the rehearsal dinner for the wedding on Saturday. Thankfully, my dad's brother was taking care of my brothers and I while Dad is off on his honeymoon for the week. At least I won't have a problem with Kaiden and Jackson this Sunday. Uncle Harley can deal with them while I live my future.

***

I sulk in the front seat of Dad's car when I wasn't allowed to go off with the band to explore the city, finding where we could go to have a victory lunch. If Dad was any other parent who wasn't so strict, I would be out celebrating with my bandmates. But instead I'm sitting in the car beside him as he drives through the city traffic.

"Rather than sitting there sulking, do you want to tell me why you took off to Mark's this morning and entered the contest without telling me?"

"Because you would have said no," I say without making eye contact with him, staring out the window. "As it is held on Friday, you would say that school is more important."

"That's right, Tessa. School is important, and I'm very disappointed you skipped school. Your grades in your school report are terrible." He slows down to stop at a red light.

"Well, I'm sorry for being a terrible student." I turn to face him. "I'm sorry for not living with the expectation of not being a straight A's student you want me to be. School just has never been an interest in me."

Dad keeps his eyes ahead, waiting for the light to turn green. His hands grip a hold of the steering wheel tightly. "I never asked or expected you to be a straight A's student. All I have ever asked you was to get good grades."

"So what if I don't get good grades? It's not like I'm going to university. Now that my band has won the contest and we have gotten a record deal, my music career is all set. Who cares about education?"

Dad chuckled, stepping on the accelerator when the light turned green. Of course he would laugh. He has never believed in my music. Sometimes I wonder what it would be like if Mum was still here. Would he be more supportive? Honestly, I can't wait once I get this deal done, graduate high school in three months, finished my final exams, and then get away from this place. Somewhere I no longer have to deal with Dad or my brothers. Mostly I just want to get away so I didn't feel so haunted by Casey's present.

"You think you can make it into the music industry?" Dad says. "Tessa, not every band will make it big. You might as well get a good education so you can get a good job."

I roll my eyes. "Whatever."

Dad slows down for another red light. "I don't understand what has gotten into you lately, Tessa. It's like you don't seem to care about anything anymore. I understood when your grades slipped a little after your mother died, but it has been eight years, Tessa."

I sigh. I was sick of this. How could he be so oblivious to what was going on in my life and not understand why I kept failing school? Oh right, because he is far too busy with other priorities than worrying about me.

"Of course you don't understand what has gotten into me lately. You're busy telling me off whenever Jackson or Kaiden do something to annoy me. You let them get away with *everything* instead of disciplining them, and blame me for their misbehaviour."

Dad turns to face me this time, narrowing his eyes at me. With one hand on the steering wheel, he points his finger at me with his other hand. "Don't you tell me how to discipline you three kids. I have to raise the three of you on my own. It hasn't been easy, Tessa. Especially when the boys were barely one year old, and I also had a job I had to juggle to keep the food on the table and a roof over our head."

"Right, Dad. All of your attention was on Jackson and Kaiden. You hardly ever paid attention to me. When I was struggling with my school work, you didn't help me when I needed help with my homework. It was all about Kaiden and Jackson."

Someone behind us honks their horn at Dad. He turns ahead to see a green light and moves forward.

Dad takes a deep breath, exhaling it slowly before speaking. "I'm sorry if you feel like I have abandoned you, Tessa. It's not like I have done it on purpose. It wasn't easy for me to take care of the twins on my own without your mother's help. If it was just one of them, maybe I could have helped you with your school work more.

Twins are a handful. Raising just one baby is a handful. Their needs were demanding and by the end of the day I was exhausted. You may not understand this, but when you have children of your own someday, Tessa, you will understand how I feel, especially if you have to do everything on your own."

I see the frustration from the side of his face. It was clearly I was pushing him to the edge, but I didn't care. I don't know why he even cares about me now. No. It's more than caring about me. It's more like telling me what to do after not parenting me for the past several years.

"Dad, I have been trying to get your attention for years, but you never paid attention. I get it. You were mourning Mum. So was I. But if everything was so much for you, why didn't you just allowed Grandma or Grandpa or even Uncle Harley and Aunt Susan to take the twins for a while so you could also have time with me? You only asked for help when you needed a break from yourself. But you never really paid any attention to me. The only person who ever cared about me was Casey. She was there for me when I needed comfort from Mum. She helped me with my school work when I needed help because I was too ashamed to ask the teacher for help. And when I asked you if I could learn how to play the guitar, it's like you only sent me to lessons to get me out of your hair for a while."

As soon as I realised I had said Casey's name, I feel the guilt rising up deep inside of me, tears prickling my eyes. Casey was always there for me, but in the end when she needed me, I wasn't there for her. *Our friendship has been over since U began getting jealous when I started dating Mark, n when I started hanging out with the band.* Why did I say those things in my last text message to her? Was Casey really the jealous one? Or was I just selfish and ungrateful?

When I don't go on to say anything for a few minutes, Dad goes on. "Tessa, I understand the stress you must be going through with your school work, along with your HSC trail exams coming up in a few weeks after the school holidays, and having Casey's death on top of it doesn't help. But it doesn't mean you can rebel and skip school whenever you feel like it. I gave you an option to stay home yesterday because I thought it would be best for you because your best friend had died. I didn't give you permission to skip school to attend a contest in hope to score a record deal that may never get you anywhere in life. Not everyone makes it in the music industry."

I roll my eyes as I cross my arms across my chest. "Whatever. Skipping was worth it because now I do have a record deal. MTripleT is going to make it big. You will see."

I wait for Dad to spit back an insult about my band. Instead he says, "When we get home, Tessa, I want you to go to your room. I also want you to be ready by four thirty for the wedding rehearsal dinner tonight."

I groan. "I'm not going to it."

"Yes, you are. You aren't getting out of it, Tessa."

"But I want no part of your and Hazel's stupid wedding."

"Look, Hazel is going to be a part of this family whether you like it or not."

"But she isn't my mother."

Dad shakes his head, slowing down at another red light. "No. She isn't your mother. I'm aware of that, Tessa. I'm not replacing her. I love your mother and I always will. But I also love Hazel, and I want you to respect my decision to remarry. Besides, you need to come. Hazel loves you and is excited to have you as her stepdaughter. She chose to have you as one of her bridesmaids."

"I don't want to be a stupid bridesmaid. I don't want to be a part of this wedding. I just..."

I didn't know how to finish the sentence. Truth be told I had no idea what I wanted. A recording contract for my band wasn't the only thing I wanted in life. For the past eight years I had wished for my family to be the same as it was before my mother had died. But mostly I wished I had fixed whatever dispute Casey and I had so we were still friends and not enemies. I wished I was with her when she was going through a rough time. The bullying I caused for her wouldn't have helped on top of the problems she had with her parents divorcing.

I wish... I wish Casey was here. I wish I had my best friend standing in front of the stage. She had promised me she will be in the front row of my very first concert. Not seeing her there today made me realise how much I missed her, and what a bitch I have been to her. If I didn't treat her like crap, she would still be here.

Without saying anything else, I unbuckle my seat belt, reaching for the door handle before the light turns green. I couldn't be in the same car as Dad. I needed to clear my mind, and I couldn't do it with Dad lecturing me.

"Where are you going, Tessa?" he demands. "Get back in the car!"

I ignore him and slam the door shut. I hear Dad's door open and then closed, horns honking from cars behind him. I don't look back at him as I walk down the street, clenching my fist. Tears threatened to fall, but my anger stopped them.

"Tessa Elizabeth Ross, you get back here this instant!"

He reaches me, ignoring the insults drivers yelled out to him for abandoning his car in the middle of the road. He grabs my arm and swirls me around. A few people stare at us as they walked pass us as I fight my dad's hand off me.

"Just let me go, Dad!" I scream at him.

Dad drops his hand from my arm. His eyes narrow at me, and the look in them terrified me. Dad had been mad at me so many times that I didn't feel any fear towards him, except laugh in his face when he gets upset with me. But this time it was like he was a different person. It was a side I have never seen before. This time my behaviour has really pushed him over the edge. And if we weren't out here in the public eye, I'm sure Dad would have smacked me across the face or something.

"Get in the car, Tessa," he scolds. "Today is not a good day to piss me off. I need you to cooperate with me. Tomorrow is a very important day to me. Now I know what you think of Hazel, and I know she isn't your mother. All I want you to do right now is get along with Hazel."

I roll my eyes. Dad has been trying a year and a half for me to get along with Hazel. I don't see our relationship ever improving.

"And all I want is for you to leave me alone," I tell him. "I'm tired of hearing about you, Hazel and the stupid wedding. For the past few weeks has been stressful for my band and I so we could make it into the contest. And Casey's death doesn't help as she is piled on all of the stress I'm going through. I just want to hang out with my friends to celebrate our win. And that's exactly what I'm going to do. I will be home later in time for your stupid wedding rehearsal."

Without another word, I turn from Dad and head down the street. Dad doesn't even try to call me back this time.

Chapter 12
Casey

I wasn't expecting to hear about Kale Ross and Hazel Franklin's engagement all over Facebook. I was expecting to hear about it from Tessa first, who I knew had a lot to say about her father dating this woman. It may have been seven years since her mother passed away, but Tessa was still very attached to her. She didn't like the idea of her father dating another woman that wasn't her Mum. I never quite understood why Tessa disliked Hazel so much or couldn't be happy for her dad. It had been hard for him and Tessa for so long when Mrs Ross passed away. It was good to see Mr Ross happy again, settling back down now that the twins were older and didn't need so much attention.

I couldn't imagine being in Tessa's position. I have no idea what it would be like if one of my parents were to start dating someone else now that they are going through a divorce. I couldn't believe how it has been three weeks already since they made the announcement. None of us have heard from Dad, and Mum was finally getting up and doing things rather than lying in bed, feeling sorry for herself. So far she hasn't been drinking, and I was thankful she wasn't, but I couldn't say for sure how long she would be sober for. I don't see Mum dating again, but Dad was more likely to find someone. If any of my parents was to find someone new, I would be disappointed at first, but I'm sure I would be happy for them. As long as they find joy in what they do, then it's what makes me happy too.

Tessa picked me up Monday morning in a bad mood. Her brothers aren't in the back seat, and my guess she had gotten into a fight with her father and decided not to take her brothers to school. She refuses to take her brothers to school whenever she gets into arguments with him in the mornings. The way she looked like she might explode, I don't dare to ask questions or say anything as we drove to school. I haven't seen her on the weekend or spoken to her as she was with Mark and also started practicing with the band, in which they named themselves M Triple T. Her bad mood wasn't because it was Monday, the day no one seems to like. She was mad because, like me, she had found out by Facebook that her father was engaged.

"I'm his daughter, for crying out loud!" she said where we stand outside on the kerb at the front entrance of the school. I have to somehow calm her down before we enter the school. For the last five minutes since Tessa had arrived, she has been ranting on and on about the news. I'm surprised she didn't call me last night, but waited until today to let go whatever is on her chest. Perhaps she was just too angry to call me last night. "I should have been the first to know. Not the stupid media."

I nod. "Yes, he should have told you."

"He didn't tell me anything until I confronted him last night when I found a news link on Facebook about the engagement. They have only been dating for four months. Four months! How can they decide to get married so early? Shouldn't they date each other longer before taking that step?"

"Everyone is different, Tessa. It took my parents three years before they decide to get married. But that was only because my mum was pregnant with Corey."

Tessa nodded. "I understand. My parents dated maybe for a year before they got married. But it's four months, Casey! How can you get to know someone in that time frame?"

I couldn't give Tessa an answer. What would I know about dating when I have never dated anyone before? I guess in a way every relationship is different. Some people move fast, others move slower.

"Maybe they felt ready to take the next step in their relationship," I suggested.

Tessa chuckled, leaning her back up against the green fence that surrounded our school. She crossed her arms across her chest. "It's more like they are engaged to make themselves look good. Maybe boost the ratings for their show."

I don't tell Tessa what I really thought, but I didn't believe that was any of the reasons why her dad and Hazel were getting married. I'm sure they're very much in love, and I'm quite happy for Mr Ross. Over the last several years I have seen how devastated he had been when his wife died, working hard to do everything on his own. I'm glad he has found someone he can settle down with.

I just wished Tessa could be happy for her father.

I glanced at my watch to see that we had ten minutes until the bell rings. "Come on, Tessa. Calm down, and let's head inside."

Tessa doesn't move from her spot. It was like she didn't even hear me, or just didn't want to take notice of what I had said. Her eyes are full of anger, and maybe if we weren't on school property, there was a chance she would have punched something or someone. Anything to let her anger go.

"I really can't believe this," she continued on ranting. "It's crazy to get engaged to someone within four months. It's like you're marrying someone you have only just met."

I don't respond to her outburst. It wasn't my place to say that two grown-ups who have decided that spending the rest of their lives with each other was something I had no say on. Maybe if they had just met I would advise them to wait a little longer, but I'm sure Mr Ross and Hazel knew what they were doing. I would never tell Tessa this, but I really do think they make the perfect couple.

"What did Jackson and Kaiden say about the engagement?" I asked instead.

Tessa clenched her jaw together. "Oh, don't get me started on those two. They can't be happier about getting a new mum. I mean, okay, they didn't know our mother, but Hazel isn't their mother. She will never be ours."

I wanted to tell Tessa that if Kaiden and Jackson wanted to see Hazel as their mother figure, then it was best that she allowed them to. I understand she was hurt, but there was no use crushing her own brothers' feelings just because they didn't remember their real mother. But I keep my mouth shut. I didn't want Tessa to let her anger out on me.

I opened my mouth to tell her to let's put all of this aside for now and head inside the school, but Mark calls out to us before I even get a word out. Tessa's face lights up as soon as she sees Mark.

Mark embraced her, pecking her lips. "How are you feeling?"

Tessa rolled her eyes. "I just want to end this nightmare."

"Try not to think about it too much. Come on, let's head inside."

Mark took Tessa's hand. He looked over at me. "Are you coming, Casey?"

I gave him a small smile. "Yeah."

I trailed behind them, keeping a distance between us. My heart sinks with disappointment. Normally I was able to calm Tessa down for anything, but today I wasn't able to. It was like she was happy about seeing Mark then she was seeing me. And usually I'm the first person Tessa would tell if something was on her mind or if something has happened. But when Mark approached her, asking how she was, I couldn't have helped wonder if he was the first to know about Tessa's thoughts on the engagement. And if he was, why wouldn't Tessa tell me, but gladly tell her boyfriend who she had only been dating for a week about the engagement of her father and Hazel Franklin. Surely that's something you would tell your best friend, isn't it?

I'm not jealous. At least I think I'm not jealous.

I brushed off the feeling. I'm sure I'm just overthinking it all.

***

Tessa and I headed to the library at lunch. The library wasn't a place she wanted to be caught dead in, but sometimes she likes to go in there when she needs some peace and quiet to write song lyrics. While she worked hard on her song, I made a start on my homework.

I glanced up at Tessa a few times as she scribbled words down in her lyric book, crossing out something she didn't like. She concentrated hard on whatever she was writing.

When it was five minutes before the fifth period bell rang, the librarian told us to pack up and to get ready to head to class. Tessa and I were seniors so we could stay behind if we had a free period, unlike the grades beneath us who had to leave five minutes before the bell. But we couldn't stay in there today as we had English right after lunch.

Tessa groans, putting her pen down between the pages. "Do we really have to go to English?"

"There isn't really much of a choice with what we have next." I pointed out, packing away my biology book.

Tessa closed her notebook with the pen as the bookmark, and stand up, swinging her bag over her shoulder. "I hate English."

I got up from the table and swing my bag around my shoulder. "You will be fine. Later we can study the questions for the book together."

"Oh, about that," Tessa said as we walked towards the entrance of the library, "I have band practice this afternoon. I don't know when I finish, so maybe don't worry about coming over to work on our homework."

I nodded, pushing open the door and walked out of the library. "That's fine, Tessa."

"Hey, Casey, do you want to come over to listen to the band? We are planning to practice in my garage before Dad comes home."

"I would love to come."

"Great," she said with a smile. "It will be great to know your feedback on what you think of our music."

We head inside the building. We weren't allowed to be inside until the bell rang, but we headed to English anyway, hoping not to be caught by any teachers.

"I would love to hear what you guys have come up with," I said. "Will you be playing the song you have written in the library?"

Tessa shrugged. "I don't know. Maybe not yet. I might play around with the chords in my room later before getting the band to play it."

"What is the song about?"

"It's about my dad and Hazel."

"Oh."

"I just... I feel so angry and hurt by them."

I put a hand on her shoulder and smile. "Hey, don't let any of it get to you so much."

"It isn't easy, Casey. I mean, ever since my mum died, Dad and I never really talked about her, or sat me down to see how I was coping. All he was worried about was how he was going to raise my brothers and me on his own. I understood at the time my brothers needed all of the attention, but it felt like Dad forgotten I was there. He only paid attention to me when teachers would ring him up to let him know my grades were slipping, or when I was in trouble for something. He didn't acknowledge me when I wasn't. And even when my grandparents helped Dad with the three of us for a short while until Dad was capable of doing everything himself, Kaiden and Jackson always got the attention. Everyone felt sorry for them because they would never know our mother."

I didn't know how I could answer Tessa. It was hard to imagine Kale Ross doing this to his own daughter. He was the TV presenter that everyone enjoyed waking up to in the mornings. He had this fun, loving, friendly personality. He was still that person I knew when I first became friends with Tessa. For a while he was a different person when his wife died. At that time he wasn't working on the morning news. That wasn't until three years later when he was offered the job. When his wife died, Mr Ross was working behind the scenes at the TV station before being in front of the camera. Over time his old personality began to show again, but Tessa began to misbehave, which is why he started to be the evil person Tessa made him out to be.

And I was glad I didn't need to say anything to Tessa, because right at that moment the bell rang for fifth period.

***

Mr Ross returned home with Kaiden and Jackson just shortly after Tessa and I arrived with the rest of the band. He was confused at first when he sees the guys setting up the band equipment in the garage. He tells Kaiden and Jackson to head inside.

"Tessa, what is this?" he questioned.

"I'm having band practice."

Mr Ross doesn't look impressed, but he nodded. "Alright. Next time let me know if you're having band practice rather than letting me find out when I get home."

Tessa doesn't say anything as her dad headed inside through the garage.

Once everything was set up for band practice, the garage door was rolled down. I sat on a beanbag in the corner, watching them as they performed quietly. I bobbed my head along to the music, enjoying every moment of it. M TripleT have only been together for a week, and already they sounded great, like they have been forming together for so long.

"You are all that I want
I don't ever want to say goodbye
Promise me nothing will ever become between us
And that you and I will always be as one."

At the end of the song I clapped, cheering Tessa and her band on.

"Well done," I said. "You guys are really good."

Tessa smiled. "Thanks, Case."

"Are you going to enter the school's talent quest next month when we return back to school?"

"We haven't decided yet," Mark answered for everyone. "We might, but we want to make sure we are excellent before we decide to perform in front of anyone."

"Well, I'm sure when you do, the audience will love you."

Chapter 13
Tessa

After the argument with Dad, my brain felt like it will explode. I no longer felt the need to celebrate our victory with the band. Even when I do eventually meet up with them, my mind was somewhere else. Everything to do with the wedding, how my life will change, and of course there was Casey, finding her way into my thoughts like she had a place there.

When I do get home, I didn't want to worry about getting ready for the wedding rehearsal dinner. All I wanted was to lie on my bed and just forget the world. I didn't want any more pressure on myself. It made me wonder if Casey was ever under this much pressure. I definitely didn't make it easy on her.

In the afternoon before we leave for the rehearsal my dad's brother, Uncle Harley comes over. He is staying with us for a week while Dad and Hazel go off on their honeymoon. I was thankful I wouldn't be left alone with my brothers for the week. Uncle Harley congratulated me for my win on the contest, which he managed to watch this morning.

After spending some time rehearsing for the wedding, it was time for the dinner. But I didn't take part in anything. I separated myself from the dining room and stepped outside in the garden that surrounded the reception. We will be here tomorrow after the ceremony.

It was freezing outside, but I didn't care. I would rather be cold than be inside with everyone else.

I walk down a path away from the building where a gazebo was beside a pond. I can hear the faint sound of the music coming from the building. I don't think anyone will notice I'm gone. I wanted Mark to come here, but he wasn't invited. Dad wouldn't allow him to come for whatever reason. Casey should be here. Hazel said to bring her along so I had a friend at the wedding. The thought of Casey being here brought tears to my eyes. Why did I ever act like a bitch to her? If I wasn't so cruel to her, she wouldn't have taken her own life, and she would be here with me right now.

I sit down on the white stone bench, looking out over the water. Sitting out here helped me to relax, and it made me wished I had my lyric book with me. I wasn't able to bring it with me and right now jotting words down for a song would be great right now. I was in a great environment that would help me with inspiration. Maybe I will jot down words on my phone.

I was just about to pull it out of my purse when a voice startles me from behind, pulling me away from my thoughts.

"Shouldn't you be inside, Tessa?" I turn around to see my Uncle Harley walking over to me. "You will be missing all the fun. Your Dad would be disappointed if you missed out on it."

I chuckle. "Trust me, Uncle Harley, but my dad probably wouldn't care less if I was here or not. When he is around Hazel, he doesn't care about me."

Uncle Harley sits down beside me. "That's not true, Tessa. Your father loves you very much."

"Bull crap he does. He never pays any attention to me."

"I know it sounds like it, Tessa, but he really does care. Look, I know for the past several years since your Mum had died, and your relationship with your father hasn't been great. But never think he doesn't love you."

"He has a funny way of showing it."

"I know he does. So anyway, your father told me about your friend. I'm sorry to hear. I'm here for you if you want to talk."

I smile at my uncle. He wasn't around most of the time since he lived three hours away. He was someone I could talk to and he wouldn't jump to conclusions like Dad would. Uncle Harley looked similar to Dad that you would think they're twins. Only Uncle Harley is five years younger than Dad and is a lot calmer than him. Maybe it was because he lived in the rural area away from the city. He wasn't married with kids. He says he doesn't think he is marriage material.

"Thanks Uncle Harley, but I'm okay," I tell him.

He doesn't believe me. Of course, he is the school counsellor at the high school in his hometown. He probably deals with a lot of crazy stuff teens get into. He would definitely know when I'm lying about what I feel about Casey. Unlike Dad, he knew when Casey and I were fighting and was no longer friends. He had wanted me to work things out with Casey, but I didn't want to.

"Tessa, what happened to Casey is very serious. You don't need to talk if you aren't ready, but I don't want you to keep everything bottled up inside. I want you to feel comfortable talking to someone. You don't have to talk to your father or me about it."

I sigh with frustration. Why does everyone think I'm not coping well with Casey's death? I'm coping fine. I don't need to discuss my problems with anyone, and it's no doubt Dad has told him everything. But at least Uncle Harley understood my need for space and wasn't expecting me to tell him exactly how I feel like Dad would.

"I don't want to talk about Casey," I answer.

He nods. "That's fine, Tessa. So, what's happening with your band now that you have won the contest?"

I smile brightly, excited to tell him everything that was happening with the band. Only he and Casey ever took an interest in my music. I had always hoped Dad would be interested, but he never was. He still hasn't congratulated me on my win personally, except for in front of the camera. If Dad doesn't want to know my music, then fine. At least my uncle is keen to know. I tell him how my bandmates and I were meeting Zane Maddox on Sunday.

Uncle Harley pats my back. "I'm proud of how far you have come with your band."

"Thanks Uncle Harley. Will you come to my first concert?"

"Of course I will kiddo. Now why don't you come on inside?"

I glance over at the building. I imagine everyone inside having a good time. Definitely no one was in a hurry to think about me or my whereabouts is at the moment, besides Uncle Harley. Dad hasn't come to find me. "I'm going to stay out here for a little while longer, Uncle Harley."

He nods as he stands up from the bench. "Okay. Well, I'm going to head back inside. Don't stay out here for too long."

***

I lie awake in my bed. I should be getting all the rest I can for the wedding tomorrow, but sleep was the last thing on my mind. I wanted to pull out my guitar to keep my mind distracted, but with it being one in the morning, I couldn't make a sound. Dad would kill me if I kept him up for his big day.

In the morning, I don't even bother to get ready for the wedding. Dad knocked on my door at five thirty to make sure I was up. But instead of getting changed into the peach-coloured dress Hazel wanted me to wear, I changed into a pair of jeans, a t-shirt and a hoodie. I couldn't deal with the wedding night now. I needed to get out of here.

I hurry down the stairs and out the door. I don't take my car. A walk and fresh air will help me to clear my mind. I set my phone to silent, knowing Dad was going to call me non-stop, asking me where I was.

I push the wedding out of my head. I didn't want to think about it. I didn't want to think about Casey either, but she is what continued to cloud my mind. If she was here, she would be over at my house to help me get ready for the wedding. She would be keeping me calm and telling me not to stress out so much. She would also tell me not to worry so much about Hazel. Casey understood how I felt about Hazel and never forced me to like her like Dad does, but she did encourage me to give her a chance. But of course I never did. I couldn't understand why I had to accept Hazel as my soon to be stepmother.

I had no idea where I was going. All I could think about is getting away for a while. I needed to clear my head before my band and I meet with Zane Maddox tomorrow. I didn't want my mind to be focusing on anything other than my music. But Casey of course wasn't going to allow me to be free from not thinking about her.

I thought back to the night when she ended her life. What was going through her head? When she went for a walk that night, did she know she wanted to go to the highway? Or was it something she just headed to without thinking? I beat myself for being the horrible friend I was. Why wasn't I there for her? Why did I turn my back to her? Why didn't I recognise the signs of her being depressed? But then again depression doesn't always have symptoms. No one is a mind reader, so there was no way of knowing what was going on in Casey's mind when she made the choice to suicide. It's like the brain tricks your emotions to act like nothing is the matter. In school I remember her trying to put on a smile, even when I bullied her.

I soon find myself at the highway. Standing on the side of the road gave me the chills. How did Casey feel when she was standing alongside the road? What was going through her mind at the time?

Corey and I texted last night. He told me that he had placed a bouquet of Casey's favourite flowers beside a tree on the side of the road where she had gotten hit. I walk along the road until I see the pink and orange lilies resting up against the tree. I ignore the traffic and everything around me as I approach the tree.

On the road I see the skid marks from the vehicle that hit her. I immediately transport myself to the night, seeing the car slam into her. The image brings tears to my eyes. When she sent me her last text, why didn't I take notice what she was planning to do? Even if we weren't friends, I could have stopped her.

I fell to my knees on the grass, letting the tears fall as I stare at the flowers.

"I'm sorry, Casey," I say in a whisper. "I'm sorry about everything."

***

"What are you doing here, Tessa?" Mark asks me when he opened the door for me, allowing me into his home. "Shouldn't you be at the wedding? And what happened to you? Have you been crying?"

Mark's house was the only place I knew I could go to as there was no doubt my family would have already left the house. I didn't have a key to get inside, and showing up at the church is the last thing I wanted to do. I don't even want to come home at all knowing how pissed off Dad will be.

"I went to the highway where Casey took her life."

Mark closes the door behind me, and then pulls me into a hug. "You should have told me to come with you, Tessa. You shouldn't have gone there on your own."

I pull away and give him a small smile. "Thanks, Mark, but I really needed to be alone."

He nods, understanding my need for space. He reaches up and touches my cheek, rubbing his thumb against my skin. "Why don't you wash your face? I will meet you in my room."

I listen to him and wander to the bathroom. I stand in front of the mirror. I was a total mess with my eyes all red and puffy. My mascara had smudged, black lines dripping down my face where tears had fallen. I looked like a clown, and I couldn't imagine what people must think when I was walking down the street.

I wash my face clean and then walked up the stairs to Mark's room. He wasn't in his room yet. I grab my boyfriend's acoustic guitar that is resting up against his bedside table. I sit down on the bed with it, strumming a chord. A tune I had in mind for a song was running through my head, so I played it out on the guitar. Later if I don't forget I will write out the notes. Maybe I could work out what lyrics will fit with it. The music instantly makes me feel better.

Mark walks in with two mugs in his hand. I put down his guitar as he sits down beside me, handing me a mug.

"I made us some hot chocolate," he says.

I take the mug, thanking him. Floating on top of the drink was three marshmallows. I take a sip. "Where are your parents?"

"Tomorrow is their nineteenth wedding anniversary, so they decided to get away for the weekend. They decided to go stay on the south coast."

The conversation I had with him the other day about this sprung to my mind. "Oh yeah. I remember you telling me about it. I completely forgot about it. And they didn't think to take you with them?"

Mark shrugs. "I didn't care. At least I get the house to myself. Plus, tomorrow we are meeting up with Zane."

I nod. As much as I have been looking forward to going to Mad Star Records for months since we found out about Battle of the Bands, now that we finally got what we wanted I suddenly didn't care about it. All I could think about was Casey. My mind wasn't on music today.

"Mark, please don't hate me, but is it possible to postpone our meeting with Zane tomorrow?" I ask him. "Just for this week only or until after Casey's funeral. I feel like everything is too much for me at the moment. I don't want to disappoint you, Tim or Travis. We have worked so hard to get where we need to be. I don't want us to lose this opportunity because I decide to postpone the meeting."

Mark puts his mug down on his bedside table. He then puts one arm around my shoulder while he stroked my face with his other hand. "Tessa, I'm not mad at you for wanting to postpone the meeting. Tim and Travis may be a bit annoyed at first, but they will understand. The last few days haven't been easy after what happened to Casey. I'm sure Zane will understand when I explain it to him."

I smile at him. "Thank you, Mark, for understanding."

He returns the smile. "It's alright. Your mental health is far more important, Tessa."

I place the mug beside Mark's and then hug him. "Do you think on Monday we could perform an acoustic version of *Forget It* for Mrs Grove?"

"What about the song we were originally going to perform?"

I shake my head. If only Mark knew what the song was really about, he wouldn't want to perform it. And I'm not planning to tell him the true meaning behind it. "I don't want to perform it anymore."

He doesn't ask questions. He rubs his hand up and down my back. "Okay, we will perform it. Why don't you rest here? I will call Tim and Travis to let them know what you want to do. I will then call Zane. When I come back, we will rehearse the song."

I thank him and he gives me a quick peck before leaving the room. I sit there for a few minutes and then grab his guitar, strumming chords.

Chapter 14
Casey

The first thing I did as soon as I woke up on Friday morning was text Tessa a happy birthday. It was the last day of school, and I couldn't wait to give the present I had for her. We have been best friends for eleven years now, and I wanted to do something special to celebrate our friendship. Growing up we were never crazy about parties, and were always happy spending our birthdays with each other or our families rather than inviting our classmates. Today I wanted to do something different than having a birthday dinner with just family and us.

I knew what I had planned for her tonight she will definitely enjoy. My only hope is that her mood doesn't change by the afternoon, and doesn't get in an argument with her father or brothers, especially when I had planned it for a month. Yet when it comes to music, I'm sure she wouldn't turn down the offer. Whatever her mood is, Tessa always says music helps her to keep calm and relax.

Tessa pulled up outside my house around eight o'clock. I skipped down the path, excited to tell my best friend the surprise I had for her seventeenth. But I had to hold my excitement when I climbed into the front seat. Tessa looked like she may scream or lose it at any moment. Her brothers Kaiden and Jackson were in the backseat with smiles on their faces. I wondered what they have done to make Tessa so stressed. At least we didn't have far to go to their school.

"Morning Tessa," I closed the door and glanced over at the boys. "Morning Kaiden, Jackson."

"Morning Casey," the twins said, innocently.

I put on my seat belt as Tessa pulled away from the kerb.

We were on the road for only a second when the twins started causing trouble for Tessa. They made fun of her for no reason at all. Tessa clenched her teeth together, ready to explode. Luckily their school was only five minutes away. I don't think Tessa would last another moment in the car.

She pulled up outside the school, and spun around in her seat. "Get out of my car, you little brats."

"I'm telling Dad on you for calling us brats," Kaiden said as he and Jackson scooted across the seat on my side.

"Whatever. Just get out of the damn car."

Jackson gasped. "You said damn."

"And I will say more bad words if you don't get out of the car."

Kaiden opened the door. "You will be in huge trouble later."

"Get out of the car before I drag you out."

"Bye Casey," the boys said as they scooted out the door. "Bye Tessa."

"Bye guys," I said. "Have a nice day."

Jackson shuts the door behind him.

Tessa waited until her brothers stepped away from the kerb, and then pulled away. Neither of us said anything for the next few minutes until we were further away from the school. I was almost afraid to speak, unsure how much time Tessa needed to cool down.

"Should I ask how your birthday is going?" I asked.

Tessa shook her head. "I'm sick and tired of Kaiden and Jackson. My Dad doesn't even do anything to discipline them. It's like he doesn't give a damn what they do to me."

"So you didn't have a great morning?"

"No. I will never have a good morning with my brothers around. Every morning they have to come into my room to wake me up. They won't even let me have at least five more minutes to sleep in. Dad doesn't even tell them to stay out of my room. Instead, he yells at me for yelling at them. Oh, and then Dad said Hazel will be coming for dinner." She sighed with frustration. "I don't want her at our place for dinner. Not on my birthday."

I smiled, not being able to hold the excitement any longer. But I will wait until we get to school. That way I don't have to worry about her crashing the car from being excited over my present for her. "What if I told you that you don't have to worry about having Hazel there for dinner?"

"What do you mean?" Tessa asked, slowing down at a red light.

"I will tell you once we get to school."

"Why not now?"

"It's a surprise."

***

Tessa found a parking spot on the side of the road outside our school. She switches off the engine and turned to face me as she unbuckles her seatbelt. "Okay, spill. What is your surprise?"

I smiled brightly, excited to see her reaction when I tell her what I had planned for her. "You know how the bowling alley had renovated several months ago, and we spoke about going to the karaoke bar they had built? Well, for your birthday I have booked a room for tonight. And as it's your birthday, the bowling alley is preparing the food for you."

Tessa's mouth drops wide opened. She squealed and then pulled me into a hug. "Thank you so much, Casey. I love you so much."

I smiled, resting my chin on her shoulder. "I knew you would like it. I thought it would be great to celebrate our eleventh year of being friends."

Tessa pulled away. "And it's a perfect way to spend it on my birthday."

We climbed out of the car, crossing the road to the entry of the school.

"Hey, Case, do you think it will be okay if I invite Mark along too? He had asked me if I was doing anything for my birthday, but I wasn't sure what our plans were."

My heart sinks in my chest. There was nothing wrong with Mark, and I quite liked him, happy Tessa had found someone. But I wanted the day to be about us, our friendship. There was nothing wrong with Tessa spending time with Mark, but since they began dating, Mark was a part of everything we did. It felt weird to have him with us when it has always been just Tessa and I. Tonight I just want it to be about us and no one else.

I smiled, not wanting Tessa to know what I really thought that could ruin this day. Now that we're in that new stage of our life where dating will become a part of our friendship, I had to adjust to it. After high school we will probably go off to do our own thing. "Sure, he can come."

"Thank you so much, Casey. I couldn't ask for a better friend." She gives me another hug.

"Hey, Birthday Girl."

Tessa pulled away from me and we turned to see Mark heading over to us. Tessa gets excited when she sees him and runs over to him. He gave her a kiss before pulling her into a hug.

"How's my Birthday Girl doing?" he asked.

"Great!"

Mark looked over at me and smiled. "Morning, Casey. How are you?"

I returned the smile. "Morning, Mark. I'm good."

"Oh, Mark, how do you feel about karaoke?" Tessa asked him.

"It's alright," he answered.

"Would you like to come to karaoke with us tonight? Casey booked a room for us at the karaoke bar at the bowling alley. Everything is set up for my birthday."

Mark nodded. "Sure. I will be happy to come. I will see if Tim and Travis are able to come if that is alright."

Tessa nodded. "Sure, they can come." She turned to me. "Is that alright, Casey? It will be a lot more fun if we had a group of people rather than the two of us."

If she wasn't dating or was a part of a band, Tessa would have been happy with it being just the two of us. But maybe she is right. Maybe adding three more people to the group will be fun.

***

Tessa picked me up after work, and we drive to the bowling alley. Mark and his friends were waiting out front. I shyly greet the guys, unsure about having them here, but I tell myself that tonight will be fun, even if it wasn't just Tessa and I.

The staff gave us our room, and told us to settle in while they prepared our food for the party. We had the room booked for two hours. It was enough for us to sing and eat until our time was up.

Being the birthday girl, Tessa went first, belting out her chosen song. I let the guys go before me. I wasn't a great singer like Tessa or her bandmates. My voice was so awful that running for the hills was the best option. I was shy at first about getting up in front of everyone besides Tessa, afraid to know what the guys will think of me, but I quickly pushed aside the fear, and belted out my chosen song. I may have been terrible, but everyone cheered me on.

Half an hour later the staff came in, setting up some finger foods. They also brought out a chocolate cake, singing *Happy Birthday*. They leave us to enjoy ourselves.

"Thank you all for coming here today," Tessa says. "Thank you especially to Casey for organising this night."

I smiled at her. "You're welcome, Tessa."

Tessa cuts the cake for all of us.

Tim then pulled out several cans of beer from his backpack that I didn't realise he had with him. As soon as I see the alcoholic drinks, my stomach twisted into knots. An image of Mum flashes in my mind, her body slumped over the table last night, wine spilled all over the floor. I didn't want this night to end with us being drunk.

"Anyone want a beer?" Tim asked.

Travis wasted no time and grabbed a can, opening it. "Thanks mate." He took a gulp of the drink.

"Mate, how did you sneak these in?" Mark asked.

"Yeah, isn't it wrong to bring your own alcohol in here?" Tessa questioned. "We are only seventeen, Tim. We might be kicked out if we can't prove that we aren't eighteen."

Tim shrugged. "I had them hidden in my bag."

"Sweet." Mark reached over and grabbed a can. "Thanks, Tim."

Tim looked over at Tessa and I. "You girls are free to have one."

Tessa doesn't hesitate to grab a can and opened it.

I, on the other hand, am the only person who doesn't dare to touch it. Staring at the cans of beer reminded me of my mother. I can see her in my mind, passed out on the kitchen table after consuming so much alcohol. I have never touched alcohol in my life, and after seeing what my mother goes through, I don't ever want to drink. The last thing I wanted to do was end up like my mother. With never touching the beverages in my life, I had no idea how well I could hold my liquor. Maybe I could be responsible; maybe I could turn into an alcoholic.

"We shouldn't be drinking this," I spoke up. "None of us are eighteen. Where did you purchase this?"

"I didn't purchase it," Tim answered. He grabbed a can. "I took whatever was in the fridge at home. My parents have been allowing me to drink since I was thirteen." He held out the can to me. "Here. Lighten up, Casey, and have a beer. It won't hurt you."

Everyone's eyes are on me as I stared at the can in Tim's hand. Tessa glanced between me and the group, biting her lip. She then looks directly at me, her eyes pleading with me to just take the drink. I shook my head. I can't take it, and I won't dare become like my mother.

"Oh, for crying out loud, Casey, just take the damn thing," Tessa said. "Who cares if we can't legally drink until next year? There is nothing wrong with having one drink."

I turned to her. She knows very well I won't ever touch it, and what I go through with my mother. So why was she forcing me to drink it now? "You know I don't want to, Tessa."

"Stop being a wimp, Casey, and drink it." She reached over and opened the can.

My heart sunk to the bottom of my stomach. Why was Tessa being like this? She would never force me to drink, not with the way I felt about my mother. Was it to impressed Mark and her bandmates?

I take a sip of the beer. The last thing I wanted was for an argument to break out at the party I had planned. The guys aren't even supposed to be here. This was meant to be a night with just Tessa and I having fun. Not getting drunk when we are not at the legal age until next year. The last thing I wanted on my best friend's birthday was to be kicked out of here for being intoxicated, or be arrested for underage drinking.

As soon as the bitter taste of the beer touches my tongue, I pushed the can away in disgust, not sure how anyone could like the taste. I reach for a bottle of water to wash out the taste in my mouth. The guys laughed at my reaction.

"Not a big beer drinker, Casey?" Tim asked. "Don't worry. Next time I will make sure to bring something special for you that I'm sure you will like."

There will be no other time, I wanted to say. *This is not how I wanted the party to go. You don't need alcohol to have fun.*

"When's your birthday, Casey?" Tim wanted to know.

"November twelfth," I answered.

"Great! Maybe I could organise your party. I will make sure I will have a variety of different alcoholic beverages for you to try," He gave me a wink.

Don't bet on it, mate, I said to myself. *You won't be invited to my seventeenth.*

I don't answer. There was no point in saying anything. No one understood the reason why I didn't want to drink. Only Tessa understood, but right now she wasn't giving a care in the world. All she wanted to do was impressed the guys. I don't know what has been going on with the band since she had joined or when she started dating Mark, but Tessa had never felt like she needed to impress anyone. She had a mind of her own. I don't understand what has changed.

***

By the end of our session in the karaoke bar, everyone was intoxicated but me. I didn't belong in the room. I wanted the night to end, and get my best friend out of here. The only trouble was I had no idea how I was going to get Tessa home. She had three beers. There was no way she could get behind the wheel. She was a red P-plater, which meant she wasn't meant to have any alcohol while driving. I didn't have a licence so there was no way I could drive us home. I had no money for a taxi. I most definitely didn't want to call Mr Ross to come pick us up. He will literally kill Tessa for drinking. I couldn't take her home so the only option I had was to allow her to spend the night at my place. Mum wouldn't mind her staying for the night.

The only person I could think of to come get us was my brother. I messaged him.

"Thanks for the invite, ladies," Tim said, climbing into the driver's seat of his car. "We should do this again sometime."

Instead of responding to his comment, I said, "You shouldn't be driving if you have been drinking."

Tim doesn't respond as he shuts the door. I have no idea if he had heard me or just chose not to listen to a word I had said. I'm not sure how much Tim has had to drink, but I don't know how he could think it was okay to drink and drive, especially with other people in the car.

"Chill, Casey," Travis said, pulling opened the door of the front passenger side. "We will be fine." He climbed into the car.

I shake my head. "No, you won't be fine."

"Who are you to tell us what to do?" Tim said with annoyance and anger mixed in his voice, winding down his window. "Mind your own damn business."

His tone startles me, and I take a step backwards, terrified of what he might do to me if I questioned him again.

Tim leans out the window glancing over at Mark who had Tessa pinned against the back of the car, one hand cupped on her jaw, the other under her shirt, while Tessa's arms were wrapped around his neck. "Hey, do you think you guys can get a room? Let's go, Mark."

Mark obeys his friend, and told Tessa he will see her tomorrow. He then climbs into the back seat. None of the guys say goodbye to me as Tim backs out of the parking lot.

"Mark is such a great guy, don't you think?"

I turned to her. "We need to get you home, Tessa."

"Yes, we need to." She patted her jeans. "Where are my keys?"

I took her hand. "Don't worry about your keys, Tessa. You're not driving home. You are drunk. You can't drive."

Tessa laughed like what I had said was all just one big joke. "Don't be silly, Casey. I'm not drunk."

She pulled her hand out of my grip, and turned to walk towards her car that's parked next to where the guys' car had been. Only Tessa doesn't make it to the car. She tripped over her own two feet and landed on her knees with her hands out in front of her. She burst into laughter and didn't care if she might have hurt herself.

I helped her up. Her palms had scrapes on them, but Tessa doesn't notice the blood on them. She is still laughing her head off.

"You're not driving home," I told her. "Corey is coming to pick us up."

"Corey?" Tessa jumped up and down excitedly, clapping her hands together. "I love Corey. Hey, Casey, did you know your brother is great in bed?"

I had no idea how to respond to her question. It's not something I wanted to answer or even cared what goes on in my brother's love life.

"Did I ever tell you that I lost my virginity with your brother?"

I stand there still, the colour draining from my face when she said it. "What?"

Tessa went on excitedly telling me how she and Corey slept with each other for the first time when we went on the camping trip a few years back. She had lied about meeting some guy from another camp just so she didn't worry me about sleeping with my brother. I had no idea what to say or how I should react. How do you react when your best friend and brother had been sleeping with each other behind your back? I wasn't sure if I should believe any of the words coming from Tessa's mouth. This is all drunken talk.

But then again, the truth speaks when you're intoxicated.

Before Tessa could respond, a car pulls up beside me. I'm still registering what Tessa had said that it takes me a few minutes to realise it was my brother's car. His friend Jett is with him, and they both climb out of the car.

"Corey, it's so great to see you!" Tessa stumbled over to him and flung her arms around his neck.

Corey doesn't answer her. He turned to me. "I hope you don't mind I brought Jett with me. He has offered to drive Tessa's car so it isn't left here."

I give him a half smile, unsure how I felt towards my brother at the moment after what Tessa had said. How could either of them not tell me they had hooked up? "Yeah, that's fine, Corey."

"Do you have the keys?" Jett asked.

Tessa removed her arms from around my brother and turned to his friend. "I don't know. I think I lost them."

I rolled my eyes, annoyed with the guys for making Tessa this way. Some bandmates they are. It makes me wonder what stuff they would get up to when they become famous. I point to Tessa's small bag around her shoulder. "The keys should be in your bag."

Tessa opened her bag and pulled out her keys. "Oh, here they are!"

She walked over to her car to unlock it, but Jett takes them off her.

"Thanks, Tessa," he said. "I'm going to drive your car back to Corey's. Corey is going to drive you home."

Corey linked his arm around Tessa. "Come on, Tessa. Let's get you home."

Tessa willing allowed Corey to lead her to his car. He opened the door to the back seat. I then climbed into the back with my friend.

"Thank you, Corey, for coming to get us," I said before my brother closed the door on me.

He returned a smile. "It's not a problem, Casey."

***

I was thankful Mum was out with her sister tonight rather than being at home. I didn't want her to see my best friend like this. She will start asking questions like where did we get the alcohol, and if I too have been drinking. She will be on the phone then to Mr Ross to inform him that Tessa had been drinking. The two of us will be grounded.

Corey had to pull over on the side of the road at one time when Tessa claimed she didn't feel too well. We pulled out front of someone's house as she vomited on the grass on the side of the kerb. She apologises to us for being sick.

Jett turned up at the house before we did, parking Tessa's car on the street. I thanked him for driving the vehicle home. Corey then helped me to get Tessa in doors. We stumbled to my room. Corey then went to fetch a glass of water for Tessa. Meanwhile I helped Tessa out of her clothes. She had a bit of vomit on her shirt which smelled of alcohol. I give Tessa a pair of my pyjamas for her to sleep in. While she changes, I picked up her clothes and head to the laundry to wash them.

I'm heading back to my room when I see Tessa and my brother through my opened door. I stand to the side of the wall so neither of them could see me. Tessa was under the blankets, lying down with Corey sitting on the edge of the bed, tucking her in.

"Have I ever told you that I love you, Corey?" Tessa said.

I don't see my brother's face as his back is to me. "No, you haven't. Tessa, don't talk about this here. I don't want Casey to hear. She doesn't know about our hook ups, and I prefer that she doesn't know."

Tessa rubbed her hand up and down my brother's arm. "I love you, Corey."

Corey doesn't respond to her. Does he love Tessa? Or does he not want to say it back in fear I would hear it? Instead, Corey stroked her hair. Tessa then grabbed his shirt and pulled him down on top of her. They kissed slowly. I watched as her arms wrap around his neck, moaning softly.

Tessa's drunken talk was true. She really had hooked up with my brother. My heart sunk deep in my chest. Why hadn't either of them told me they were together? I don't even know how I feel about them. Maybe I would have been okay if they had told me, but they kept the relationship hidden from me.

What hurts the most is that Tessa, my best friend of eleven years, couldn't tell me about her feelings for my brother. Nor could she tell me she had lost her virginity to him. If she had told me, maybe I would have been okay with them dating.

Corey is the first to pull away from Tessa, getting off the bed. "We need to stop, Tessa. I can't let Casey see us."

"I miss you, Corey."

"I miss you too, Tessa. But we can't talk about this here. Not when Casey could hear us."

"She won't know."

I chose that moment to walk in. I put on a smile, pretending to not have heard their conversation or see them make out. "Your clothes are in the washing machine."

Tessa doesn't thank me. She had passed out even though just a few moments ago she had been talking to my brother.

"I will leave you alone," Corey said. "Jett put a bucket on the floor in case Tessa needs to vomit during the night."

"Thank you, Corey."

I wait for him to confess to me about his secret relationship with my best friend, but he doesn't. He said goodnight and then leave my room. I wanted to shout out to him to tell me the truth about what really happened between Tessa and him.

My stomach feels like it had been kicked, and maybe it has been. I turned to Tessa who is fast asleep in my bed. It was too late to make them confess anything. I will talk to them about it in the morning when Tessa is sober.

Chapter 15

Tessa

Home was not the place I wanted to be, but I stay with Mark for most of the day before I headed to my place. No one was there, and I have no idea how long the reception will go for. But when it does, I don't want to know what my punishment will be. Dad and Hazel won't be leaving for their honeymoon until tomorrow, so tonight there will be a lot of screaming and yelling for why I didn't show up for the wedding.

I had no key to get in through the front door, so I had no choice to go around the backyard where I hoped my bedroom window was unlocked. I climb up the drain pipe, and onto the roof of the veranda. The window to my room is opened ajar, and I'm thankful that no one had closed it.

I crawl through the window. I lie down on my bed, turning on my phone where I had turned it off earlier so I don't have to worry so much about Dad contacting me. My home screen was greeted with twenty missed calls – fifteen from Dad, two from Hazel and three from Uncle Harley – and eight text messages – four from Dad, demanding where I am, two from Hazel asking if I was okay and wanted me to contact her as soon as possible, and another two from Uncle Harley, wanting to know where I was and if I was okay. I ignore everyone's message but my uncle's, texting him to let him know I was okay, and where I was this morning. I told him how I needed to clear my head about Casey.

I figured my uncle couldn't get back to me straight away, but he messages me back within seconds. ***I'm glad to know you're alright, Tessa. Everyone has been worried when you walked out without an explanation. Later when I get home I will talk to you. But I will warn you now that your father is extremely furious with you.***

I honestly didn't want to face my father when he returns home, but I knew I would have to eventually. It was either tonight or when he came back from his honeymoon.

I pick up my guitar, and began playing a tune that has been stuck in my head all day while I was at Mark's. I think of Casey as I played. I randomly think of lyrics that I thought would go well with the music.

> *"I'm sorry for all of the things I have done*
> *And I would do everything that I could*
> *To make it all right again*
> *To see the smile I once knew*
> *To hear your voice and your laugh once again."*

I stop playing the chords, setting the guitar aside, and then grab my lyric book from the top drawer of my bedside table. I jot down all of things I have been keeping about Casey inside. I couldn't tell anyone that I'm responsible for killing my best friend. Casey killed herself because of me.

Tears fall as I write. Eventually they blur my vision, and instead of wiping them away, I buried my face in my pillow. I should have done more to help Casey rather than make her feel like she wasn't worth living anymore. She never made me feel like that, so why did I make her feel like that?

***

"TESSA!"

I wake to a dark room a couple of hours later, unaware that I had fallen asleep. Dad yelled out my name, his tone of voice terrifying me. I think to my uncle's text message where he had said how furious Dad was. Now was not the time to act like a total smart ass to him like I always do. I don't even want to know what he is planning to do to me. Would he even accept the reason why I needed to get away?

I sit up just as Dad walks into the room, switching on the light. I'm blinded for a brief second from the light, but my eyes quickly adjusted to the brightness. Dad stands at the door frame, giving me the same expression he had yesterday when we were on the street in the city. The way his eyes were filled with anger and the way his nostrils flared, it was like he was a totally different person and not my father. I couldn't recognise the man standing in front of me.

"Where the hell have you been, Tessa?" he yells at me.

I open my mouth to speak, but no words came out.

Dad slams the door shut and repeated the question.

"I needed to clear my head," I say.

"You needed to clear your head? And you couldn't tell me this or ask if you could leave the house? Have you forgotten what today is?"

"I didn't say a word to you because I knew you wouldn't let me take a walk to clear my head."

"Of course I wouldn't, Tessa! Today is a very important day for both Hazel and I. It's our wedding day! It had been stressful getting ready and hoping nothing would not go wrong. But rather than worrying about the wedding, all I could think is where you have wondered off and if you were safe. I almost called off the wedding to search for you, but your uncle told me not to, that you will come home."

I roll my eyes. That was typical of Dad, always putting his own needs before me. I no longer felt terrified of him. It was clear it wasn't just about me missing the wedding. It was more like how Dad would look at his wedding. I imagine what paparazzi or what the media would say about him when I didn't show up.

"Of course, Dad," I say. "It's all about you, right? You don't give a damn about me. All you care about is your wedding with Hazel. And with me not turning up there, it doesn't make you look good."

Dad clenches his fist together as he strolls across my room. He stands in front of me, raising his arm. I flinch, thinking he was going to hit me, but he doesn't. He only points his index finger at me.

"Don't you dare speak to me like that, Tessa," he says through his teeth. "You know how hurtful it was to not have you there?" He put his arm down by his side. "How worried I was that something could have happened to you when you disappeared?"

"Nothing is going to happen to me, Dad."

Dad rubs a hand over his chin, thinking of what to do with me. "You know, Tessa, I don't want to deal with you right now.

All I want right now is to settle down with my new wife before we go off to our honeymoon tomorrow. So starting from now, you're grounded until Hazel and I return home. You aren't allowed to leave the house, not even to see Mark. And don't think about trying to work around your Uncle Harley because I will make sure he doesn't. Now, there will be no dinner tonight for you. I want you to go straight to bed. If you complain, you will be grounded for another week."

Without another word, Dad leaves the room, slamming the door shut. I sit there for a moment, thinking of what he had said. Tears then hit me, wondering what Dad would think of me if he knew I was responsible for Casey's death. He would think low of me; maybe disown me for bullying my best friend.

***

I wake to a text message in the morning, thankful Dad didn't take my phone from me last night. Mark had message me to let me know that Zane Maddox still wants to see us today even though I had requested to cancel the meeting. We weren't recording any songs, just signing a contract and talking about our future with Mad Star Records. The meeting wasn't until one o'clock. Being grounded, I had no idea how I was going to be able to go. My only hope was that my uncle would understand how much this contract means to me, and he will bend my father's rules.

Hating the idea of getting out of bed and leaving the room in case Dad was still around, I walk downstairs to find my uncle. My brothers were in the lounge room watching the morning cartoons.

They paid no attention to me, and I was surprised they hadn't come into my room this morning. Maybe after what happened last night with Dad and I, they were too scared to enter my room.

Uncle Harley was in the kitchen, sitting at the table reading something from his tablet. He looks up when I come in. "Good morning, Tessa."

I stand at the end of the table, leaning on the chair as I greeted him. "Has my dad left yet?"

Uncle Harley nods. "I drove Hazel and your father to the train station an hour ago."

I smile, glad that I don't have to see my father's face for the week. Soon he and Hazel will be sailing across the South Pacific Ocean to New Caledonia for their cruise. At least a week away from each other will do us good. "Uncle Harley, as you know that I won the contest on Friday, so my band and I have a meeting with the producer of Mad Star Records later today. I know Dad said I'm grounded, but I cannot miss this meeting."

He nods. "Yes, I know this meeting is important to you. I don't know what your dad will say, but since I'm in charge for the week, I'm allowing you to go. But I want you to make sure you come home right after the meeting."

I promise my uncle I will. Why couldn't Dad be more like his brother? Calm and understanding instead of strict. "Thanks, Uncle Harley. You're the best."

"Hey, I'm taking your brothers out for breakfast this morning. Would you like to come along with us?"

My stomach grumbles loudly at the mentioned of food. I could not say no after not eating anything last night.

"Go and get ready so we can head out," my uncle says.

I turn to leave when Uncle Harley calls my name. I turn to face him.

Uncle Harley gestures to the chair I had been leaning on. "Take a seat for a minute, please. Let's chat for a bit before we head out. I won't keep you long."

I listen to my uncle, and sit down. Sometimes I hate how my uncle is a counsellor as he always wants to get you to talk about what is going on in your life. But at the same time, I was thankful I could talk to him about anything, and he will listen without giving me a hard time. Unlike Dad, who will yell at you for your mistakes.

But I knew the one thing I could never do is admit to my uncle that I may be responsible for Casey's suicide.

"Is this about yesterday?" I ask.

Uncle Harley closes the cover on his tablet setting it down on the table before speaking. "Yes, it is about what happened yesterday. You don't have to talk to me about yesterday if you don't want to. But I want you to know that I will not yell at you. Not like the way your father did. I know he isn't good at understanding things. Do you want to start with what made you disappear in the morning rather than getting ready for the wedding?"

I sit there without making any eye contact with my uncle, twiddling my thumbs. "I just felt like I was under a lot of pressure with everything that is going on. My ex-best friend died, to make sure my band wins a record deal, making sure the final assessments are done before the school holidays start in two weeks, and with Dad's relationship moving so fast with Hazel. I mean, they dated for about four months before getting engaged. Although I know Kaiden and Jackson doesn't understand what really goes on, but I just feel so angry that I didn't get a say in all of this, how I felt about

Dad dating again and if I felt comfortable with Hazel becoming my stepmother."

Uncle Harley nods. "Yes, I agree that this is a big step that your father should have discussed with you first to know what you think. I know it has been difficult for your father to raise you three kids, but he needs to think how this affects you too."

"He doesn't think about me."

"When your father returns home, I will talk to him for you. Then, I want the both of you to sit down and talk. It's something you both really need to do."

I chuckle. "That will never work."

"Well, I'm going to make him. It has been eight years since your mother died, and you both really need to talk about your differences. I hate seeing the both of you fight."

I give my uncle a smile even though I knew there was no way Dad would want to just talk.

"So do you want to talk to me about Casey?" he goes on. "Did you manage to clear your head?"

I sit there, not really sure what to say. "I took a walk and ended up where Casey ended her life."

My uncle is quiet for a moment. "I'm sorry, Tessa."

Sorry. That's all everyone seems to know how to say. If anyone should be sorry about what happened to Casey it should be me.

"Tessa, I want you to come to me or to anyone who you feel comfortable with when you're ready to talk about Casey. If you don't want to talk to anyone then use your music. The last thing I want is for you to keep your emotions bottled up inside."

I give my uncle a small smile and then stood up from the chair. "Thanks, Uncle Harley. I'm going to go and get ready now."

Without another word, I head to my room.

Chapter 16
Casey

I don't think I slept at all that night. Besides being up half of the night as Tessa threw up in the toilet, not bothering to use the bucket Corey had left for her, I kept replaying in my head what happened between my best friend and brother.

How could I have been a fool to not know what was going on between them? When I think of it now, it made sense Corey was the guy Tessa had been seeing. We were the only campers. I never once saw another human being when we were at the lake. It hurts knowing neither of them had come forward to let me know there was something going on between them; especially it has been a secret for two years. Okay, I understand why they didn't say anything. They were afraid of what I would say or maybe their relationship would impact mine and Tessa's friendship. But still, I would rather know their secret beforehand instead of finding out through a drunken moment.

Truthfully, I have no idea if I really approve the two of them together. But at the same time, it shouldn't be up to me if they decide to date. Though it would be awesome to have Tessa as my sister-in-law if she and Corey were to get married. Times may have changed now, so who knows if Tessa will still be dating Mark in the next few months. Corey is currently not dating anyone.

I let Tessa continue sleeping in the morning. She will wake up soon. The first thing I do is fetch some pain killers and then head to the kitchen to grab a glass of water for her. Corey is in there cooking eggs and bacon.

"Good morning, Casey," he greeted me. "Did you get much sleep?"

I grabbed a clean glass from the rack on the sink, letting out a yawn. "No, not enough." I turned on the tap, filling the glass.

"Is Tessa up yet?"

I shook my head, turning off the tap once the glass was half full. "Not yet, but I'm going to go and wake her."

Corey nodded, flipping a piece of bacon over. "I have breakfast if you girls would like some."

"Thanks, Corey. I will be out soon."

Taking the glass of water and the pain killers, I head back to my room, setting everything down on the bedside table. I then open the blinds in my room, letting the sunlight sweep in. Tessa groaned at the slightest bit of sunlight, burying her head under the pillow.

"Close the blinds, Casey," she groaned.

I sat down beside her and removed the pillow from her. "Come on. It's time to get up. Corey is making breakfast for us."

"I don't want to get up. Not because it's Saturday, but because it feels like someone is hammering my brain with a jack hammer."

"I know. That's why I left some pain killers and a glass of water for you." I point to the bedside table.

Tessa raised her head to see, but only to groan and put her head back down. "I'm never drinking again."

I tapped her arm gently. "Come on, sit up and take the pain killers to make you feel better."

Tessa doesn't move at first, but after a few minutes she sat up, reaching over to grab the glass and the tablets. Once she swallows the two tablets I had given her, she drank the rest of the water.

I sat there watching her, wondering if she will say anything about what she remembers from last night, but doesn't say a word. I doubt she will say a word to me about her secret relationship with my brother.

Tessa placed the glass on the bedside table and then used her index fingers to rub her temples. "Why did I allow myself to drink so much?" She stopped rubbing them and then jerked her head up at me. "I didn't do something I shouldn't last night, did I?"

Yes, I said silently to myself. *You spill your secret to me about hooking up with my brother. And then last night you made out with him.*

I shook my head. "No, you did not do anything you should. The only thing you did was have your head in the toilet for most of the night."

I should have right there made her confess everything. But I decided not to just to keep the peace. The last thing I wanted was a screaming fight with my best friend first thing in the morning. The screaming wouldn't help Tessa's hangover. I also didn't want my neighbours knowing what has been going on either. It's bad enough they hear my parents fighting.

"Oh, God." Tessa rubbed her fingers over her temples. "My head won't stop throbbing. I shouldn't have drunk so much last night. One should have been enough. I'm sorry, Casey, for keeping you up half of the night."

I gave her a small smile. "It's alright, Tessa. I'm just glad you're feeling okay now, besides having your hangover.

"I should have said no to Tim and listened to you. I know I shouldn't be drinking until next year, but I just wanted to impress the guys, especially Mark."

Of course that's why she went and called me a wimp last night, completely disrespecting my wishes to not drink. I didn't know why she felt like she had to impress Mark or any of his friends. She never had to before she started dating Mark.

"Let's not worry about last night," I said. "The main thing is you had a great birthday. Now I really need to get dress for work. Why don't you take a shower and freshen up, and then join Corey in the kitchen for breakfast?"

Tessa agreed and then left me to get changed.

But Tessa didn't end up going in the shower. Instead she was sitting at the table with Corey with a plate full of fried egg, garlic tomatoes and bacon in front of her. As soon as I saw the two of them together, I lose my appetite. I'm not saying they can't be together, but I just wished I was informed about it. I have to get out of here and think. I couldn't be here with my brother or best friend.

"I'm going to head off to work early," I said. "Thanks for breakfast, Corey. I will see you this afternoon."

"Wait," Tessa said with her mouth full. "Let me drive you to the shopping centre."

I shook my head. "No, Tessa. I don't want you to drive me. What if you pass a police car along the way and you get pulled over for a random breath test? You will be in trouble for drinking. You're a red p-plater, which means you can't drive at all if you choose to drink."

"Nonsense, Casey." Tessa stood up. "I feel fine. I can drive you to work."

"No, Tessa. Alcohol will be in your system for twenty-four hours. I can't let you drive me."

She only laughed. "Relax, Casey. I'm not going to get caught by the police. They won't be around at this time of the morning."

"I don't want you to be in trouble for drink driving or for drinking underage. How would it look with being the daughter of a TV presenter?"

Tessa rolled her eyes. "Who cares about what it looks like for my dad? Just give me a minute, Casey, and I will drive you."

She gets up, leaving her breakfast half eaten on the table, and heads to my room.

"Are you alright this morning, Casey?" Corey asked me. "You seem to have something on your mind."

You know exactly what is on my mind, Corey! I wanted to scream out. *You know exactly what you did two years ago, how you and Tessa have been sneaking around my back. Why didn't either of you tell me what went on between the two of you? If you had told me straight out, I could have felt okay with everything. But knowing it has all been a secret for so long, I don't know what to think of you both.*

"I'm fine, Corey," I answered instead. "I'm going to go. I will see you later. Tell Tessa I said bye."

"I won't be home tonight," he said. "Jett and a couple of my friends are going out."

"Okay, bye."

Without saying anything else, I hurried out of the house before Tessa came out with her car keys. Once out the front door I ran down the front path and down the street before Tessa came after me.

***

I don't talk to Tessa for the rest of the weekend. I don't even contact her to come pick me up after work. I only sent her a message to say I had to work back and I wasn't sure how long I would be. Tessa replied back with an okay, but doesn't question me to why I had walked out on her this morning. She was probably with Mark or was at band practice.

Or maybe she was with my brother? Do they both still see each other secretly behind my back?

Monday morning, she pulled up outside my house to pick me up for school. I was still feeling hurt from the other day, and when I saw her I really didn't know what to think. When I greet her as I climbed into the front seat of her car, my tone of voice wasn't happy to see her. It wasn't like I wasn't pleased to see her; it's just that I still didn't know how I was supposed to feel about her secret.

And I couldn't bring myself to say what I knew. Once I do, our relationship will never be the same again. I can feel it in me of how awkward it will become between us.

Tessa must have sense something was on my mind. As soon as she dropped her brothers off at school, she turned to me and said, "Is something wrong, Casey?"

"I just have a lot on my mind," I answered.

"Do you want to talk? I haven't heard from you since you left for work on Saturday."

"I'm fine. Really."

"Are you sure, Case? You left in such a hurry, even when I said I will drive you."

"I just had to get out of the house and think."

"Is everything okay at home? Have you spoken to your dad?"

I shook my head. "No. I have tried to call him, but he doesn't answer."

"I'm sorry to hear that." Tessa turned into the street our school is on. "You know you can talk to me about it."

I wanted to believe Tessa. I thought I could tell her everything, but it was obvious she was lying to herself. She couldn't even tell me that she had slept with my brother.

Tessa found parking on the street, and together we head towards the entrance of the school where Mark was waiting for us. He greeted his girlfriend with a hug and kiss. He greeted me as well, and then put an arm around Tessa's waist, strolling through the entrance.

I told myself not to be jealous or feel any envy towards Tessa. I have no reason to be. I should be happy for her that she has found someone to be with. Only I wished she wasn't leaving me in the dark. It feels like she was drifting apart from me each time now that she is dating Mark. It's like we never were friends or we were just acquaintances. When I want her, she isn't available because she is with Mark. Or when I plan something with her like on Friday night, Mark has to be a part of it all. I'm sure someday when I began dating I would still want to make time to spend with my best friend. I mean, I know when you start dating that person is the most important thing in the world to you, but so is your friends and family.

For the rest of the day I try to keep my focus on my school work, but my brain felt like it might explode. At lunch Mark and his friends sat with us, but I honestly didn't feel like I belonged within the group. They talked about the weekend, and the music they had been practicing yesterday. No one ever seemed to want to acknowledge me.

"Are you up for studying this afternoon?" I asked Tessa as we leave English for the last period of the day.

"Oh." There's disappointment in her tone, like she wasn't expecting me to come over to work on her homework like we always do whenever we have English during the week. I also help her with maths as both of them are her worse subjects. My maths skills weren't great, but I did okay. "I forgot about you coming over today, Casey."

"What do you mean you forgot I was coming over?"

"Chill, Casey. There is no reason for you to get upset. It just slipped my mind, okay?"

I stopped walking and turned to face her. "But we do this every Monday."

"Well, sometimes things happen and plans change."

I crossed my arms across my chest. "Really? Is that how it is now that you're dating Mark? Or when you joined your band?"

Tessa stared at me with a shock expression across her face. It then turned to a frown. "What is that supposed to mean, Casey?"

"You know exactly what I mean, Tessa. You have been spending more time with them instead of spending it with me. I'm not saying there is anything wrong with you being with them. All I ask you to do is spend some time with me too. We hardly do anything with each other anymore."

She rolled her eyes. "Oh, stop being dramatic, Casey. I don't need your permission with who I want to hang out with."

I started walking backwards to get away from Tessa, still facing her as I spoke. "Whatever. Just forget about me and hang out with Mark. He must be more important than me. I will just do my homework myself, and you can ask Mark to help with yours."

I bumped into someone and they scold at me for not looking out where I was going. I apologised to them and turned the right way, hurrying away from Tessa.

But I don't get far until she is beside me again, walking down the stairs to the first floor.

"What is your problem? I thought you were happy for me and Mark? Why all of a sudden are you against me?"

I don't answer her until we reach the bottom of the stairs. "I'm not against you, Tessa. I'm hurt that you much rather spend more time with Mark than with me."

"Well, I'm sorry that I have a boyfriend and you don't. I'm also sorry that I'm a part of a band and you aren't. But there is no reason for you to get so pissed off with me."

Without another word, Tessa stormed off. I eventually follow her from a distance. But rather heading to her car, I decided to walk home. There was no way she will let me get in the car after our disagreement. It wouldn't be good if we were sitting in a closed space together.

I had only walked a few metres away from the school when a car pulled up alongside me. I didn't turn to see who it was and was about to break out into a run in case it was someone ready to abduct me. But I relaxed when I hear the familiar voice.

"You know something, Casey?" Tessa yelled out to me from her car. "I really don't know why you're so jealous about Mark. You are acting like you own me, which you don't, Casey."

I stopped walking and turned to face her. She hits the brakes on the side of the kerb, her hands on the steering wheel, narrowing her eyes at me. "You think I own you? That's not what this is about, Tessa."

"Then what is this about?"

"I want you to not leave me out of everything instead of always putting Mark first."

"I'm sorry, but that's how it is when you date someone, Casey. You spend some quality time together to get to know each other. Yes, I'm going to choose Mark over you, but that doesn't mean I have stopped being friends with you. We can still do things together."

"It doesn't feel like we are doing things together anymore."

"What do you mean, Casey? Of course we have been spending time together. We hung out on my birthday last Friday."

"Yes, but we weren't alone, were we? Everything we do now has to have Mark with us or even Tim or Travis. Whatever happened when it was just the two of us?"

"Sometimes things changed, Casey. But I never left you out of anything. And if I want Mark or his friends to join us in our activities, I'm allowed to. I want them apart of our lives too. Maybe you should get yourself a boyfriend so you can understand how I feel now that I'm dating Mark. I'm sure once you start dating you wouldn't want to spend any time with me. Oh wait; you don't even know how to talk to guys without getting all tongue-tied. You will never get yourself a boyfriend if you can't talk to them." Tessa chuckled.

Tessa's words stabbed me in the heart. Tears were on the verge of falling, but I hold them back. I can't cry here. It will show I'm the weak one. For years Tessa had always tried to encourage me to talk to a guy I liked, the same way I would encourage her to talk to Mark and make the first move if he doesn't ask her out. Now she was using a weakness to why I was so shy around guys. Is this true to why I don't have a boyfriend? To why I have never even been kissed? Because I was shy, so quiet that no one ever noticed me, or because I got all tongue-tied when around boys I liked?

Tessa winds up the window, which meant this conversation was over. She pulled away from the kerb, leaving me to cry on the side of the road.

Chapter 17
Tessa

A limo swings by my house just as Zane had promised it would to drive us to Mad Star Records. For a few minutes I spent some time alone to think in the limo, my mind completely in all of this special treatment I was receiving. I imagined how much Casey would have loved being inside this vehicle. When it pulls up outside of Mark's before moving onto Tim's then to Travis', I try my best to be thrilled, but my heart just wasn't in it.

At the studio we take a seat in Zane's office, discussing what we were going to do for our first album. He understood that I wasn't going to record anything today. He definitely wanted us to record *Forget It*, and wants to get it done as soon as possible so we could give the world a taste of our music, making them want more. He is also working to get us onto a talk show, or one of those searching for new talent shows where we can perform live on there. He wanted to know what other songs we had and which ones did we think will be great on our first album. I have no idea how many songs we had written, but there were several of them. We probably will come up with more once we start the progress of putting the album together. Zane gives us a week to come up with a list of songs we can record, and books the studio for next Saturday.

Next Saturday will be my birthday. Was that enough time for me to recover from Casey's death in order to be able to perform my best? Her funeral was on Friday. Zane may have been nice enough to let me recover for the week, but I wasn't sure it was enough to fully grieve. Was grieving for a person ever really gave you enough time to move on? I know I have said so many times before that I didn't care if Casey was dead. Deep down inside, those harsh words I had told myself were eating me up. Right now I just want to get through the week and not feel any guilt for what I have done to Casey.

I shake Casey out of my head, because I can't be thinking about her right now. I need to keep focus on my future. Zane discusses with us on any other songs we may have for him and if we could have a list of songs ready to be recorded by next week. We promised to have it ready by then.

***

If I wasn't grounded, I would have gone over to Mark's right after our meeting. But instead of going straight home once the limo dropped me off, I felt the need to disappear for a while even when I should be going home. I head to Casey's. I wasn't sure if it was the place I should be hanging out in after what happened between Corey and I the other day. But it was the one place I thought to visit to see how Casey Roland's mother was doing since I didn't see her there the last time. Visiting her should be okay.

I message my uncle to let him know what I was up to. He replies back saying it was fine and to be back before dinner.

Mrs Roland answers the door. Her eyes are weary liked she hadn't slept in days. Her face lighting up when she sees me. She opens the door and pulls me into a hug.

"It's good to see you, Tessa. Corey told me you came to visit the other day."

I pull away from her. "It's good to see you, Mrs Roland. I have been so worried about you and Corey when I came by to see you. But you were resting in your room. I didn't want to disturb you."

She rests her hand on my shoulder. I see the sadness in her eyes. Casey had the exact same ocean blue eyes as her mother. I try not to let the colour make me feel down. I needed to be strong when around Casey's mother.

"The last few days hasn't been easy," she says. "I'm happy to have Corey help me out. I don't think I could cope with all of it on my own. And I'm also no longer Mrs Roland. I go by my maiden name, Emerson, now that I'm divorced."

I didn't know Casey's mother had changed her surname. But then again of course I wasn't aware of it since I stopped talking to Casey for so long.

Ms Emerson invited me inside, leading me to the kitchen where she was making tea. She gestures me to the table and tells me to sit down while she prepares a tea for me. I wasn't much of a tea drinker, but I accept her offer.

"Thanks for the tea," I say as she sets it down in front of me.

She smiles as she sets her cup down on the table and sits down beside me. She had also placed a plate of cream biscuits. "It's no problem, Tessa. It's a nice change from the wine or any other alcohol I would drink. The night Casey had ended her life I was completely unaware she had left the house. I had drunk a whole bottle of vodka, and had passed out on the couch when the police appeared at the door. I didn't want to believe what had happened. I tried reaching for another bottle to forget the pain, but Corey wouldn't allow me to. He took all of the alcohol in the house and tipped it down the sink so I couldn't drink myself to death. He also took my wallet and hid it from me so I couldn't buy anymore. My mind is going crazy, and I badly want a drink."

I reach out and place my hand over hers, giving her a smile. "You can do this, Ms Emerson. Both Corey and Casey had been trying to get you to stop drinking for a long time."

She nods. "It hasn't been easy, Tessa. I have been completely lost after I had the miscarriage. It put such a strain on the entire family. I turned to drinking for comfort. I know it's not something I should have done, but for a while the pain did go away. And then my husband left, and I drank more. Both of my children have been helping me to give the alcohol up, but I never did listen to them even when I knew I should have. The morning after Casey had died, the first thing I did was grabbed a glass of wine. The pain of losing a second child was way too much for me. Before I could pour myself a second glass, Corey snatched the bottle from me, disposing it. He told me that drinking is not what Casey would have wanted me to do." She inhales a deep breath before continuing on. "Corey is right. Casey would not want me to drown my sorrows with alcohol. After the funeral on Friday, I'm going to sign up to a support group to help me to quit drinking."

I smile at her, proud of what she was doing. I remember when Casey would tell me how she desperately wanted her mother to stop drinking, terrified she would wake up one morning to find her unresponsive. I told her to keep encouraging her, and that's what Casey had done. There was that one time on my seventeenth when I called her a wimp for not wanting to drink alcohol. I knew she was affected by what she had seen her mother go through that she vowed she never wanted to end up like her mother. To avoid doing so, she never touched alcohol.

"Casey always believed you could do it, Ms Emerson."

She smiles, and then removes her hand from mine, placing it on her cup where her other hand was. She takes a sip of her drink.

The front door then opens and closes again. "Mum?"

"In here, Corey!"

I can hear his footsteps walking across the carpet. I didn't turn around, but from the corner of my eye I could see him standing at the door frame. I close my eyes for a second, feeling Corey's hands and breath on me from the other day. I shouldn't be thinking about him. I'm with Mark, and I don't ever want to lose him because I cheated on him.

"Oh. I wasn't expecting to see you today, Tessa," he says.

The way he says my name makes my stomach do a somersault. I tell myself silently that I shouldn't feel this way about Corey anymore.

I force myself to look at Corey, and when I do, I see the lust in his eyes. I give him a smile. "I came over to see how your mother is doing."

He returns a smile, which sends my heart racing for joy. He then walks over to the counter where he had two bags full of groceries.

"Thank you, Corey, for going shopping," Ms Emerson says.

"It's no problem, Mum." He takes out the loaves of bread.

"Oh, honey, leave the groceries there. I will unpack them after my tea."

"I don't mind unpacking."

Ms Emerson allows him to unpack the groceries. I keep my eyes on my tea so no feelings could stir up inside me. But it doesn't work. My body aches for him. I tell myself that I'm not here for Corey. I'm here to check up on Casey's mother. But those old feelings had other plans.

"Tessa."

I force myself to look up from my tea and turn to him to where he was standing behind his mother.

"When you finish your tea, could I see you in my room, please? I want to talk to you about something."

I give him a half smile. "Sure."

He leaves the room. Ms Emerson and I sit there in silence as we finished our tea. When we finish, she gets up first to clear the table. I offer to clean, but she tells me there is no need for me to.

I get up myself to go and see what Corey wanted.

"Are you coming to the funeral this Friday, Tessa?" Ms Emerson asks me before I leave the kitchen. She stood at the sink.

I didn't want to go to the funeral. But I knew I should go to pay my respects for my former best friend. I give Ms Emerson a small smile, promising I will be there.

I leave the kitchen and head to Corey's room. His room is across from Casey's. Her door was closed. Walking passed it gave me an uneasy feeling in the pit of my stomach.

I turn to Corey's room and knock on his door. He opens it, pulling me inside before closing the door behind me. He then pushes me against the door, pinning his body against mine as he smashes his lips on mine.

At the back of my mind, I tell myself that this is wrong. The other day when Corey and I made love on the couch was once off. It was something we both needed to escape the pain we felt towards Casey, and to make a closure between us when we had stopped talking. I wasn't sure what this was between us right now. Were we trying to make up for lost time? Was there something between us that we didn't want to admit? Or was this all to take away the pain?

I push those thoughts out of my head as Corey moves his lips to my ear. He whispers, "I haven't been able to stop thinking about you."

I wrap my arms around his neck as his lips found mine again. He moves his hands down my body, resting them on my thighs. He then lifts me up so I could wrap my legs around his waist. He moves me over to his bed and lays me down on it. I reach for the zipper of his hoodie, and help him take it off. I reach for the hem of his shirt and we break the kiss so we could pull it off, throwing it to the floor.

Our lips reconnect, my hands running along his bare chest. But as Corey's hands find the hem of my long sleeve shirt, pulling it over my head, the guilt kicks in. I didn't want to cheat on Mark. I still had feelings for Corey, but my heart was with Mark now. When we were together the other day, it was only to keep my mind off Casey. I didn't want to make this a habit and hurt Mark by continuing to cheat on him. Casey may be gone, but it didn't mean Corey and I had the right to hook up now that she isn't here.

I push Corey off me before he had the chance to unclasp my bra.

Confusion spreads across his face. "What is it, Tessa? Why did you tell me to stop? Did I do something wrong?"

I shake my head, biting my lip. A lump forms in my throat as I fight back the tears. "I can't do this anymore, Corey."

He strokes my face. "Do what?"

I gesture between us. "This. Us."

Corey sits up straight on his knees. "What do you mean, Tessa? I thought you wanted this as much as I did."

"I will always love you, Corey." I'm unable to hold the tears back, and I let them flow down my cheek. "But I can't keep sneaking around."

Corey leans towards me, stroking my hair. "We don't have to sneak around anymore. Casey is no longer here. We can be together now."

"It's not about Casey, Corey. I have a boyfriend who I really love."

He removes his hand from my hair and sits back on his knees. My heart crumbles when I see the disappointed look on his face. For the past few years, I had dreamt of getting back with Corey, hoping he would forget the whole friendship rule about dating your sister's best friend. Or hope that Casey would allow us to be together so we didn't have to worry about sneaking behind her back. But then Mark came into my life, helping me to recover from my heartbreak. The feelings for Corey are still there and always will be, but Mark is who I want to be with. The way he cares for me, he helped me to feel something after I lost Corey. He has always made me feel good about myself, especially after a fight I might have had with my dad. He hasn't stopped checking up on me since Casey passed away. How could I go behind Mark's back like this after what we have been through together for the past year? I can't stand to see what I am doing to him right now. I don't want him to know I have hooked up with someone. I couldn't bear to lose him. What will happen to our band if we broke up? I allowed myself to hook up with Corey just once, something I thought I needed, but I didn't want to keep doing it all the time.

"I don't understand, Tessa. I thought you wanted to be with me. I thought you still had feelings for me. What happened on Thursday?"

I didn't look at him, and stare at the blue abstract of his bed sheets, wiping my eyes. "I was in pain, Corey. I hadn't seen you in so long since Casey and I stopped being friends. When I saw you the other day, all of the old feelings came back to me."

"Oh. I see." He gets off the bed. "You came over here to use me?"

I shake my head. "No, Corey. I didn't use you. I-I love you. I never stopped loving you."

"So you decided to make love to me even though you have a boyfriend?"

"I told you it was alright. I needed it, and you needed it. I thought this will be the only time we would do it and we would never see each other again."

Corey sits back down on the bed, running his hands through his hair. "When I kissed you on Thursday, it was like I was kissing you for the first time." He turns to me. "The memories from two years ago flooded my mind. I couldn't stop thinking about you all weekend, Tessa. And the song you performed, it reminded me of what a jerk I was to you and I wished I could take it all back. I wished we could go back and confessed our feelings for each other to Casey, to beg her to allow us to be together. Maybe you and

I could still be together. And maybe..." In a soft voice he says, "Maybe Casey would still be here."

Corey bursts into tears, hiding his face behind his hands. I move over to him, wrapping an arm around his shoulder and moved his hands from his face. I place my hand on his chin and make him face me.

"Don't blame yourself about what happened to Casey," I tell him. "Even if she had approved us being together, she probably would have still ended her life."

He nods. "You're right. I just wish I knew what was going through Casey's head at the time. I wished she had come to me if there was something bothering her. I would have helped her the best way I could even if I was busy with work and uni. I would have dropped everything to help her."

"I wished I knew what was going through her mind as well." *Maybe then I wouldn't have bullied her. I wouldn't have left our damage friendship the way it was. I would have done everything I could to repair it so we could be friends again. Would Casey then be alive if I hadn't put her through hell?*

I think back to my last text message I sent her just before she took her life. Did she think we had a chance to be friends again? What could I have done if I knew she was going to run into oncoming traffic? If I had just wrote that I would like to put everything in the past aside, start fresh and be friends again, maybe Casey would have had second thoughts.

If only I knew the damage I was causing, I wouldn't have bullied her.

"Did you notice that anything was wrong with her?" Corey asks, interrupting my thoughts.

I shake my head. "No. I haven't spoken to her since we had a fight last year right after my birthday."

Corey is surprise to hear this. "Really? Casey never mentioned that you had a fight. When you stopped coming around, I thought maybe you had a job or something."

"We ended our friendship. She was jealous that I was dating Mark, and that I was spending too much time with him instead of with her."

"What if not spending enough time with her wasn't the only thing?"

"What do you mean?"

"Did you notice how quiet and distance she was the day after your birthday? It was like she was lost in thought about something, and didn't feel like talking. She just wanted to be alone."

I try to think back to that day, but everything was a blur. This Saturday will be my birthday. Who remembers what they did a year ago? For my seventeenth I was so drunk that I don't even remember what happened that night.

"What happened on the night of my birthday, Corey? Do you remember anything from that night?"

He nods, and I hold my breath as I wait for him to recall everything that happened. He tells me how he had come to pick Casey and I up from the bowling alley because I had drunk too much and couldn't drive. As much as I thought it was alright for me to drive, Casey had called her brother to come get us. His friend Jett had driven my car home. Corey then tells me that we had made out on Casey's bed while she had gone to place my dirty clothes into the washing machine. Just a few minutes after we had pulled apart, Casey had walked in.

My stomach twisted into knots. The secret I had kept from my best friend wasn't so much of a secret like I thought it was. Corey and I had tried so hard to keep it from Casey, but in the end she had found out about it.

I don't meet Corey's eyes as I say, "Does that mean she could have seen us?"

"It could have. She never addressed it to me, but the vibe she was giving me the day after, I would say she knew."

It made sense now for the way Casey had been acting. She knew about Corey and I. She was mad because we had kept it a secret for so long and left her in the dark. So when she did found out, it was all a bombshell to her.

"If she knew about us, why didn't she say anything?" I wanted to know.

Corey shrugs. "Maybe she wanted us to come forward."

I nod, thinking that's exactly what she had been doing. She had been waiting for us to confess our secret. I wonder on the day we fought about me spending too much time with Mark, was she also mad about Corey and I?

"Was there anything else I should know about that happened to Casey? After our dad walked out, she kept quiet and I want to know if she ever spoke to you about how she may have felt. I know you ended your friendship, but did she ever say anything to you with what was going on in her life? Perhaps you have seen something?"

I look down at the floor so I don't meet his eyes. What will he think of me if he knew what kind of friend I was to Casey? I knew of all the terrible things what was happening to her because I was the one who caused it. I encouraged others to hurt her, and I never did anything to stop it.

"There was one time Casey came home from school crying," Corey goes on. "What happened, Tessa? What broke my sister? Especially on New Year's Eve. When my mum was in the hospital, Casey was hurt bad. Her face was covered with bruises and cuts, and she somehow broke her ribs. She claimed she had fallen down stairs, but I don't believe her. Tell me what happen, Tessa."

Instead of answering him, I get off his bed, grabbing my shirt, and walk out of the room. Even when he is calling me, I don't turn back to look at him. If he knew what I did to Casey, he will never speak to me again.

Chapter 18
Casey

Whenever Tessa and I fought, we would make up the same day or the next day. Once we tell our parents what had happened between us, they shared their advice, and then we make up. Our fights were usually over stupid unnecessary things, stuff I don't even remember what they are anymore. You know how it is in kindergarten or primary school. I'm not going to be your friend because you did this and that.

We were no longer in kindergarten or primary school. We were high school students who were graduating next year. We weren't fighting over unnecessary things anymore like you lost my favourite toy or I'm not talking to you because you didn't show up to my birthday party or whatever younger kids fight over. No, we were fighting over things that could easily wreck our friendship for good. Everything was due to jealousy or who can do this before graduation. Nowadays it was all about peer pressure, and if you weren't a part of the "It" crowd, you were nobody. Tessa has experienced more things than what I have done in my teenage years, and she made me feel bad for why I wasn't doing it too. She had a boyfriend, lost her virginity, and these days a lot of kids were disrespectful to their parents with the attitude that you can't tell me what to do anymore. I didn't have the latest phone or whatever new gadgets there were. Me, I wasn't the kind of girl anyone wanted to date. I haven't even kissed a boy, let alone lost my virginity. I respected my parents, and would never talk back at them if I didn't agree with them on something like the way Tessa was with her father. Sometimes Tessa does give me a hard time for always listening to my parents.

Our fight was about jealousy over a boy. We didn't speak to each other for three days. My heart ached in my chest when I saw Tessa at school hanging with Mark and his friends. It was like she preferred to be friends with them and not me. We didn't even sit with each other in English. It made me wonder how long will our fight last for. Or why we were fighting over something stupid anyway. I mean, I never said Tessa couldn't date. I just wanted her to still include me into things, make time with me also. Those three days felt weird with not talking to Tessa. We spoke every day, and the silence between us was driving me mad.

On Thursday night I started typing a text message to apologise to her for the things I had said on Monday. I never sent the message. I was too terrified to speak to her face to face, as well as a text, afraid she may not forgive me at all. So I deleted it.

Friday morning I was surprised to hear a knock at the door just as I was getting ready to leave for school. For the past three days I have been walking to school. Whoever was at the door, I really hoped they wouldn't keep me for too long. Hopefully whoever was at the door will be for Mum and I could get going to school. The last thing I wanted was to be late.

But the person standing at the door wasn't for Mum. It was for me. I wasn't expecting to see Tessa here.

She smiled shyly at me, unsure how I would react to her present after our fight the other day. "Hey, Casey."

I returned the smile. "Hey. What are you doing here?"

"I came to apologise for the other day. I also wanted to give you a lift to school."

I opened my arms and embraced Tessa. "I'm sorry too. I shouldn't have gotten so upset with you."

Tessa pulled away. "No. You have been right, Case. I have been spending a lot of time with Mark and my bandmates. We haven't spent a lot of time together, and I'm sorry for giving you a hard time about being jealous."

"It's alright, Tessa."

"This is such a stupid fight."

"Let's put it aside."

So we did. I follow Tessa out to the car to where her brothers sat in the back seat. Kaiden and Jackson greeted me, excited to see me.

Once the twins are dropped at school, Tessa excitedly said, "You will never guess what I heard yesterday."

"What?"

"I overheard that Max Downing likes you!"

My stomach does a somersault. It seemed too good to be true for Max Downing to even like me. I'm sure he doesn't even know I exist. I may have had one class with him, but I have never even spoken a word to him. But still hearing that he does like me in return excited me.

"He does?" I asked, interested to know more what she had heard about Max. "Who did you hear it from?"

"I heard Max say it himself at lunch yesterday when Mark, Tim, Travis and I sat near him and his friends. Isn't it great, Casey? You have been crushing on Max for so long, and he also has the same feelings for you." She turned to me to give me a quick smile before turning her eyes back to the road.

"If he likes me, why hasn't he asked me out or why hasn't he spoken to me?"

Tessa shrugged. "Maybe he is shy just like you are, or he is waiting for the right time to ask you out. Hey, why don't you ask him out today?"

The excitement I felt quickly faded. The whole idea of walking up to Max and asking him out terrified me. I have never asked a guy out on a date before. The scenarios in my head didn't help as I wondered to myself with what would have happened if he said no. I would be humiliated in front of him and others.

I expressed my fears to Tessa.

"There is nothing for you to be scared about, Casey. Max likes you, and I'm sure if you went up to him, he will say yes to a date. I will be right with you so you won't feel so scared."

I give her a small smile, thanking her.

We are outside of our school now. Tessa found a parking space underneath a tree out front and pulled in.

She cut off the engine and turned to me, unbuckling her seat belt. "Everything will be okay, Casey. I mean it. When you see Max today, just stroll up to him and say, 'Hey, Max'. Start some small talk with him, and then ask him out."

I was surprised to hear how much Tessa knew about asking a person on a date, especially when she had never gone up to Mark herself. He was the one who asked Tessa out. She wouldn't even do it herself when I had suggested it.

"Since when have you become an expert in asking someone on a date?"

"I'm not. But I figured this is something you could do. You have to start somewhere, Casey. If you don't show Max that you're interested, then you might never go out with him. He will never be your boyfriend. You don't want him to find another girl, do you?"

I shake my head. "No, I don't."

"Then take the chance and ask him out. You won't know what happens until you ask him." She smiled at me. "Remember, I will be there for you, Case."

***

I saw Max in the corridor as I walked from my first period to second period class. Tessa wasn't with me as she had Music for first period while I was on the other side of the school building in Visual Arts. My heart races a million miles per minute when I saw him.

He is with two of his friends, his white school shirt half tucked into his grey trousers. His hair is dyed dark blond, the roots of his natural brown hair showing. I didn't like much of the blond in his hair, but it was still a great look on him. I battle in my head to whether or not if I should walk up to him now and asked him out without Tessa's help.

My mouth feels dry as soon as I approached him. I was afraid I wouldn't be able to speak. But I keep in mind of what Tessa had said earlier how I didn't know what would happen if I didn't approached Max. The least he can do is say no. Only could I handle him saying no?

"Hey, Max," I said.

Max stopped talking to his friends where they were chatting about some football game, and turned to me. He is surprised to see me, and smiled, which causes the butterflies to flutter around my stomach. "Hey."

"H-how are you today?"

My heart pounded loudly in my chest. I feared that if I could hear it, then Max and his friends could most likely hear it too. Max stared at me strangely, like he had no idea who I was.

And that's exactly why he was staring at me strangely.

"Do I know you?"

His question startled me. I wasn't sure if I should act confused or embarrassed for approaching him in the first place. My cheeks grew hot. How could he not know me? Especially when Tessa said she heard him say he liked me.

"My name's Casey Roland," I said, shyly.

It takes him a few seconds to register my name. "Oh, yes. Tessa Ross' best friend, right?"

I nodded, biting my lip. *Come on, Casey. You can do it. You can ask him out.* "I was wondering if you would like to go out with me sometime."

Max's friends making an oohing noise and then burst into laughter in the most immature way, like me asking him out was a joke. Or maybe they were just making fun of him because I asked him out instead of him asking me. Was it wrong for me to approach him like this?

I waited for him to answer me. The longer I wait for his answer, the more I became anxious. His friends weren't making me feel any better. Max doesn't even tell them to stop.

"Casey, you're a nice person," Max said. "But I already have a girlfriend. I'm dating Amelia Smith."

My heart sinks deep in my chest, and my cheeks feel even hotter now. I didn't understand why Tessa would tell me Max had a crush on me when he was already dating someone. I wasn't aware of him dating anyone at all. Of course he is dating Amelia Smith. She was tall and thin with long wavy brown hair. She was no doubt prettier than me so I could see why Max liked her. What was I thinking that Max will ever like me?

I swiftly walked past them and heard the guys laughing behind me. What a fool I am for approaching him like that.

My eyes prickled with tears, but I hold them back the best I could. The last thing I wanted was for people to ask me what happened, or for Max to laugh at me. Most of all I wanted to know why Tessa had told me he had liked me in the first place when, really, he didn't. He was already dating someone else.

I didn't pay any attention in class. All I could think of is what a fool I am. The thing I couldn't understand is why did Tessa say Max liked me when he doesn't? Or maybe it was all just a misunderstanding. Tessa might have misheard everything.

The time couldn't past by any slower. All I wanted was to find Tessa and talk to her about what happened.

As soon as the bell rang, I gathered up my things and hurried out of the classroom. I waited for her at our usual lunch table. I waited for like maybe five minutes until Amelia Smith walked over to me. She stood in front of me, crossing her arms across her chest.

"Who said you could ask my boyfriend out?" she demanded.

I don't meet her eyes. "I'm sorry. I didn't know he was dating anyone."

"Well, now you do. Don't ever speak to him again, you hear me?"

I nodded, a lump forming in my throat. I try so hard to fight the tears that threatened to fall. I waited for Amelia to leave before I do let them fall. Why was everyone giving me a hard time for something I didn't know about? I didn't always keep track of who was dating in my grade. I wasn't even aware of Max dating anyone.

"Are you alright, Casey?" I heard Mark's voice.

I glanced over at him as he and Tessa walked over to me, hand in hand. Tessa let go and hurried over to me, embracing me. She then took my hand, telling Mark we will be right back, and then lead me away from the shelter area so we could be alone. We stood behind a building, hoping no teacher will bust us for being in an out of bounds area.

"Tell me what's wrong, Casey."

I wiped my eyes and face Tessa. "Did you know that Max Downing is dating Amelia Smith?"

Tessa's mouth drops opened. "He is?"

"Yes, he is. I asked him out while I was walking to my next class. He told me he couldn't go out with me because he already is dating someone."

"I'm sorry, Casey. I really thought he liked you."

There was something in her voice that showed me she had known. She was hiding laughter, and I realised that Tessa only said this to humiliate me in front of the guy I really like. It wasn't like her to do that, so why would she? We have been friends for so long. We would never play a cruel prank on each other like this.

"You knew about Max dating Amelia, didn't you?"

Tessa gave me an innocent look. "I didn't know. I swear, Casey."

"Well, why did you tell me you heard him say that he likes me when he was dating someone? You do realise what a fool I look like to when I approached Max? And just not long ago, Amelia comes up to me to warn me to stay away from him."

"Case, I swear to you that I heard him say it."

"Bull crap, Tessa. Just tell me the truth. Why did you tell me he liked me when he doesn't?"

She doesn't make eye contact with me as she said, "I just thought it would be fun to play a harmless prank on you."

"Harmless? Tessa, I looked like a fool in front of him!"

"Sorry. I thought you will chicken out and wouldn't talk to him. You always chicken out when talking to guys."

"And what were you trying to prove by doing that?"

"It wasn't to prove anything. I just did it for fun."

"You think humiliating me in front of the guy I really like would be fun?"

"It was just a joke, Casey."

"It's not a joke. How would you feel if I did the same thing to you about Mark?"

Tessa looked away for a second before turning back to me. "I did it for a laugh, okay? Yes, I knew Amelia and Max were dating. They have been dating for a week."

"But it doesn't make sense to why you would do that, Tessa. I thought we were friends. Friends don't play cruel pranks on each other."

"And the last time I look, friends didn't get jealous if one of them started dating."

"I'm not jealous, Tessa. Why would you do this to me? I thought when you came over this morning it was to apologise. You then told me the guy I like has a crush on me, and you told me to ask him out. And when I do, I find it is all a lie."

"Well, it hurt me a lot, Casey, when you told me how you didn't want me to be hanging around my own boyfriend."

I let out a frustrating sigh. "Seriously? You're still worried about that? Tessa, I never said you couldn't hang around Mark. All I wanted was for you to also spend some time with me. Do things like we used to."

Tessa started to back away from me. "There's no doing things like we used to because we can't be friends anymore. I can't be friends with someone who is always jealous of me for being with my boyfriend. I humiliated you for a laugh."

My heart crumbled to pieces. "So you did this to get back at me?"

She shook her head. "No. I did it for a laugh and to end our friendship."

Without another word, Tessa walked away. I stand there trying to register everything that had happened. None of it made sense at all. Especially how this morning I thought Tessa came to my house to apologise to me. It wasn't anything like that. All she wanted to do was make fun of me in front of the guy I really like. Why did she have to do that? If she wanted to end our friendship, then why didn't she just say she didn't want to be friends instead of humiliating me?

The tears flowed down my face, but I don't do anything to stop them. Instead I decide to leave the school grounds. I'm not the kind of person who would jig school, but I didn't want to run into the girls' bathroom to wash my face where the smokers hung out during lunch breaks. I don't want anyone to start asking me questions. I also couldn't face Amelia, Max or Tessa. I couldn't bear to wonder what they must think of me.

I made a run to the school's entrance before I was caught by any teachers. I walked as fast as I could to get home. Both Corey and Mum were home when I get there. My brother is sitting on the couch watching TV while having one of his study books on his lap as he works with the television on. That's how Corey has always been. He could never do his homework in silence. He had to always have music or the television on. Me, on the other hand, I have to do my work in silence.

Corey looked over at me as I rushed through the door. "What are you doing home, Casey?"

But I don't answer him. I hurry to my room. I heard him get off the couch, asking me what had happened. I slammed my door shut before he could ask me more questions or before he could follow me into my room. Right now I just needed to be alone.

I dropped my bag on the floor and threw myself on the bed, burying my face into the pillow as I sobbed loudly, ignoring both my brother and mother as they knocked on my door, concerned with what had happened. After a few minutes they got the message how I didn't want to talk, and left me alone in peace.

The only sound I could hear was the sound of my own sobbing.

Chapter 19
Tessa

I switch off my phone once I get home to avoid the texts and calls Corey kept leaving me. After what happened back at his place, I couldn't deal with him. I needed to go somewhere to think things through, somewhere that was far from here. Somewhere I could be alone.

But right now I couldn't disappear somewhere to be alone. Not when I was grounded. I didn't want to get into an argument with my uncle. It's not something I could deal with right now.

Uncle Harley suggested that my brothers and I should have a games night, but I declined his offer. It sounded fun, but I wanted to be somewhere quiet to think. Plus, with Kaiden and Jackson being young, they always cheated with board games. I couldn't argue with them, or my uncle, all because my brothers don't exactly understand the rules of the game. I have other things on my mind to worry about than that. So the best way for me was to separate myself from them.

I lock myself in my room, blocking out the sounds from downstairs. I grab my lyrics book and guitar, sitting down on my bed with it. I write what I thought about Casey, and how I have been feeling for the past few days. I strum chords for what seemed forever. I didn't stop until a knock came from my door.

I sigh with frustration. "Who is it?"

"It's just me," my uncle says from the other side. "Can I come in?"

I set the guitar down and open the door for my uncle.

"Its eight thirty, and I'm putting your brothers to bed. Could you keep it down in here? And please don't stay up too long."

"I won't."

"Your music sounds good. How did it go today?"

I nod. "It was good. We mostly discuss what we will be doing for the album. We are going to be recording songs next weekend."

He smiles proudly. "That's good to hear, Tessa. I'm really proud of where you and your band has ended up. You guys are going to do great. I will leave you now. Please don't stay up for too long."

He says goodnight and then leaves me to go back to what I'm doing.

***

I stayed up most of the night writing the song. I tiptoed down to the garage in hope the guitar wouldn't make too much noise and wake anyone up. I didn't care that I didn't go to bed until past midnight. All I wanted was to get the song done so I could perform it to my bandmates during practice this afternoon.

I don't think I got any more than four hours of sleep. I hit the snooze on my alarm as soon as it rings in the morning with no energy to get up for school. As much as I wanted to sleep in, I have no choice but to get up. I had my assessment to complete for Mrs

Grove today, and I didn't want Mark or I to fail because I didn't want to show up to school. But for me there was no such thing as sleeping in. After giving me four days of space in the morning because of Casey, my brothers wandered into my room to make sure I was out of bed.

Once having a shower to freshen up, I walk into the kitchen to make myself a cup of coffee. The caffeine should keep me alert for a few hours. I wasn't in the mood to have breakfast, but Uncle Harley made sure I sat and ate before heading off to school. The good thing was he was taking my brothers to school instead of me.

I open the door to leave when I find Corey standing there, his arm in mid-air, ready to knock.

"Corey, what are you doing here?"

He put his arm down at his side. "I need to talk to you."

I shake my head. "Not now, Corey. I have to get to school."

"I know. It won't take too long. I promise."

I glance behind my shoulder. I hear my uncle telling my brothers to get ready for school. I step outside on the veranda and closed the door behind me. "Fine. Let's talk over near my car."

He follows me down the steps and down the path to where my car was parked behind my uncle's.

I place my bag on the ground beside my feet, and then lean my back up against the car of the driver's side. "What do you want to talk about, Corey?"

It's a question I didn't need to ask him. It was clear he was here to talk about what happened between us yesterday. His eyes stare back at me, begging to be forgiven for everything that has happened between us.

"I just want to apologise for yesterday," he says. "Since you wouldn't answer any of my calls or texts last night, I thought coming here was the only way I could get you to talk to me."

"There's nothing to really think about, Corey. We basically used each other to somehow cope with our grieving for Casey by bringing up old feelings."

Corey shakes his head. "No. I don't think we used each other because we were grieving. When you kissed me on Thursday, it spun up feelings and memories of us. It made me think how stupid I was to give you up like I did, to think it was okay to date someone else without telling you. I couldn't be with you because you are my sister's best friend. I used you for my own pleasure. I was afraid to admit to my sister how much I liked you. But I let the fear get to me, pretending that nothing ever happened between us. I'm in love with you, Tessa. I had always have been. It just took me three years to realise what I have done."

The way he had said he loved me made my stomach do a flip, and sent my heart doing a crazy dance. I too had felt all of the feelings I had for him come back to me. Our hook up was only meant to be one time. It wasn't supposed to mean anything. We were just two ex-lovers who were grieving their loss for someone we loved dearly, and it was also a closure to forgive each other for what happened in the past. It's not meant to be anything more than that.

"I have a boyfriend, Corey," I remind him. "I had loved you. You were my first kiss, first time. You were also the first guy to ever break my heart. I really thought we were going to be something. I wanted you to make it official that we were together. I wanted us to tell Casey the truth. Instead after four months of sneaking behind her back, you decide its best we pretended whatever we had between us never happened by bringing a girl home with you who wasn't me. When I started dating Mark, I swear it was so damn hard at first to push you out of my head and start a new beginning with someone else who I truly love."

"I was sixteen, Tessa. I was immature and didn't think how this would make you feel. And I'm sorry that I was selfish for what I did. I wish I could take it all back. I really wish I could. I was terrified of my own feelings. I had dated other girls, but none of them compared to how I felt about you. I was afraid to tell Casey how I felt in case she didn't agree for us to be together."

"You should have told me that this is how you felt."

"I know I should have."

"Look, Corey, what we did on Thursday was something we both needed. We were hurting and for a moment having sex with you was a way to escape the pain I felt about Casey. I wanted her off my mind. Seeing you for the first time since we went our separate ways and I started dating Mark brought up old feelings. What we did was only meant to be a one-night stand. I wasn't planning to see you again until the funeral."

I see the hurt in his eyes when I mentioned how hooking up with him was meant to be a one-night stand. I used to want so much more from Corey, but all of that has changed now. My heart now belonged to Mark and that's who I wanted to be with.

"I don't believe you that it was a one-night stand," he says. "The way we made love, I could feel the old connection between us from when we used to be together. It made me realise what an idiot I was for letting you go."

I couldn't deny it that I felt our old connection. But everything has changed between us. We were two different people. Corey wanted to be a scientist while I wanted to be a musician. It could never happen between us, even if we tried to make it work.

"We just can't be together, Corey," I tell him. "Casey may be gone, but that doesn't mean we should be together."

"Give me one good reason why we can't?"

I give him a *'what do you think?'* look. "You know very well, Corey. I have a boyfriend now. I can't just ditch him to be with you. I wanted you when I was fourteen. Where were you then, Corey? Screwing some other girl? Where is she now? You aren't screwing anyone at the current moment so you think it's okay to start sleeping with your sister's best friend? Especially now that she is dead?"

Corey narrows his eyes at me. "And yet you were the one who came onto me, Tessa. You're the one who came over to ask me how I was, and then brought up the past before making the first move. You say you love your boyfriend, but then you screw your ex-boyfriend behind his back? All because you were a total mess after what happened to Casey. You accused me for taking advantage of you in the past for being a virgin. But here you are taking advantage of my feelings. Yet, you said our hooked up was only about sex, to forget about Casey for one moment. But honestly, Tessa, when we made love on my couch, it was not just sex. I could feel the connection we previously had."

I look down at my feet, biting down on my lip. *But would you really want to be with me if you knew what I had put Casey through?* I wanted to say, but the words don't leave my mouth.

Corey steps closer to me. He reaches out and rests his hand on my chin, making me face him.

"I understand the pain you're going through," he says. "Being with you helped me to keep my mind off my sister. I can't stop thinking about you, Tessa. I'm a fool for letting you go. And I also understand if you don't want to be with me. I promised you that after the funeral I will disappear."

I nod, but don't say a word. We both knew that was the best thing for us. It hurt for me to know I may never see him again, but I couldn't be with him if it brings old feelings and memories. Mark is who I want to be with now.

"I should let you get to school," Corey says.

I nod. "Yes, I need to go or I will be late."

But he doesn't move away so I could get into my car. His body is still close to mine, his hand that was resting on my chin was now resting on my cheek, his thumb stroking my skin. I should push his hand away, but I liked the feel of his hand on my skin. His breath is warm against mine, sending my heart racing. He watches me carefully, waiting to see what I would do. We may not be able to be together, but we knew our heart desired us to be together.

Corey connected his lips with mine. I closed my eyes, wrapping my arms around his neck instead of pushing him away. But before Corey and I could take the kiss further, I hear Mark's voice cursing behind me.

Corey and I pull away from each other, turning to see Mark standing at the end of the driveway. His hands are clenched beside him as he narrows his eyes at Corey.

I curse softly to myself when I see my boyfriend standing there. So much for keeping my hooked up with Corey a secret.

"What are you doing here, Mark?" I ask.

He walks up the driveway with his hands still clenched together. "You didn't answer your phone last night, Tessa. So I thought I would come by to see if you were okay in case something happened. But I see why you didn't answer the phone. You were busy screwing Casey's brother."

Mark takes a step towards Corey, but I step in between them, holding up my hands to stop Mark.

"No, Mark. I wasn't screwing Corey. I had turned off my phone to work on a song." *I also had it off so Corey couldn't contact me.*

"Bull crap you were, Tessa."

"Mark, listen to me. I was not with Corey last night."

"Listen to her, man," Corey speaks up. "She wasn't with me."

Mark turns from me to Corey. His facial expression terrified me as he looked like he was going to kill someone. And that person was definitely going to be Corey. He pushes me aside and then swung at Corey, hitting his jaw with his fist. He allows Mark to hit him and doesn't do anything to stop him.

I squeal for Mark to stop. Mark listens, but doesn't take his eyes off Corey. His jaw clenches tight.

"You keep away from, Tessa," Mark warns him. "I'm sorry that your sister died, but that doesn't mean you can come onto my girlfriend."

"Mark, let me explain," I say.

Without looking at me he tells me to shut up while his eyes stayed fixated on Corey.

"Hey, don't tell her to shut up," Corey hisses at Mark.

"Don't tell me what I can and can't do," Mark spits back. "I'm not the one who is hooking up with someone else's girl."

"I didn't steal her. Tessa and I were a couple a few years back. Did she ever tell you that?"

Mark takes another swing at Corey. This time Corey blocks his punch, and takes a swing at my boyfriend. They don't stop there. Mark threw another punch and Corey tackled Mark to the ground. I scream for them to stop, even tried to pull Corey off Mark, but I was only knock to the ground.

I hear footsteps running on the pavement, follow by a male's voice yelling at Corey and Mark to stop. I don't register the voice at first as I watched the guys roll around until I see my uncle pulling Mark off Corey.

"Knock it off, the both of you!" Uncle Harley scolds at them. "I don't know what is going on here, but I want you to stop it now."

Mark's lip is bleeding. Corey gets to his feet, and I see the blood pouring from his nose, the blood dripping down and onto his white top underneath his grey hoodie.

"Sorry, Mr Ross," Corey apologises. "This wasn't supposed to happen. I'm sorry."

Without another word, Corey took off down the driveway to where his car is parked on the street.

Uncle Harley lets go of Mark, and then look between the two of us as I get to my feet. "Do I want to know what just happened?"

I shake my head, afraid to open my mouth and explain everything, knowing I will break down into tears right here. A lump form in my throat as I fight back tears. This is it. My relationship with Mark is over. I don't want it to be over all because I made a stupid mistake.

My uncle stares at me for a long time, wanting me to open up to him, but could see I didn't really want to say anything at all. He turns to Mark. "Get yourself clean up before you and Tessa head off to school."

Mark shakes his head angrily. "No. I'm going to just go and get out of here."

"Mark, clean up inside the house."

He listens to my uncle and then turns to the house. My brothers are standing on the veranda, wondering what happened. Knowing Mark would not want my company, I follow him anyway to avoid questions ask by my uncle.

Mark stands at the sink in the bathroom, washing his face. I stand in the door frame. He doesn't know I'm there until he glances at himself in the mirror. He narrows his eyes at my reflection. Redness was just under his left eye and I knew later it will bruise.

"Go away, Tessa," he scolds at me. "I don't ever want to see your face again."

I disobey him and enter the bathroom, shutting the door behind me.

"No. Let me explain everything, Mark."

"What is there to explain, Tessa? You cheated on me!"

Tears prickle my eyes. I blink them back so they couldn't fall. Mark is right. What is there to explain? I cheated and broke the trust of our one-year relationship. Mark glances back at me, waiting for me to answer. The look in his eyes scared me the most, like he could break something at any moment. I have never seen him this furious before. We have never ever fought until now.

"You weren't supposed to find out about this."

Mark rolls his eyes. "Of course I wasn't meant to. But I did, Tessa. I found out about it."

"We were only meant to hook up once. That's it. No strings attached."

"Well, it seemed like you were attached to strings."

"I was a mess on Thursday."

"Oh, so right after you screwed me you decided it was okay to screw someone else? Tessa, I know how hard it was for you on Thursday, but it doesn't mean you can use Casey's death as an excuse to why you cheated on me."

I nod. He is right. I shouldn't have done that. At the time I didn't care how Mark would feel if I had slept with someone else. All I wanted was to forget the pain I felt, and being alone with Corey brought on the old feelings.

"I'm sorry, Mark. I didn't mean to hurt you."

Mark curses. "Of course you hurt me. Didn't you think how it would make me feel?"

"Please forgive me, Mark. I will make it up to you. I promise. After this week I will be having nothing to do with Casey's family. I may check in on her mother every once in a while, but I will have no contact with Corey."

Mark scoffs. "This isn't something I can easily forgive you for, Tessa. You can do everything you can to make it up to me, but your trust is something that will take a long time for you to make it up to me."

I open my mouth to speak, but a knock at the door interrupts me.

"Mark, Tessa, could you please finish your conversation later?" Uncle Harley calls out from the other side. "You don't want to be late for school, and I need to leave in a sec to take the twins to school."

"No problems, Mr Ross," Mark calls out. "We are about done."

Mark pushes me aside and opens the door.

"Mark, please," I pleaded with him before he walked out. "Please forgive me."

He looks back at me, and for a moment I thought he was going to say something to me. Without a word, he heads out of the house. I stand there staring at the open door. My heart crumbles to pieces in my chest. I tell myself to hold it all together that when Mark cools off, he will talk to me again. He couldn't stay mad at me forever, could he?

My uncle comes to the door. Before he could ask me anything, I burst into tears, sinking to my knees and cover my face with my hands. Who am I thinking that he wouldn't stay mad at me forever? He may not have said anything, but it was clear that we had broken up, all because of something stupid I did.

Uncle Harley kneels beside me and pulls me into a hug. He rubs his hand up and down my back.

"Is Tessa okay?" Kaiden asks.

"Did something happen with her and Mark?" Jackson adds.

"Boys, give me a few minutes alone with your sister," Uncle Harley says. "Wait for me in the car."

I hear my brother's footsteps as they leave.

Uncle Harley waits for a few minutes before pulling away and removes my hands from my face so I could look at him. I don't even want to know what I look like, but I was glad the fight happened here and not at school. Dad would kill me if he knew I was involved with a fight.

"Do you want to stay home today?" he asks.

I shake my head as I wipe my eyes. "No. I can't stay home today. I need to be at school today. I have an assessment to complete."

He nods. "Okay. Do you want to talk about what happened? We can talk after school today?"

I shrug, not really sure how I will feel later today once my band finishes practice. That is if we still have a band by the end of the day. Would Mark even want to be a part of it if we don't sort things out and get back together? What will Travis and Tim say about this?

"It's all depending how I feel after band practice today."

"Alright. Well, you better get going to school before you're late. Are you okay with getting to school? You don't need me to drive you?"

"I'm fine."

Uncle Harley gets off the floor and then helps me up. He pats my shoulder. "It will be alright, Tessa. Mark will eventually forgive you."

I wanted to believe his words, but the way I saw the anger and hurt in Mark's eyes, there was no way he would ever forgive me.

Chapter 20
Casey

I hadn't realised I had fallen asleep until the grumbling sound of my stomach woke me from skipping lunch. I didn't expect to sleep for too long either. The time on the clock on my bedside table was 4:29pm.

Forcing myself out of bed, I head to the bathroom to wash my face. Before I went to the kitchen, where I could smell potato bake being cooked, I checked my phone to see if maybe Tessa had texted me. Hopefully to apologise for what she did or see if I was okay. My heart sank in my chest when I saw that there were no messages from her or from anyone.

I put my phone away and walked to the kitchen. Mum was getting whatever she was cooking out of the oven and setting it on the stove. My brother was nowhere to be seen.

Mum looked over at her shoulder and smiled. "Oh hey, Casey. It's good to see you're awake. I wasn't sure if I should leave you sleeping or if you would like dinner. I called your boss to let him know you weren't feeling well. He said he will hopefully see you tomorrow."

I gave my mother a small smile. I completely forgot about work and was thankful Mum had called Freddy for me. After what happened today, I don't think I could work. "Thanks, Mum. I will have dinner."

Mum returned the smile. "Why don't you set the table and I will plate the food? It's just us eating tonight. Corey left to go out with friends."

I set the table for the both of us. As I do, Mum asked me how I was. It was something I didn't want to talk about or want to think of the humiliation. The words Tessa had said ached my heart.

"I'm fine, Mum," I told her, grabbing two glasses from the cabinet, and then set it down on the table.

Mum didn't believe me. "You didn't look fine when you came home this morning. Is everything alright at school?"

I don't answer her as I grabbed the pitcher from the fridge full of water, and poured into the glasses.

"Besides Tessa and I having a fight, something happened to me that was really humiliating."

"Let me get dinner on the table and then we sit down at the table to discuss it."

I mumbled okay and sat down at the table, waiting for Mum to sit down with me to eat.

Taking a few deep breaths to hold myself together, I told Mum everything that happened today. She listened carefully to what I had to say.

"Oh, sweetie," Mum said, reaching over to rest her hand on mine. "I'm sorry that had happened." She gave me a small smile. "I'm sure everything is a misunderstanding. Maybe Tessa misheard it."

I shook my head. "No. That's the thing. I thought she misheard as well, but then later on she told me it was a prank."

"You and Tessa are best friends. Why would she pull that kind of prank?"

I shrugged. If only I knew the answer to that. "I thought we were best friends too, but now we aren't. She'd much rather spend time with her boyfriend than spend time with me. She then told me I would never get a boyfriend if I couldn't talk to a guy without chickening out. I go all shy when I talk to them."

"Boys will always come between your friendship. You both are in your fifth year of high school. You are both going to be exploring new things where you won't do much with each other like you did when you were younger. You have a job and there will be somethings you might miss out on because of the job. Tessa has chosen to start dating, which will mean she is going to want to spend more time with her boyfriend. It doesn't mean she is not going to want to spend time with you, Casey."

"But it feels like she doesn't care about me. Everything is about Mark. He has to be a part of everything we do."

Mum nodded, putting her knife and fork down on the table and took a sip of her drink. "I understand, Casey. You got used to it being just the two of you, but now a guy is involved. There is nothing wrong with him being a part of your activities. If you or Tessa decide to get married someday you might want to spend time all together, especially if you have kids."

I saw where my mother was coming from. Have I really been acting jealous like Tessa had said I was?

I often imagine what mine and Tessa's life will be like in the future, to what we would do once we graduate high school, and how we would fall pregnant at the same time so our kids could grow up together and be the best of friends like us. But of course that was no longer happening. We had thought that once our HSC was over, we would travel the world. Now it was more likely she would travel with her bandmates once their music career kicks off, and I would be forgotten. Tessa wouldn't worry about asking me to come along with them.

And if I had no idea how to properly speak to a guy then I guess I will never have a boyfriend. I may never get to experience what Tessa will have.

"I don't think I will end up dating anyone," I said.

Mum shook her head. "Never say you won't, Casey. Even if you won't find someone now, you could find someone later on. You're still in high school, and the only thing you need to worry about is your school work. I know in high school you're expected to date and lose your virginity by the time you graduate, but you honestly don't need to worry about what others do, Casey. Tessa chose to date. Don't bring yourself down because you don't have someone. Your day will come, Casey." She smiled at me. "And I'm sure you and Tessa will make up once you have sort out your differences."

I nodded, not sure if I wanted to believe the last part about Tessa and I being friends again. I had a feeling it wasn't going to happen.

***

I went around to see Tessa once I finished dinner. I played out in my head how I was going to apologise for being wrong and how I wanted to be friends again. My hope she would listen to me. She can't hate me forever, can she?

I can hear the TV when I step onto the veranda. It's dark now and I hoped I wouldn't be in too much trouble for coming here too late. I wonder if Mr Ross knew anything about what is going on between Tessa and I. Yet, I wouldn't be surprised if he didn't know, since Tessa rarely ever spoke to him. Not without getting into an argument.

Mr Ross answered the door. He smiled when he saw me standing there. "Casey, it's great to see you. I haven't seen you all week."

I returned the smile. "Yeah, I have been busy with work and with other things. I have the afternoon off today. I wasn't feeling too good."

"That's no good. I hope you feel better soon."

"Thank you, Mr Ross and congratulations on your engagement. Sorry, I haven't had the chance to say it to you."

"Thank you, Casey." He moved aside and gestured me into the house. "Come on in. Tessa is up in her room."

I entered the house and headed up the stairs, silently praying to myself that Tessa will accept my apology. I'm not even sure why we said our apologises this morning when it didn't mean anything. So hopefully this time it will be a real one instead of a fake.

I heard the chords of her guitar coming from her room. I hated the idea of interrupting her. Taking a deep breath and exhaling it slowly, I tapped on the door.

Tessa groaned when she heard my knock, mumbling "What now?" I heard her footsteps walking along the carpet, fiddling with the lock and opened the door. She frowned when she saw me. "What do you want?"

"I want to apologise for everything. I spoke to my mum and she said that I may have overreacted just a little about you being with Mark. I'm sorry, Tessa. I shouldn't have acted the way I did."

Tessa laughed. "You needed your Mum to tell you that?"

My heart crumbled in my chest. "Why are you being mean to me, Tessa? I apologised to you."

"That's doesn't mean I have to accept the apology, Casey. Just because I'm dating Mark doesn't mean I wouldn't still hang out with you. We could organise days where I could be with Mark and other days with you. But no. You wanted me all to yourself, like I belong to you when I don't. I'm sorry you don't have a boyfriend, but you can't stop me from liking anyone. Now get out of my face, Casey. I don't ever want to see you again."

Without another word, Tessa closed the door on me. I stood there staring at the door, unsure how I was supposed to fix any of this. The eleven years of friendship with Tessa was gone.

Chapter 21
Tessa

Getting through the day wasn't easy knowing Mark was mad at me. My biggest fear was knowing what Travis and Tim might say when they find out what I did, and then I would be kicked out of the band. I didn't want that. Not with how far our band has come.

Mark and I had music first period. Mrs Grove gets us to perform our song first thing before moving onto the next part of the lesson. During class Mark and I would sit together, but this time we don't. While I sat at the back of the classroom, he sat at the front.

At recess I feared I might not be allowed to sit with my friends, but it seemed Mark hadn't told Tim or Travis anything. He was quiet as he munched on a packet of salt and vinegar chips. To ease the tension between us, I show my bandmates the song I had written about Casey.

"This is incredible," Tim says once he had read it.

I give him a smile. "Thanks. I played some chords last night, but I thought that maybe during practice today that we could play the song. Maybe even record it when we go into the studio next week."

Travis nods in agreement. "Yes, we should definitely play around with the music and record it for the album." He turns to Mark. "Have you read Tessa's song yet? What do you think of it?"

Mark doesn't look in my direction. "It's good. It would be interesting to hear how it sounds."

I give Mark a smile, but he doesn't see it.

"Do you have any other new songs we could put music to before we hit the studio on the weekend?" Tim wants to know.

"I have a few," I answer. "Maybe we could play all of our songs this afternoon and see which one we should put onto the album."

My bandmates agreed to the idea, and I hoped by the afternoon that Mark will be talking to me again. We couldn't keep ignoring each other like this. It wasn't good for the band, and I didn't want to be the blame if our band breaks up before it even starts.

***

I head to the local coffee shop on my way home from school before heading home, deciding that coffee is what my bandmates and I need. I order my coffees, almost not recognising Max Downing from behind the counter as he served me.

"I didn't know you worked here, Max," I say.

"I started working here two months ago," he answers.

"That's great."

"Hey, I haven't gotten the chance to say this to you, but I'm really sorry about Casey."

I give him a sad smile. Should people really be saying sorry to me with the way I treated her? "Thanks."

"I feel bad that I didn't know her all that well," he goes on. "You would think spending six years of high school you would know everyone in your grade, but Casey wasn't someone I knew. When she approached me, asking me out, I felt ashamed for not knowing who she was."

I nod. "Casey was so quiet and distant herself from everyone that you would never realise she was there."

"I wished I could have gotten to know her. If I wasn't dating Amelia, then I would have gone out with Casey."

I smile at his words. I wish Casey was here to hear this. I could imagine her blushing, gushing to me later about going out with him while also getting tongue-tied.

I think back to the time I told Casey that Max liked her. We hadn't spoken for a few days, and I know in some way I should have forgiven her for our stupid fight. I knew our friendship was important, and Casey was right. I was spending more time with Mark and my bandmates that I wasn't exactly spending much time with her. When I did, I wanted Mark and the band to hang with us. I wanted the five of us to spend time together. But I didn't realise that Casey wanted some alone time with us too.

I'm not even sure what I was thinking. Selfish thoughts I guess occupied my mind, telling me what I needed, and not what Casey needed. What did I need exactly? More alone time with Mark instead of being with my best friend who needed me more than anything with the problems her home life was causing? I told myself I didn't need her. I wanted to devote my time with my bandmates so we could make it big someday. Also, spending more time around Mark was a way I didn't have to go over to Casey's and see her brother.

Max was in my maths class, and one day I just had this evil thought of tricking Casey into thinking Max liked her. Of course he didn't because everyone knew he had started dating Amelia

Smith, which Casey wouldn't know because she isn't the kind of person to listen in on gossip. I thought maybe I could pull this prank in a way to end our friendship. The right thing to do was to just say it that I didn't want to be friends anymore. But I thought playing a cruel prank will be better. What I was getting out of this, I wasn't sure. It wasn't like me to do something this cruel to Casey, but I wanted her to leave me alone.

So, I told her I had heard that Max liked her. The way her face lights up knowing that this guy she has been crushing on for so long caused my stomach to twist into knots.

This isn't right, I told myself. But I did it anyway.

Casey shyly expressed her fears of asking him out, and I encouraged her to go up to him. I honestly didn't think Casey would do it, that she would chicken out like she always did whenever she was around guys, getting herself tongue-tied. I was walking to my next class when I spot her in the corridor, and I stood nearby watching her. The way Max looked at her with confusion, and I wondered what Casey had said. Then his friends burst into laughter, and I couldn't help to laugh out an evil chuckle knowing that my plan had worked, and I made Casey humiliate herself in front of the guy she liked. There was something about the way I saw the humiliation on her face that I wanted to hurt Casey more. To get her back for the way she made me feel for hanging around with Mark more than her. But why did I needed to do that? Because I didn't want to admit she was right about me spending too much time with my boyfriend. Casey needed me. Her Dad walked out, her brother was hardly home anymore, and her mother was an alcoholic. She needed me to help her to get by.

And all I did was become a terrible friend and pushed her away.

This isn't the kind of person I am. How did I become so damn selfish to think that hurting Casey was okay?

Without saying goodbye to Max, I step aside for the person behind me to be served. Why did I trick Casey into thinking Max had liked her when I knew he was already dating someone else? What kind of friend am I? Casey would never have done that to me with Mark.

Now that I think about it, what was I getting out of this prank? Nothing. I don't even know why I came up with the idea for it. Casey wouldn't have done that to me with Mark. And if I had wanted to end my friendship, I should have said it to her. Not humiliate her in front of her crush and his friends.

Tears prickle my eyes, but I blink them back. I couldn't cry right here.

Once my order is called, I take the tray and head to my car and let the tears fall before heading to my place.

Chapter 22
Casey

The world was crumbling around me, and I felt like I was in the middle of it all, waiting for the ground to open up beneath me, swallowing me whole.

I do my best to keep busy at work and not to worry so much about Tessa. But it wasn't easy to forget about what happened between us. I was lost without her. There has never been one day since we became friends when we weren't without each other. If we ever did have our differences, we would only fight for one day and make up the next day like nothing ever happened. But fighting with Tessa for almost a week now made me wonder what to do without her. My heart ached in my chest, wishing Tessa would forgive me for making one stupid mistake. I didn't mean to upset her.

Amelia and her friends were at the shops the next day on Saturday. It has only been a day since I humiliated myself in front of Max, and seeing Amelia made me want to hide and forget what I had said. They weren't the kind of girls I didn't think enjoyed reading, but they did enter the bookstore. I have never once seen them with a book and something told me they weren't here to purchase anything. I wasn't even sure how they knew I was working in this store. Maybe they had seen me on my lunch break or something. I'm stacking some new releases onto the shelf when they walked into the store. I watched them from the corner of my eye where they stood at a stand of memoirs, picking up a random book to flip through. I heard them whispering and laughing.

I glanced over at them. Amelia gave me a death stare before her and her friends turned away. Whatever they were talking about had to do with me asking Max out. I already felt humiliated and did not need her to make it worse. Amelia then told her friends it was time to leave. They leave the store while appearing over their shoulders, whispering.

Throughout the day I checked my phone, hoping to find a message from Tessa asking me how my day was like she always does. But there was nothing. Not even a message to say to let's forget all about this fight and be friends again.

It has only been a day since we ended our friendship, and I have no idea how I was going to get by without Tessa.

***

Days turned into weeks and eventually into a month with Tessa not talking to me. Mum was back to drinking when one of her friends saw Dad with another woman. She was doing well being sober and had found a new job. I don't know why she allowed Dad to get to her and bring out a bottle like alcohol was the solution for all of her problems.

Most nights I was alone with Mum as she drank her sorrows. I do my best to hide the wine and vodka bottles from her, but she always found them again or purchased new ones. Corey was hardly around, always with his uni friends or he was at work. Even during the holidays, he was off doing things, leaving me to deal with Mum. But since the night Tessa was drunk and I had seen the two of them kiss, it was like he was trying to avoid being home in case Tessa was here. I haven't told him how we had ended our friendship. I haven't even told Mum about it. Not even at the time when she asked me how Tessa was and wondered why she hadn't been coming over. I told her she was busy babysitting her brothers or had band practice, which is probably not a lie.

I spent recess and lunch alone, often disappearing to the library. I saw Tessa in the hallways and she would walk past me like I didn't exist. In English she sat away from me. When our teacher asked us to pair up for an assignment, Tessa looked straight over at me. We loved it when teachers assigned us into pairs because we never had to think who we should join up with. I thought maybe she would change her mind and come over to me when she stood up from the chair, walking over to me. But my heart sank from the hope she had given me as she made her way over to Mark's cousin Eileen who sat behind me.

I try not to let Tessa see I was hurt. I glanced around the room to see who I could pair up with. Everyone else had already found a partner. Eventually my teacher paired me with Darren Winters.

***

November came around. As my birthday approached, I kept hoping Tessa would talk to me or say she has planned something big to celebrate. But on the day I turned seventeen, I celebrated my birthday for the first time without Tessa. I kept glancing at my phone on the day, hoping she would forget everything that happened between us and would text me a happy birthday. Better yet, I wanted her to come around and say it personally to me, maybe even spend the evening with me like we have always done for each other's birthdays.

But this year, I wasn't important enough to her. And with the way my family was falling apart, my birthday felt like it wasn't worth celebrating.

By December it had been six months since Tessa stopped talking to me. There was still that hope I had where I wanted to believe she would want to be friends again. But when the bullying started, I knew then that our friendship was definitely over.

I'm in the bathroom when I saw what was written on the walls of the stall that was filled with racist comments about students in the school, comments that hurt even if it wasn't talking about you, but you felt the empathy of what that person must feel if they saw their name on these awful comments. In capital letters, written with a black ink permanent marker were the words "CASEY ROLAND IS SO FAT THAT SHE LOOKS LIKE A WHALE."

I stared at the words, reading it over and over again. I recognised the handwriting straight away. I remember once flipping through her lyric book she had accidentally left at my place. I never told her that I had flipped through it to see what she had written. She would have killed me if she knew I had read it. One thing that stood out when I read it is how she wrote the Y in my name. She always looped the tail when writing in capital, as well as when she is writing it in smaller print. This was indeed Tessa's handwriting.

I stare at the words for so long that tears prickled my eyes. I don't understand why she would write something like this. I haven't always been skinny like Tessa. I had a bit of body fat around my hips and tummy, but it wasn't something that ever really worried me.

There have been a few times when mean girls would have nothing better to do and pick out my flaws. Guys are jerks sometimes when they would say I'm fat. Tessa would always stand up to those bullies and tell them to leave me alone, that there was nothing wrong with my weight. Now Tessa was the bully.

I stepped out of the stall, wiping my eyes. I didn't want someone to walk in and see me crying. I wonder how many girls in our school have seen what Tessa had written. Whoever read it, did they know who I was?

I stared at my reflection in the mirror. I heard Tessa's voice in my head, telling me how I looked like a whale. I eventually turned away, not wanting to look at my reflection anymore.

For the rest of the day everyone stared and whispered about me. No doubt it was about what was written on the bathroom stall. People can't possibly believe those words, do they?

When school ended for the day, I hurried to find Tessa. I wanted to find out why she was being horrible to me. I get it. We aren't friends anymore, but that didn't mean she had the right to bully me or spend rumours to make me look bad, or take every insecurity I had to hurt me.

I found her at the front of the school with Mark, Travis and Tim. She stood close to Mark who had his arm around her waist. I wander over to them.

"I saw what you wrote in the girls' bathroom," I said to her.

Tessa turned to me, innocently. The guys turned to me also, wondering what I was talking about. "I didn't write anything in there."

"Don't act dumb like you don't know what I'm talking about, Tessa. You wrote how I looked like a whale. Why did you write that? You wouldn't like it if I had written it about you."

"I didn't write it."

"Bull crap. It's in your handwriting."

"That doesn't mean I had written it. I'm sure someone in this school has a similar handwriting to me."

She had a point, but I know it was Tessa. Why would it be anyone else?

"If Tessa says she didn't write it, Casey, then she didn't do it," Mark said. "She would never write something like that. Make sure you know who wrote it before you start pointing fingers."

I stared at Mark, wondering why he was sticking up for her. I get it. Tessa is his girlfriend and he wants to believe she is this nice innocent person who wouldn't write nasty stuff about people on the bathroom walls. I wanted to believe Tessa wouldn't do that. And for a moment half of me wanted to tell Mark about the night of Tessa's birthday where I witnessed her kissing my brother. But I keep my mouth shut because then that will show I'm no better than her.

I turned my attention back to Tessa. "Really, Tessa? You need your boyfriend to defend you for something you know you did do?"

Tessa frowned at me. "I told you, Casey. *I did not do it*."

"Then who did, Tessa?"

She pulled away from Mark, throwing her arms in the air. "I don't know, Casey? What do you want me to say? That an invisible person walked into the toilets and wrote it? I swear I did not do it. Why would I?"

"I don't know why you would. The same way I don't understand why you stop being my friend because of some stupid squabble we had over something we didn't need to fight about. I said I was sorry, Tessa, but that doesn't mean you get to act like a total bitch to me, thinking it's okay to be doing what you are doing." I nodded my head in Mark's direction. "And don't try to act innocent and think your boyfriend can get you out of what you did."

Tessa narrowed her eyes at me. Putting her bag down near her feet, she shoved me hard in the chest. "Don't ever talk about Mark like that!"

I set my own bag at my feet, and shoved Tessa back. "Then stop covering your innocent up."

"I'm not!" She pushed me again.

"Stop pushing me!" I returned the shove.

Tim told us to stop, but we don't listen to him.

This time when Tessa shoved me, I tripped over my bag, hitting the ground hard, the back of my head banging against the pavement. I don't have time to think about the pain as Tessa's foot is shoved hard into my stomach as I tried to get up. Mark tells her to stop it, but she doesn't listen.

She is on top of me now. The palm of her hand slapped me hard against my left cheek. Tessa screamed at me to say that this is what I deserved for accusing her for writing on the bathroom stall, and for being mad at her for spending too much time with Mark instead of me.

Before Tessa could go to slap me again, I reached for her hair that's pulled into a ponytail, and pulled on it. She screamed, pulling my hand away then she pulled the strands of my hair that's loose around my shoulders. She tugged on the hair so hard that I thought the roots would come out. She doesn't even let go as I begged her to stop. The tears prickled my eyes as the throbbing at the back of my head worsens as Tessa bang it a couple of times against the pavement.

There's a ringing in my ears. Around me I can hear other students chatting about what was happening. I can hear Mark, Tim and Travis telling Tessa to stop. I can hear Mrs Grove's voice who is currently on bus stop duty, telling students to move away, and even told a student to put their phone away who had been filming the fight, threatening them if they don't delete the video that she will send them to the principal's office. She yelled at Tessa to stop what she was doing to me. Tessa's hand let's go of my hair. I then hear her voice as she kneeled on the ground, her face appearing over me so I was glancing up at the blue sky.

"Casey, are you alright?" she asked me.

I nodded, which was something I wished I didn't do as pain shock right through my head.

She helped me up and then march both Tessa and I to the principal's office.

***

Tessa was sent into Mr Kelman's office first while I sat outside with an ice pack to the back of my head. He wanted to speak to us separately. He hadn't mentioned anything about calling our parents, and I feared that he would. Bringing Mum into this was the last thing I wanted. I didn't want her to know I was fighting with Tessa. I mean, she knows we are having problems, but she wouldn't like us using our fists to solve our problems.

After about fifteen minutes talking to the principal, she stormed out of his office. She glanced at me, frowning and then mumbles "I hate you". Hearing her say that stabbed my heart. But before I could say a word as Tessa walked away swiftly out of the office to head home, Mr Kelman called me.

I followed him into his office. He closed the door behind me, gesturing me to the chair in front of his desk. I do as he says and sat down, still pressing the ice pack to the back of my head.

Mr Kelman sat down in his chair. "Tessa has told me her side of the story. Now I want to hear yours. Do you care to tell me what went on between you two?"

"What did Tessa tell you?" I wanted to know before I answered him. I knew she would somehow lie to get out of trouble, to make it look like I was the bad guy who started the whole thing.

He straightened up in his chair. "I want to hear your side of the story, Casey, before I make the decision on who is guilty."

I nodded and told him what I had found in the bathroom, how I had approached Tessa this afternoon to confront her about what she had written. I didn't do it to cause a fight. It wasn't supposed to lead to that at all. I just wanted to know why she had written what she wrote on the wall. I wanted to know why she hated me so much.

Mr Kelman doesn't answer me at first once I finished explaining my side of the story, processing everything to mine and Tessa's story. I wonder what she had said and if he would tell me. "Do you have any proof that Tessa Ross had written this?"

I shook my head. "No, I don't."

"Then how do you know she had written it?"

"It was in her handwriting."

I stared at him puzzled. What kind of proof do I need to catch Tessa out? The bathroom stall walls are full of racist and nasty comments that can put anyone's self-esteem down, even if it's not written about you. Of course Mr Kelman wouldn't know what is written on our school bathroom walls. He never would have step foot in there. He doesn't care what does on in there.

"Why do you need more proof when I clearly know it's her handwriting?"

Mr Kelman sighed with frustration. Clearly, he just wanted to get out of here instead of dealing with more student drama. "Thousands of students in this school have written something on the walls. Anyone could have written it unless you have seen Tessa do it."

I really could not believe the principal of this school wasn't doing anything with what Tessa had written. Okay, he had a point. I didn't see her write it. But that's how it is, right? You never know who writes on the walls. I didn't see Tessa with the black permanent marker, scribbling her cruel words on the walls. I just knew it was her. Why would it be anyone else? I'm fighting with Tessa. No one else. She wrote those things to hurt me.

"If there isn't anything else you need to report, Casey, then we are done here," he told me when I didn't respond to whether or not if I have seen her do what she did. "But before I let you go, I have to give you a punishment."

"A punishment? For what? I didn't do anything."

"Don't try and make it out that you're completely innocent, Casey. Since there is only three weeks left of school, I would hate to suspend you and Tessa for fighting. So for a week I will be giving you after school detention. I will be sending a letter home to your parents to notify them with what is going on."

I nodded, unsure what I should say back. I know I shouldn't have shoved her back. I should have walked away, and I wouldn't be sitting here in the principal's office. But I don't understand why I'm in trouble for fighting, and Tessa wasn't getting punished for what she had wrote on the bathroom stall wall, only because I didn't have proof she had done it.

Mr Kelman dismissed me, telling me he will be sending a letter home to my mother tomorrow, and my week of after-school detention starts tomorrow. It was the very first detention I have ever had. Tessa was more of the kind of person to get detention. She was always getting one when she spoke back at her teachers. I can imagine the argument she will be getting in with her father tomorrow.

Right now as I left the principal's office, I don't want to know what my mother would say when she hears about this.

Chapter 23
Tessa

My bandmates and I work on the song all afternoon. We didn't even work on any of our other songs and decided to practice playing them another day. I fight back tears as I hear the song come to life with the drums and bass guitars other than with my acoustic. If Casey knew I had written the song, she would cry when she hears it.

Mark still wasn't talking to me, but he had spoken a bit as he helped with suggestions on what chords should be used. I guess that's a good thing so far.

As we played the song over and over again, I soon realise I needed to confess to both Ms Emerson and Corey for what I had put Casey through. I couldn't keep lying to them with what I had put her through, how I was the one who was responsible for her death.

We kept working on the song until Uncle Harley walks into the garage to let us know it was six o'clock. I honestly didn't care about the time or that it's dinner. All I wanted to do was work on the song until I thought it was perfect.

"The song you wrote about Casey is good," Mark says to me when it was just us standing alone in the garage, where Tim and

Travis had walked out to the van. He looks my way as he zips up his guitar into its case. "She would have loved it."

I thought about the day when Casey promised me she will stand in the front row once our band have gotten our first break. Whenever I played my music, Casey always had this huge smile on my face, proud of what I have written even if she knew nothing about music. Even when some days I got frustrated with writing my music, unable to find the right chords, or I couldn't figure out what lyric to use, she always gave me a suggestion that could make the song better. I wondered to myself that despite us no longer being friends, would she still have gone to my big break to support me, keeping her promise.

I imagine my band on the stage, singing this song. Casey stands at the front of the stage. Maybe I would have invited her onto the stage, announcing to the audience that this song was dedicated to her. I could picture the tears in Casey's eyes as I begin to sing the song.

Mark's right. Casey would have loved it.

And I wish she was here to hear it.

***

Once my bandmates left, I told Uncle Harley I needed to see Corey. He wasn't sure about letting me go after what went down earlier today with Mark and Corey, but I said it was important I go to sort some things out. He allowed me to, just as long as I wasn't out for too long.

Corey answers the door when I get there. He greets me with a smile, but I knew once I start talking, he won't be smiling.

"Tessa, it's great to see you," he says. "I wasn't expecting to see you after what happened this morning."

"Is your Mum here?" I say straight out, not wanting to talk about this morning. "I need to talk to you both about something important. Something you both should know."

Corey shakes his head. "No. Mum isn't here. My aunt took her out for the evening. But whatever you need to talk to us about, I will pass the message onto her later." He stands aside. "Come on in, and sit down. Would you like a drink?"

I shake my head as I walk into the house. "I'm fine thanks, Corey. Besides, I don't think I would be here long enough to have one."

"What are you talking about? You're always welcome here." He gestures to the couch. "Come take a seat."

I stare at the couch, the same one where Corey and I had sex on the last time I was here. I turn back to Corey and shake my head. "No, I rather not sit down. You are not going to want me here after I tell you this. You might never want to speak to me again."

Corey's face turns serious. "What do you need to tell me, Tessa?"

I inhale a deep breath, holding it as long as I could before exhaling it. I can tell him this. I need to take responsibility for my actions for what I have done to my best friend. "I killed Casey."

Corey stares at me for a long time, confused and shock as he opened and closed his mouth. "W-What?"

"Well, I didn't physically kill her, but I mentally did."

"I don't understand, Tessa."

"I bullied her, Corey. I bullied her so much that it made her want to end her life."

Corey shakes his head. "No. I don't believe you. Why would you do that, Tessa? You're best friends."

"We *were* best friends. We stopped being friends in June last year. She was jealous that I was spending too much time with my boyfriend and not with her. I got so mad at her that I told her that our friendship was over. I don't even know what made me start teasing her. I was just so angry with her."

It takes Corey a minute to register what I had said. "Why would you do something like that, Tessa? What kind of friend are you? You aren't the kind of person who would bully someone."

"I didn't mean to bully Casey."

"Bull crap, Tessa," he raises his voice. "Whatever issues you both had, you didn't need to bully her. It's never the answer to anything. How would you feel if Casey was to do the same thing to you?"

I don't answer him because I knew what he was saying was true. How would I feel if Casey was to do the same thing to me? Would I like it? Of course I wouldn't. No one likes to be bullied. It's never the answer to anything.

"I'm sorry, Corey. I'm sorry for everything. I know apologising is not going to bring Casey back, but I understand if you don't want to talk to me ever again. I wish I could take it all back for what I did to her."

Before Corey could say anything, I open the door and run out of the Rolands' home.

Chapter 24
Casey

Mum grounded me for the week when she received the letter from Mr Kelman. I never explained to her about the reason why Tessa and I fought. I just told her we had a disagreement. It then followed onto a lecture how it was wrong to use violence and how Mum had taught me not to fight. I knew what I had done wrong, but Tessa was the one who provoked me.

I do my best to avoid Tessa for the week so I don't get in any more trouble than what I am already in. But it wasn't all so easy when I saw her in the halls or when I had English and P.E. with her. At least on Thursday and Friday afternoon I didn't have do detention with her. Mr Kelman gave me permission to not to attend those two days as I had work, but I was able to make those days up next week.

But getting through the week avoiding Tessa was the least of my worries. Around school my classmates would whisper or look over at me, talking behind my back like I didn't exist or didn't know what they were saying about me. They spoke about Tessa and my fight, for the reasons why we were no longer friends. The words that hurt the most were the ones Tessa had written on the bathroom stall wall. The girls who had seen it began making fun of my weight. It wasn't just them, though. No. Guys were in on it too.

During P.E. on Friday afternoon, I heard some girls whisper, laughing at me while we played soccer. It wasn't the sport for me, and most of the time I don't participate in it. 'She looks like a whale' are words that are playing over and over again in my mind. Thinking of those words made me feel fat. And because I wasn't running up and down the oval for the game, I could imagine what others must think of me for not taking part in the sport. I caught sight of Tessa, who was hanging out with Amelia and her friends while our teacher gave us a short break before we picked up the game. She looked my way, smirked and then turned back to her new friends. Seeing her with them made my heart sank in my stomach. It was nice to know how important I have always been to her.

When P.E. was over, I couldn't wait to get into the change rooms to get back into my uniform to get out of school for the day. At least when I'm at work after this it will help me keep my mind off everything.

I hid in one of the showers to change. I stripped down to my underwear. But as I go to grab my skirt, I realised it wasn't amongst my stuff, neither was my shirt. Who would have taken it?

There was only one person I knew who would play this kind of prank on me.

I stepped out of the stall in my underwear to find Tessa. Other girls stopped what they were doing as I walked pass them until I find Tessa standing with Amelia on a bench near a large mirror on the wall. They turned to me, both laughing.

"Well, isn't it the whale," Tessa laughed. "Where are your clothes?"

I frowned at her. "Stop calling me names, Tessa. It's not nice of you to be saying those things. You wouldn't like it if I called you that."

"Then don't call me it."

"Where are my clothes, Tessa? Give them back, please."

Tessa gave me a smirk. "Oh, what's the matter, Casey? Did you misplace your clothes?"

Amelia and a couple of girls standing nearby chuckled. I do my best to ignore them and keep my focus on Tessa.

"I'm not leaving until you give me back my uniform."

Tessa glanced through her bag where she had her P.E. clothes in there and her sneakers with the laces tied together. She had her skirt on as well as her shirt that wasn't buttoned up, showing off the white lace bra she had on. She then looked up at me. "I'm sorry, Casey, but I don't have your uniform. I don't know where it could be."

I don't believe her. "I know you took it, Tessa. No one here would take it. You're the only one who has something against me."

Tessa chuckled. "Do you know how ridiculous you sound, Casey? What could I possibility want with your uniform?"

I crossed my arms across my chest. "I don't know. You tell me why you would want to take it. Maybe you did it to get back at me or something."

"Well, I didn't take it so don't blame me for anything."

I shook my head at her and then head back to where I was to change. I had no choice but to change back into my P.E. uniform. But when I returned back to the stall, I saw someone had placed my uniform on top of my P.E. uniform. I glanced around to see who might have dumped it there while I had gone to speak to Tessa, but it could be anyone. Some girls nearby laughed at me. Without staying another moment in this changed room, I threw on my clothes and ran out of it before I bumped into Tessa.

***

I stood in front of the mirror in my room, wearing only my underwear. I stared at my reflection for a long time, wondering if what Tessa had said was true. Was I overweight?

I wasn't super skinny like Tessa, but I didn't think I was overweight either. I was a size fourteen. That shouldn't worry me as I wasn't so big like Tessa claimed I was. But the voice at the back of my head wanted me to beat myself up, tell me that everything Tessa said was true. It didn't take me long to believe the words that played over and over again in my mind.

I turned away from my reflection. I couldn't stand to see how ugly I was in the mirror.

***

The Christmas holidays couldn't come fast enough. I was glad to be able to get out of school for the year so I could forget everything that had been going on. Tessa wasn't making things easy for me at school. Every day she would make my life hard with insults, anything to put me down. It still made me wonder what made her do this to me. I understood if she was mad at me for how I didn't like her hanging with Mark all the time, but why did she feel like she needed to bully me?

With it being the holidays, I picked up extra shifts at the bookstore. Working kept my mind off everything. As it got closer to Christmas, I had high hopes that Dad would return home, surprise Corey and I with something. But of course, that was just wishful thinking. He never called, sent a letter or a parcel. It was like we were dead to Dad.

I wanted to believe Tessa and I would prepare our relationship by Christmas Day, but that didn't happen either. Sometimes I would walk by her house and hear her band playing music from the garage.

If I knew how to fix things, I would. But it felt like nothing will ever be fixed. I don't understand why everything in the past six months turned out to be like this. I hated myself and I wanted everything to go back to how it used to be when my parents were together and to when Tessa and I were still best friends. There was no Mark and there was no band. Back to when it was only us dreaming about the future and what we will do together.

***

The day after Boxing Day I was surprised to see Tessa walking into the bookstore. My heart danced for joy in my chest, thinking that maybe my Christmas wish was going to come true. Tessa was here to apologise for everything and we will be friends again.

I smiled at her. "Hey, Tessa. What can I do for you?"

Tessa doesn't return the smile. "What are you doing for New Year's?"

I think for a moment. "I'm working until five thirty, and then head home to be with Mum. Corey is heading into the city with friends to watch the fireworks."

"Would you like to come to a party that Amelia Smith is hosting on New Year's? Her parents will be out of town so she will have the house to herself."

"Oh." My heart sank with sadness where I had been hoping Tessa would tell me to forget everything that has happened and that we could spend New Year's Eve starting over. But that's not what she wanted at all. She wanted me to attend a party where she knew I didn't quite fit in with that scene. Tessa knew I prefer to attend parties where it was just us two. "I don't think Amelia would want me there."

"Of course she wants you to come, Casey. It's going to be a small party."

Half of me wanted to say yes, the other half reminded me what had happened at Tessa's birthday. I didn't want a repeat of the last time. And I was surprised with how much time Tessa was spending with Amelia. I remember the days when she never liked her, always saying how she was a snob. Now she acted like they were best friends ever since the time Amelia approached me when I asked Max out.

"Aren't you spending New Year's with Mark or any of your bandmates?" I asked.

She shook her head. "No. They all have plans with their families, and there is no way in the world I will be spending the New Year with my family. Hazel is spending the night there."

"Thanks, Tessa, but I don't think I will come along to it. You know I don't really fit into parties."

Tessa rolled her eyes. "For crying out loud, Casey, just come. Stop being so ridiculous, okay? Why do you think I was your only friend? It's because you don't socialise with anyone."

Her words stabbed me in the heart. Did she really think like this when we were friends? "I can't help that I'm shy."

"Look, just come along, Casey. It's not like you will be in a room full of strangers. You will know everyone there. They are just girls from our grade who are friends with Amelia. Besides, I'm sure it will be better than spending the New Year at home."

I didn't mind spending it at home. It's what Tessa and I have always done. It was the one day of the year where we were allowed to stay up until 12.30am to watch the fireworks. And since this New Year's Eve will be the first without my dad, I didn't want to leave my mother alone. I fear how she would be tonight. She will drink until she passes out. In the morning, I will be the one to clean up her mess since Corey will not be there to do it. He is never around when Mum drinks too much.

"Tessa, I really can't. It's the first New Year's Eve without my dad, and I don't want to leave my mother alone."

She signed with frustration. "Seriously, Casey? You're worried about your Mum? She is a grown woman. I'm sure she will be alright being on her own. And I'm sure she will be fine without you there, telling her whether or not if she can drink."

I wasn't sure how to respond to her, not sure if it was an insult. Tessa knows how I feel about my mother drinking, so why tell me that my mother much rather not have me around without telling her if she should be drinking?

So I said yes to her invitation even though it was something I really wasn't sure about.

Chapter 25
Casey

"Will you be staying at Tessa's tonight?" Mum asked me when I said goodbye to her. She was already on the couch in front of the TV drinking a glass of wine. I wonder how many she will be having tonight.

I shrugged. I honestly had no idea what was going to happen tonight. Tessa never mentioned if we were going to be out all night. "I will probably spend the night at Tessa's."

She smiled at me. "Alright. You have a good time, Casey."

"Are you sure you will be alright by yourself tonight?"

Mum nodded as she took a sip of her wine. "I'm good, Case. Go have a good time."

I gave her a kiss on the cheek, and then head out. Tessa told me she would be picking me up to drive us to Amelia's. She pulled up in front of my home just as I closed the door behind me.

"Thank you for inviting me to the party," I told her as I slipped on my seat belt.

"It's fine," Tessa pulled away from the kerb. "Amelia thought I should invite you. After the New Year her family is moving up to Queensland."

"Oh. I wasn't aware of her moving. Is she still with Max?"

"Why do you want to know? So you can date him once she is gone? Max will not date you if that's what you're thinking. He and Amelia are trying the long-distance relationship."

I nodded without saying anything in case I say something that will make Tessa say some kind of insult.

For the rest of the car ride, we sat in silence. It was strange how in just six months we had become strangers with nothing to say to each other. When there is something to say, it ended with insults.

The sun is starting to set when we reach Amelia's house. I followed Tessa to the front door where Amelia opened it for us. She smiled brightly when she saw Tessa, but it quickly faded when she saw me. I understood she was mad at me for asking her boyfriend out, but I didn't understand why she had to continue to hate me.

Amelia greeted us with a happy New Year and led us through her house to the kitchen, where three of her friends were sitting around the island. Pop music played from someone's phone. Amelia announced to her friends that Tessa and I had arrived. The three girls looked up from where they had been giggling and talking about something while popping snacks into their mouths. Katie-Lynn had long wavy blonde hair and blue eyes while her twin sister Beth's hair was also blonde, but in a pixie haircut and had green eyes. Their facial features also were different that you could easily mistake them as not being sisters.

Parker Knight was Amelia's other friend. She was the only red head in our grade.

As soon as the three girls turned to us, I feel their eyes mainly on me instead of Tessa. It made me feel small, and a voice at the back of my head screamed at me to get out of there, that I did not belong here at all.

"What is Casey doing here?" Beth asked.

"Remember I said I will bring her along to the party?" Tessa answered.

"Yes, I remember."

Amelia turned to me, and smiled. It was a smile I could see was fake as she tried to act friendly to me. "Take a seat at the island, Casey, and have as much food as you want."

"But not too much or you will look like a pig," I heard Katie-Lynn mumbled softly, but it was still loud enough for me to hear.

I pretend I don't hear what she had said. Tessa sat down on a stool next to Parker, whose eyes are on the screen of her phone. As I go to sit on a stool on Parker's other side, the doorbell rang. She almost knocks me off my feet as she leaped off the stool. She doesn't even apologise to me, pushing passed me to run to the door.

"Jace is here!" she squealed, running past Amelia to the front door.

I sat down on the stool beside Parker's empty one. I felt the twins' eyes on me as they looked up from their phones every few seconds. Half of me wanted to scoot across to where Tessa was, to close the gap between us, but I wasn't sure if we were even friends or why I'm really here. Tessa wasn't paying attention to me. She was busy talking to Amelia as she took out a jug of peach iced tea from the fridge. The four of them ignored me like I wasn't even there.

It's not too late to leave, is it?

Parker returned with a guy who is a few inches taller than her. I didn't recognise him from school and guessed he must be from another high school in our area. In his hands are two cases of beer. My stomach dropped at the sight of it. No. I can't go through what happened at Tessa's birthday again. Maybe I should leave and spend the night with Mum. She would appreciate my company.

I got off the stool. "Well, thank you for inviting me over, but I really need to go."

Everyone looked at me weird.

"What's the hurry, Casey?" Amelia asked. "You have only just gotten here. The party has started."

"She doesn't drink beer," Tessa spoke up without looking my way. "Actually, she doesn't drink any kind of alcohol. She is too afraid of turning into her mother, who is an alcoholic."

The way Tessa said it sounded like it was a crime because I didn't like alcohol beverages. All because of how I see what my mother goes through and I didn't want to turn out to be like her.

"Seriously?" Beth chuckled. "You don't like beer?"

"You're missing out on the good stuff," Katie-Lynn added. "It's the best drink ever."

"But none of us is eighteen yet," I answered.

"Jace is eighteen." Parker looked up at her boyfriend. "Aren't you, babe?"

He smiled at her and kissed her passionately.

"Guys, please get a room if you're going to make out," Amelia said, pulling a disgusted face.

Parker pulled away and turned her attention to me. "Would you mind moving? Jace is going to sit there."

I didn't want to argue, so I moved out of the way. Parker took a seat while Jace placed the cases of beer on the kitchen counter. There were no more stools so Amelia told me to grab a chair at the dining table. So I did and set it down beside Tessa, who was texting Mark. He was vacationing on the Gold Coast with his family.

"So who is this chick?" Jace gestured his head towards me as he opened the case of beer. He took a few cans out.

"Casey is Tessa's friend. She also tried to steal Max from me." Amelia took a few cans and then turned to everyone else. "Okay guys, who is up for a game of Never Have I Ever?"

Everyone at the island agreed. Amelia handed everyone a can before grabbing her own and sat down next to me. Jace handed Parker a can before sitting down beside her. I stared at the can in front of me. Everyone opened their drink except me.

"Everyone ready?" Amelia asked.

Tessa and the others responded with a nod or a yes.

"How do you play this game?" I asked. My cheeks heat up knowing everyone is going to look down at me for never playing this game. It's clear they have all played it before.

"You're kidding, right?" Parker sighed heavily. "You have never played Never Have I Ever?"

I shook my head. "I have heard of it, but I have never played."

Tessa chuckled. "Don't be surprise, you guys. There are a lot of things Casey hasn't done."

I looked at Tessa, wanting to ask her what that was supposed to mean, but Amelia spoke first.

"The rules of this game are simple," she explained. "A person says something they never have done before. If someone has done something you have done, then they take a sip of their drink. The next person who is beside you will continue on with the game. But if no one response to what you have said, you have to drink. Get it?"

I nodded. "Can I have a glass of water instead, please?"

Tessa let out a frustrating sigh. "It's not going to be a drinking game if you aren't going to drink the same thing as us. Sure, we don't have to play this game with alcohol, but we are choosing to. So suck it up, Casey, and drink the beer. Stop being the wimp you are and have some fun. No one said you will end up like your mother if you drink. You just need to know how to control your liquor."

I should have right there stood up and left. The voice at the back of my head screamed at me to leave. But I worried of what they will all say about me. Part of me wanted Tessa to change her mind and say she is sorry about what she had said, and tell me I didn't have to play this game with alcohol if I didn't want to. I also wanted her to stand up and tell me that the two of us are going to ditch this party and get out of here.

But who am I kidding? Tessa was never going to do that for me. She was Amelia's best friend now. Not mine.

"The game would not be fun if you don't get drunk with us," Amelia said.

"But you can have fun with this game without being drunk," I answered.

"Oh my gosh!" Katie-Lynn said with impatience in her voice. "Who are you and what planet are you from? Can't you just play this damn game the way we want to play? Act like a normal person, will you? There is nothing wrong with drinking."

I closed my mouth. There was no use to keep arguing. It was clear no one here will respect my views. Not even my former best friend who knew how I felt about alcohol. I opened my can and wait for the game to start.

"I will start off," Amelia said. "Never have I ever ran away from home."

Parker picks up her can and took a sip.

Katie-Lynn goes next. "Never have I ever done drugs."

Jace picks up his can and from the corner of my eye I saw Tessa pick up hers, taking a sip. When I saw her do it, I had no idea how to think. For as long as I have known her, she would never have touch drugs.

"When did you start doing drugs?" I asked her.

Tessa rolled her eyes as she placed her can back on the table in front of her. "Why? So you can start telling me it's wrong? Tim offered me and the rest of the band some weed a couple of months ago. It was just one time. It was no big deal."

Beth is next. "Never have I ever failed a subject in school."

Tessa takes a drink.

Jace and Parker said their confessions next. No one picked up their drinks when Jace said he never cheated on anyone. He then took a drink. The twins and Amelia drank on Parker's confession when she said she had never been on a plane.

Tessa is next. "Never have I ever gotten a speeding ticket."

Jace drinks.

It's my turn now. I had no idea what I should say. I was afraid to even say anything in case I was laughed at. I said the first thing that popped into my head. Or maybe I shouldn't have said it. "Never have I ever kissed someone or been kissed."

No one drinks. Instead they laughed at me. It was clear they were all in relationships or had been in one. I was the odd one out. I didn't even fit into this crowd that Tessa was hanging out with now.

"You seriously have never kissed anyone?" Katie-Lynn said, like it was such a big deal.

"Why are you taking this like it's a big deal?" I asked. I keep in mind what Mum had said how it didn't matter if I had a boyfriend in high school, or if I met someone later on in life. "I'm sure there is a ton of students in our grade who has never kissed anyone. I mean, some don't end up being in relationships until after high school. Perhaps I will find someone then."

Tessa laughed. "That's if you ever do talk to a guy without freezing up."

The others all laugh, saying when they received their first kiss, and all I wanted to do was just hide away, forget I even came here. And with Tessa I just didn't know why she would make fun of me like she is. She would always encourage me that I would find someone. Now she showed off with what she had and I didn't.

I get up from the chair and headed outside to the backyard where there was a pool. Everyone asked me where I was going, but I don't answer them. Someone yelled out that I'm a buzz killer.

The air is still humid from the hot day we have had. I take off my shoes and sat down on the edge of the pool, dangling my feet in the water. There I let the tears fall. I can hear the laughter from inside. It made me wonder why Tessa brought me here. I didn't belong in this crowd. I liked it when Tessa and I were friends, and didn't know why everything had to change between us. Had she wanted to stop being friends with me for a long time?

I should leave. But then I remember how Mum was so happy for me when Tessa had invited me to the party, that maybe we had fixed our friendship. And I hated the idea of heading home early to tell her the things that has been happening here. She would be devastated to hear how truly damaged Tessa's and my friendship was. How could an eleven years friendship end like this?

Chapter 26
Casey

The game went on for half an hour and no one seemed to care at all that I was still sitting beside the pool. Nearby neighbours were letting off fire crackers, which caused dogs to bark over the noise, and there's the loud music from parties. In half an hour will be the nine o'clock fireworks. Everyone around me seemed to be having a great time, celebrating something worthwhile for what this year had brought, and what the new year will bring.

For me I had no idea what my new year will bring. Next year I will be graduating high school. It was a time Tessa and I talked about so many times. How we were going to dress for the formal and what we will do once we graduate. Now that was all just nine months away, I had no idea what I will be doing without Tessa. And within those nine months I wonder how it would go for my family. The divorce was finalised last month, which led Corey and I losing all hope of seeing our parents getting back together. Dad still hasn't been in contact with us or even requested to see us since he had walked out. It was like Corey and I were never his kids, nor were we a part of his life. But I guess the New Year was a chance to start new.

And I tell myself that even if Tessa and I were no longer friends, maybe when school starts at the end of January I will make a new friend.

"You know you can come back inside."

I turned to see Jace walking over to me with a can of beer in his hand. From inside I could hear pop music playing. "I don't want to play the game anymore."

"We are no longer playing." He sat down beside me, putting the can beside him. "We played for twenty minutes and then eventually got bored. We decided to dance before we watch the nine o'clock fireworks."

"I think its best I stay here out of everyone's way. I want to go home, but I don't want my mum asking me questions to why I'm home early."

"Your name is Casey, right?"

I nodded. "Yes."

"Come on inside, Casey. Don't sit out here on your own. Don't let those girls get you down because of some teasing they did. Come in and dance."

I gave him a half smile. "Thank you, Jace, but I'm alright out here. Besides, I can't dance. I don't want to make a fool of myself in front of the others."

Jace chuckled. "Trust me, I don't think it matters if you make a fool of yourself. The girls are all drunk after playing the game."

"I'm okay out here. It's a nice night."

"It sure is."

"So do you go to our school? I have never seen you before."

"No, I attend a different school. Parker and I live on the same street. I actually graduated this year."

"That's great. What are you planning to do next year?"

He shrugged, grabbing his can and taking a sip. "Work, I guess. I just finish thirteen years of schooling. I do not want to do more."

I laughed. "Not unless your job requires a certificate or degree, then you will have to do a course."

"I will make sure the job won't involve doing that. So how long have you and Tessa been friends for?"

I turned away from him, looking down at the water. "We aren't friends anymore, but it was eleven years."

Jace let out a low whistle. "Eleven years is a very long time. I don't think I have had any friendships that have lasted that long."

I gestured to the house. "You should head back inside. I'm sure Parker is looking for you."

Jace finished the rest of his drink, crushing the can before setting it down beside him. "I don't mind being out here with you."

I wanted to tell him that I wanted to be out here by myself, to be alone to think, and maybe figure out how I was going to sneak out of here without anyone seeing me. It wasn't like they would even notice if I'm gone anyway. They would carry on with the party like I was never here.

My thoughts are interrupted when I felt Jace's hand on my knee. I glanced down at his hand as he slowly runs his hand up my thigh. Before he could move his hand under my dress, I grabbed it and moved it away from me.

I looked up at him. "What are you doing?"

He doesn't answer me. He grabbed my face roughly and placed his mouth over mine. My heart raced in my chest as a thousand things ran through my head. What was I supposed to do? Do I go along with the kiss? What is Parker going to say?

I don't return the kiss. I put my hands on his shoulders to push him off me.

"Jace, no!" I cried between his kiss.

He doesn't listen. His hands are still cupped around my jaw like he was afraid of letting me go. He didn't even care that I wasn't returning the kiss. I can smell the beer on his breath. I wondered how much he has drunk since arriving here. And why would he kiss me when his girlfriend was only a few metres away in the house?

I put my hands on his arms and moved them away from my face. This time he pulled away from me. He doesn't seem angry at me for pushing him away. Instead he gave me a smirk and there was something in his eyes that told me I was in trouble. I don't even want to know what Jace was planning to do to me. I don't understand why he would come onto me when he had a girlfriend.

"I see you're playing hard to get," he said.

"Is that what you think I'm doing?" I shook my head. "No. I have no interest in you. I just want to sit by the pool in peace and quiet."

I removed my feet from the water and go to get up, but Jace grabbed my arm.

"Are you nervous about your first kiss?" He ran a hand through my hair. "It's okay, Casey. Just relax."

He leaned in to kiss me again, but I pulled back.

"What about Parker?"

"Don't worry about her."

He smashed his lips against mine. I refused to return the kiss. I pushed against his chest, but he would not get off me. It's not until we heard someone cursing that he had pulled away. I was thankful for that person for choosing to walk out here at the right time. I didn't want to know what would have happened if no one had walked out to find us here.

"What the hell are you doing, Jace?" she demanded, as she walked over to us.

Jace got to his feet. "Parker... it's not what it looks like."

Parker stood in front of him. "What does it look like then?"

"I tried to stop her, but Casey was the one who came onto me."

I stood up just as Parker laid her eyes on me. She looked like she wanted to kill me. She took a step towards me.

"He is lying, Parker," I tried to tell her. "He is the one who came onto me."

She narrowed her eyes, raising her hand and strikes me across the face. My skin burned when her skin made contact with mine. I put my hand over my cheek. Why did she hit me and not her boyfriend? How could she believe him and not me?

"How dare you put your hands on my boyfriend!" Parker scolded at me.

"But I didn't kiss him! I swear I didn't, Parker! I would never do that to you." I glanced over her shoulder at Jace. He doesn't even seem one bit ashamed for lying. I also spot Tessa and the other girls walking out to see what all of the commotion is about. Great. Just all of the attention I needed. "Tell her, Jace. Tell her I didn't kiss you."

"Don't try to get out of it, bitch. Just because you don't have a boyfriend, doesn't mean you can steal mine."

"Seriously, Casey?" Amelia said as she walked over to us with the others behind me. "Are you going to be stealing everyone's boyfriend like you tried to steal Max from me? Why can't you find your own?"

"But I didn't kiss him." I turned to Jace. "Please, Jace. Tell them the truth. All I did was come out here to sit by the pool, and then he sat with me. We talked for a bit and then he came on to me."

It didn't matter how much I explained this to everyone, no one wanted to believe me. Even Tessa didn't want to believe me. I don't even understand why Jace would frame me like this, especially when I only have just met him. If he didn't want to be caught picking up another girl than he shouldn't have been doing it with his girlfriend nearby. Jace wasn't doing anything to own up for what he had done.

"Why can't any of you know that I'm telling the truth?" I asked.

Parker crossed her arms across her chest. "Why should I believe a word you say?"

How could I get them to see I wasn't lying?

I looked at Tessa who wouldn't meet my eyes where she glanced down at her feet. "Tessa, tell them I'm telling the truth. You know I would never lie about something like this."

Tessa doesn't say anything in my defence.

When Tessa doesn't respond, I realised at that moment that it was my clue to leave. I don't thank Tessa for inviting me. I picked up my shoes that are sitting on the edge of the pool. I go to move, but Parker blocked my way. When I tried to go around her, Amelia, Beth and Katie-Lynn surrounded me while Tessa and Jace just stand there together, watching.

"Where do you think you're going, Casey?" Parker asked me. "Did we say you could leave?"

I ignored her question. "Please let me go. You don't want me here and I don't want to be here, so it's best I leave to save you time with kicking me out. I'm sorry to be a burden. And Parker, if I were you, I would find another boyfriend. Jace isn't a very good guy."

"And why should we let you leave?" Amelia asked. "So you can leave here and steal someone else's boyfriend?" She shook her head. "No. You have already tried to steal Max from me, now you're going after Jace. Whose boyfriend are you going after next?" She smirked. "I bet next you will go after Tessa's boyfriend. Isn't that the reason why you two aren't friends anymore because you want Mark Brady?"

I looked over at Tessa, who is looking everywhere except at me, trying to avoid me.

"I'm not trying to steal anyone," I told her. "Please, just let me go, and I promise you won't hear from me again."

I tried to pushed passed Parker and Amelia, but they blocked me. Parker shoved me back, making me stumbled backwards into the twins. They shoved me back. My heart pounded in my chest wondering what was installed for me. If these girls do anything, would Tessa stop them or would she be a bystander?

"What do you think we should do to her so she knows it's not okay to flirt with our boyfriends, Parker?" Amelia asked.

Parker smirked at me. "Whatever it takes for this loser to understand that it's not okay to do what she does. It's no wonder Tessa stopped being her friend. I would never want to be her friend. Or be caught dead being around her."

And with that she pushed me hard in the chest, knocking me into the twins. One of them tugged my ponytail so hard that I feared my hair would be pulled out by the roots. I let out a sharp cry, begging them to leave me alone. Jace and Tessa watched on as the other twin shoved me into Amelia, making the twin pulling my hair to let go. Amelia then shoved me to the ground. I hold out my hands to prevent me from smashing my face against the concrete. My palms scrap against the ground, tears pickled my eyes. I cursed at myself for not leaving sooner.

But mostly I regretted allowing Tessa to talk me into coming to this stupid party. Why did she bring me here? Did she know Amelia and her friends were planning to do this? Why would Tessa be friends with these girls?

Before I had the chance to get up or recover, someone's foot slammed in my back. Someone's hands rolled me onto the side. The toe of someone's shoe kicked into my stomach. Another foot kicks. I couldn't breathe for a moment from the blow. I was kicked in the back next. I cried out stop to them, but they only spat out insults at me.

I snuck a quick glance at Jace and Tessa. Jace was filming the fight on his phone, while Tessa just stood there. She looked like she wanted to say something to them to stop, but hesitated. I couldn't understand why she would hesitate stopping them from beating me up like this. She knew what they were doing so why did she let it be okay?

"Tessa, tell them to stop," I begged her. I tasted blood in my mouth where someone had kicked my jaw. "Please."

Tessa stared at me, her fingers on her bottom lip as she bit at her nails. Why is she just standing there? Why isn't she helping me?

Amelia kneeled down in front of me, grabbing my chin to make me look at her. "Don't ask her for help. Tessa isn't going to help you. You brought this on yourself."

"What did I ever do to you?" Some blood spits out of my mouth.

"Besides trying to ask my boyfriend out? Nothing. I never liked you. No one here does. You're someone who has always been invisible to us. I'm so happy that I'm moving schools so I don't have to see your face. And don't even think about flirting with Max once I'm gone. My friends will make sure you stay away from him. Anyway, Max would never date a girl like you. You are just not pretty enough. Maybe that's why you don't have a boyfriend."

The others laughed.

"Why did you ask Tessa to invite me to your party if you don't even like me?" I wanted to know.

Amelia shrugged. "I thought it would be fun to invite you, and see what we could do to tease you."

"Beating someone up because you don't like them is wrong."

I expected Amelia to answer back, but instead she let go of my chin and stood, addressing her friends that they should head inside and leave me out here. Someone spits on me as they walked by.

I lay still on the ground, unable to move. My body ached so much that I wasn't sure how I was going to be able to get up and head home. Why didn't I listen to the voice in my head earlier to get out of here rather than staying here at the party? I wasn't wanted here. Tessa didn't want me here either. She tricked me into coming here.

I turned my head slightly to where Tessa was standing. While everyone headed inside, saying nasty comments about me, Tessa just stands there staring at me. I saw the concern in her eyes, like she wanted to see if I was okay, apologise for everything getting this far, but she was also looking scared. I had no idea why she needed to be scared for. She had the power to stop Amelia and the others from bullying me. She too could stop doing what she was doing, and become friends again, forgetting everything that has happened to me.

Tessa glanced back at the house, waiting for everyone to go inside. When everyone had disappeared, Tessa hurried over to me and helped me sit up.

"I'm so sorry, Casey," she said. "None of this was supposed to happen. They were only meant to tease you, not beat you up."

"Why are you friends with them, Tessa? Why did you ditch me for them? They are horrible. They aren't your friends."

"I have been hanging out with them for a bit, but I'm not friends with them."

"Why are you doing this to me, Tessa? I know I have upset you, and I'm sorry I got upset with you. But why do we have to make a big deal out of the whole thing? Why can't we be friends again?"

I wait for Tessa to answer me, to tell me she wants to be friends again, but she doesn't.

Instead she said, "I'm sorry, Casey. You better go. I'm really am sorry."

She helped me to stand on my feet and then hurried inside, leaving me to wonder how did our friendship come to this.

***

I had no money to call a taxi or an Uber, so I had no choice but to walk home. There was the option of calling up my brother, but he would no doubt be drunk and wouldn't like me disturbing him on his night out with friends. Every part of my body ached and I wasn't sure how I was going to be able to walk home. What was a fifteen-minute drive from my house was probably a half an hour walk or more. And at the pace I was walking, no doubt it was more than half an hour.

The ground is warm from the hot day as my feet touched the pavement. I held my shoes in one hand where I just didn't care about putting on my shoes again. I couldn't even bend down to put them on. With any other hand I clutched it on my left side, where the pain was unbearable. I couldn't breathe right, and I feared I may have broken a rib. I had no idea how I was going to explain any of this to Mum or to Corey.

Fireworks were going off, but I pay no attention to them. I just want to get home and forget this night had ever happened.

I don't know how long it took me to get back home, but I felt relief to get through the front door. The television was playing with New Year's Eve celebrations down by Sydney Harbour.

It's then I spot my mother lying on the floor between the couch and coffee table, a spilled wine glass lay beside her, red wine staining the carpet.

Chapter 27
Tessa

I pulled out the old shoe box I had hidden in the back of the wardrobe, full of memories of Casey and I. We may not have been friends anymore, but I kept what I cherished the most, things I couldn't throw away, even when I was mad at her. I sit down with it on my bed, opening it up.

Inside were photos and objects. I pick up a blue and green beaded bracelet with five white beads with black letters spelling out my name. Casey had given it to me the very first time when we became friends. She made one for herself also with red and orange. *"No matter what happens to us, as long as we have these, we will be friends forever,"* she had said. My heart ached thinking of that memory. Unfortunately, we didn't stay friends forever.

I put it back into the box. There were a few shells we had collected when our families had gone to the beach together one summer. It was the very first time when she told me she couldn't swim. We were both six then, but Mum had been taking me to swimming lessons so I had a fair idea how to keep afloat. Casey on the other hand didn't know how to stay afloat. She had lessons, but for whatever reason she didn't feel comfortable in the water. So I took her hand, and walked her to the water. We didn't go far in. We stood where the water had just come up to our knees. I didn't push her to go fully into the ocean. We both had floaties on just in case, but even with them on Casey was terrified of the water.

There's a picture to go with that day. I had on a rainbow one piece swimsuit while Casey's was pink with strawberries printed on them. She had on pink floaties on her upper arms to match her swimsuit while I had on green ones. We stood in front of a sandcastle we had made while Corey stood at the back of us.

Another photo showed us outside the function centre where we were attending our Year Six formal. One photo was us in our matching school uniform on our first day of Year Seven standing outside of the school's entrance.

As I flipped through the box a little longer, I wonder what went wrong in our friendship. It shouldn't have ended up the way it did. Casey was right about what she said to me on New Year's Eve. I didn't need to be a bully, or hang around someone who was or even needed to turn completely against Casey and treated her like dirt, all because of a misunderstanding. Yes, I was mad at her because she didn't like me spending too much time with Mark. She had apologised to me, and I didn't accept her apology. And then the cruel prank I pulled on her about Max. Being the bystander when Amelia and her friends beaten her up only because they never liked her. Amelia also wanted to get back at Casey for asking Max out. We had planned to hurt her so much that night. I didn't even want to invite Casey to the party when Amelia said to bring her. I don't know why I even agreed to bring her along and ruin her night. I just stood there as the girls kicked her, bashed her like she was nothing. I didn't do anything to help her when she pleaded for my help. I was afraid to step in, afraid they would turn on me next. I shouldn't have been afraid, but I was.

Why did I become friends with Amelia and her friends anyway? How could I even say they were my friends? I didn't keep in contact with Amelia once she moved, and I didn't stay friends with the others. Not after the way I had let them treat Casey. My parents never raised me to be a bully. So why did I become one?

I remember the day I planned the prank with Casey. Amelia approached me later that day where we had a class together. She strolled up to me with a frown.

"Hey, Tessa, tell your friend Casey to stay away from my boyfriend," she said. "Better yet, tell me where I can find her. I will make sure she stays away from Max."

I curled my lips into a smirk. "Don't worry. I don't think Casey is going to do it again."

After that day, Amelia and I started talking more. Other students were starting to realised something was going on between Casey and I. We were no longer the inseparable. I saw Casey in the halls, looking lost without me. She would sit at lunch on her own. Every now and again, our eyes would catch each other from afar, and for a moment I would feel horrible for what I was doing to her. But then I remind myself for why I stopped being friends with her.

She said she was sorry, Tessa, I argued with myself.

I know she is sorry, but I can't be friends with someone who is jealous for not wanting me to be with my boyfriend.

Days went on, and I was spending more and more time with Amelia and her friends. If I wasn't with her, I was with Mark. When I was with Casey, she was an excuse for me to get out of the house when I was fighting with my dad or whenever Hazel was over. Now, I spent my days going over to see Mark.

The day before New Year's Eve, I was supposed to be baby-sitting my brothers. Instead I argued with my dad about it, and walked out, escaping to Amelia's. Her friends Katie-Lynn, Beth and Parker joined us. Amelia and I sat on her bed while the other three sat on the floor. Beth was braiding her sister's hair, while Parker had pulled out her vape.

"Parker, how many times have I told you not to vape in my room?" Amelia scolded her. "If my mum finds out, I'm dead."

Parker blew out the smoke. "Relax, Amelia. She's not going to find out." She turned to me, holding out the vape to me. "Want to try, Tessa?"

I stared at it in her hand. I have never touched a cigarette in my life, nor vapes. There was that one time I have tried a joint though, but it's something I don't want to do again. Smoking isn't for me.

I shook my head. "No, thanks."

Parker shrugged. "Your lost." She took another puffed of it before putting it back in her pocket.

"So, my parents won't be home for New Year's Eve," Amelia announced. "I'm thinking of having a party." She looked over at Parker. "Hey, Park, do you think you can get Jace to bring the beers?"

Parker smiled at the mentioned of her boyfriend. "Of course I can get him to do that."

Amelia turned to me. "Tessa, how about you bring Casey along?"

I stared at her, wondering why she wanted her to come along. I knew Casey wouldn't come. Parties just wasn't her scene, especially if there's drinking involved.

"She won't come," I said.

"Why?" Beth snorted from where she tied her sister's braid with an elastic band. "She doesn't like to party?"

"Why do you even want to invite her, Amelia?" Katie-Lynn asked. "She's an outcast. She also tried to steal Max from you. Why do you think Tessa stopped being friends with her? She probably tried to steal Mark."

She would never try to steal Mark from me, I wanted to say, but kept my mouth shut. *Casey is not that kind of person to steal someone else's partner. She would not do that to me or to anyone.*

"I just thought it was a nice gesture." Amelia turned to me. "So can you invite her, Tessa?"

There was something in Amelia voice that told me I couldn't trust her. It made me wonder what she was planning to do, and if inviting Casey was really a nice gestured. It was bad enough Amelia and her friends suggested I wrote those nasty words about Casey's weight on the bathroom wall at school. I never wanted to hurt her like that. But a part of me was afraid of what my new so-called friends would do if I didn't listen to them. So I wrote them, knowing if Casey ever saw the words, she would be devastated. She didn't deserve it. For a while, teasing her was supposed to make me feel good, but eventually I had no idea why I was doing it. I wanted to stop, somehow beg Casey for forgiveness, but I didn't know how to stop being the horrible person I was becoming. Even when Casey approached me that afternoon, asking why I had written those cruel words, I didn't want to admit the kind of person I was for writing it. I didn't want my boyfriend or my bandmates to know what I was becoming when I was hanging around Amelia and her friends.

And I wished I never invited her to the stupid party.

That night, even though I joined in with the cruel jokes, deep down I felt sick to the stomach. In my head, I'm trying to figure out how do I stop this? And when we stepped outside to find Parker arguing with Casey about coming onto Jace, right then I knew I should have said something. I watched as Amelia and her gang beat Casey up. It was clear now why Amelia wanted me to bring her along. Though, I'm not sure if beating her up was one of them, but teasing her and putting her down was something Amelia had planned.

When it was just Casey and me standing beside the pool, and the others had gone inside, I was torn on what I should do. I wanted to be with Casey and make sure she was alright. I told myself to ask her if she was hurt and volunteered to take her home, but I couldn't bring myself to ask her that. Cause deep down inside, I was afraid of what Amelia and her friends would do to me next if they even saw me out here talking to Casey.

It's time to end this rivalry, I told myself. But I couldn't find a way to tell Casey how sorry I was. Everything has gone too far and I feared our friendship will never be the same again.

Leaving Casey outside, I went to join the others. When I entered, everyone was laughing at something, and I don't know if it's because of what they had done to Casey. I grabbed another can of beer, but as I opened it and took a sip, I recalled the concerned look Casey had given me. Or maybe it was fear. I don't know exactly, but I know how she felt whenever she is surrounded by alcohol. I also shouldn't have told her to stopped being a wimp, when I know what she is going through with her mother. But all I did was humiliate her so I could fit in with Amelia and her friends.

Each passing day that went by, I kept telling myself to make up to Casey, to check on her after what happened, but I didn't.

After Amelia moved states, it's just me with Katie-Lynn, Beth and Parker. After that night on New Year's Eve, I don't know why I was still hanging around with them. I didn't belong with their friend group. I belong with Casey's. Sometimes I drove past her street, tempted to show up to her door and ask her for our friendship back, but I didn't know how to. Eventually I withdrew my friendship with Amelia and her friends. I never told them I didn't want to hang out with them because of what they had done to Casey. So I told them I needed to hang out with my band. It wasn't a complete lie. In four months we were going to enter the contest, and all I could think about is the record deal. We needed all of the practice we needed in order to get it, and it paid off in the end.

Closing the box up and setting it on my bedside table, I curled up into a ball and cried. Casey, if you can hear me, please forgive me for what I have done to you. If I could take it all back, I would.

I could have stopped the bullying. Maybe then Casey would still be here.

I especially could have given our friendship a second chance that night when she texted me. I remember staring at my phone, and thinking to myself that Casey didn't deserve me as a friend because I knew deep down inside, I damaged our friendship. I didn't deserve a second chance from the horrible friend I have become. She was better off without me. So I wrote back to her saying our friendship was over for a long time.

But I didn't know what she had planned to do. I didn't know that she was reaching out to me, hoping that I would change my mind about everything and we will be friends again. She was in pain and begging me for help. Casey needed me, and I chose not to help her. All because I was a selfish bitch. I should have responded back and said, "Yes, I want to be friends again."

Because that's what I want. I want us to be friends again, even if I didn't think I deserve a second chance with Casey, but she was giving it to me.

And I blew the opportunity.

"I'm sorry, Casey," I whisper over my sobs. "I'm sorry."

***

I move my fork around the spaghetti Bolognese my uncle had made. I had a few bites of the food, but my appetite wasn't there. My brothers were almost finished their dinner, sauce around their mouths. I could feel Uncle Harley's eyes on me, but he doesn't say anything in front of Kaiden and Jackson.

"Is everything okay, Tessa?" Uncle Harley asks me once the twins leave the kitchen, heading to the lounge room to watch something on the television.

I wanted to tell him I was fine, but then I would be lying to myself. Knowing my uncle, he would keep asking me how I am until I finally open up and talk about Casey.

I let my fork drop on the plate with a clutter, and turn to my uncle who had already finished his meal. "Have you ever done something you shouldn't? You could have stopped it when you had the chance, but regret it later when it's all too late to fix?"

Uncle Harley stares at me for a minute before answering. "Yes, I had a few things that I wished I didn't do and if I could go back to change anything, I would."

"What was your regret?"

He doesn't answer straight away, getting up from his chair and taking his cutlery and plate to the sink. He stands there for a moment before sitting back at the table. "Have I ever told you how I almost lost my life when I was twenty-one? Or did your father ever mention it to you?"

I shake my head, pushing my plate away from me. I was surprised this story has never been mentioned. Not unless, of course, Dad felt like this was something my brothers and I never had to hear. There were stories he and Uncle Harley would share, but the near-death experience was not one of the stories.

"On my twenty-first birthday, I got into my friend's car after going to a pub for a few beers," he explains. "Your father suggested I take the taxi home, but I didn't. My friend was too drunk to drive, but we both thought it was okay and it should be fine if he drove me home. I didn't live too far from the pub and neither did he." He pauses, placing his hands around his empty glass.

"Unfortunately, we were wrong, and if I only had listened to your dad, everything would have been fine. My friend ended up crashing into a telegraph pole. I escaped with a few cuts and bruises, but my friend wasn't so lucky. His legs were crushed underneath the dashboard. His right leg was badly damaged and it had to be amputated. I often wonder to myself that if I had listened to my brother and talked my friend out of driving that night, would he still have his leg."

I didn't say anything for a long time, not even sure what I should say. So I didn't respond on my uncle's situation. Instead, I blurt out about what I did to Casey.

"I killed Casey." The tears burst out before I could even stop them, a lump forming in my throat. I tell him about the bullying that I had done that lead to Casey taking her own life.

Uncle Harley gets off his chair and pulls out the one beside me, sitting down. He embraces me and I rest my chin on his shoulder, instantly feeling better as he rubs a hand up and down my back, telling me it's okay.

I hear footsteps running into the kitchen.

"Is Tessa okay?" Kaiden says.

"Why is she crying?" Jackson adds.

"Tessa is upset about Casey, that's all," my uncle replies. "Now why don't you boys head upstairs. When I finish talking to your sister, I will come upstairs to make your bath before you go to bed."

My brothers don't leave straight away. Instead, they walk over to me and wrap their arms around me. I let go of my uncle and return my brother's hugs. I don't remember the last time we have ever had this nice moment without trying to kill each other. I mostly never accept any kind of affection from them. They then leave the kitchen so Uncle Harley and I could be alone.

"Don't blame yourself for it, Tessa," he says.

I stare at him with a puzzle look. "How can you tell me not to blame myself? I tormented her, treated her like she was nothing, and I did nothing to stop it."

He nods. "I know you did, and what you did was wrong. But maybe the bullying wasn't the only thing that made her end her life. She could have been going through other things that you weren't aware of, and the bullying on top of it could have taken a toll on it. She may have felt too that no one would listen or have the support she needed to get through whatever she was going through."

It made sense to what he was saying. I started tormenting her at a time when she needed me the most. I couldn't imagine what must have been going through her mind when her parents divorced. Her father wanted nothing to do with her, her mother was an alcoholic, and her brother wasn't always around because of university or work. And there's me – her best friend of eleven years who completely turned against her. For what? All because I was mad at her for telling me I was spending too much time with Mark rather than being with her? I guess she was right. I could have split my time between them both, but I wanted to be with Mark more.

Being mad at her because of Mark wasn't the only thing I was angry about. In fact, I shouldn't have ever gotten upset with Casey. The whole fight we had was stupid, something I didn't have to be all over-dramatic about like it was the end of the world. I was frustrated with Dad, especially with his engagement to Hazel. My grades were slipping and that led to constant arguments with my dad. I used music to escape my problems, and was glad to be made the lead singer of M Triple T. I was able to write down how I feel in my songs. With all of the frustration I felt, I took everything out on Casey, like it was her fault for everything. I was more concerned about my own problems than with Casey's.

Why was I so damn selfish to her?

"We don't know what is going through someone's mind," Uncle Harley continues on. "We have to be aware of our words and actions, because they could hurt someone. I don't know what went on between you and Casey, but it sounded like she really needed you, Tessa. I understand you stopped being friends, but I believe she still wanted you to be there, and you chose not to. You didn't know Casey had chosen to take her own life, Tessa. No one did. Casey had a choice to call for help. Maybe she did reach for help, but felt like no one was there for her. Just keep in mind, Tessa, to think before you say or do something to someone. If you feel like you might have offended someone without realising it, apologise to them. Be there for someone when they need something. You may not be able to change what you did to Casey, but you can change the future. You can prevent the same thing to someone else, maybe save a life."

I take in every word my uncle said. I couldn't change what I did to Casey, but next time I could help someone else going through the same thing as her.

There's a knock at the door at that moment. I get up to answer, but before I could go answer, Uncle Harley calls me back.

"I know you and your dad has a lot of issues to work out, but when he returns home, I want you to talk to him. You will never know what could happen tomorrow, and the last thing you want is to leave this world regretting you never sorted things out with your father, just like what happened with Casey."

I couldn't imagine having a better relationship with my dad, but Uncle Harley was right. If we didn't try to fix our relationship now, we may never do it and I don't want to regret for never apologising the things I have said to him if something was to happen to either of us. And if I couldn't make things right with

Casey before she died, the least I could do was make it right between Dad and I.

I promise my uncle that's what I will do, and then leave to answer the door.

To my surprise Corey was standing there, holding a copy of *To Kill a Mockingbird* in his hand.

"What are you doing here?" I ask, closing the door behind me as I stepped out on the veranda. "I didn't think you would want to talk to me after what happened this afternoon."

"I don't know how I feel right now," he explains. "I just don't understand how you could put Casey through this. I need a few days to process everything you have told me. I have decided not to tell my mother what you did. It will hurt her, and I'm afraid to know what she will do if she knew the reason why Casey took her life."

I nod. "Whatever you decide to do, Corey, I don't blame you for not wanting to speak to me ever again."

Corey sighs. "It's not that I don't want to speak to you again. I'm still processing everything. I want to continue seeing you. I'm crazy in love with you, Tessa, but I know I can never be with you. I wished I never ditched you like I did. But I'm not here to talk to you about what we should have done in the past. I'm here to ask you if you would like to give a speech at Casey's funeral on Friday. It will be held at nine thirty. I know you and Casey stopped being friends, but I think she would want you to speak at her funeral."

I wasn't expecting Corey to ask me after what I had done, but I was glad he had asked me. I hated public speaking, but I will do this for Casey.

"Also, I want to give you this." Corey hands me the book. I take it from him. "I know you aren't much of a reader, but I think Casey would have wanted you to have it. She brought her own copy of the book after you read it in class. She spoke about how much she loved the book, and it's one of her all-time favourites."

I stare at the title in my hands, instantly taking me back to when I used to constantly complain to Casey about why we had to read it for English. I smile at him. "Thank you, Corey."

He returns the smile. "I will see you on Friday." He kisses my cheek and then walks off the veranda, down the driveway to where his car was parked on the street. I watch him get into his car until he drives off.

I head back inside. Uncle Harley called out from the kitchen, wanting to know who was at the door. I told him it was only Corey. He then asks me to do the dishes while he made a bath for my brothers.

Once the dishes were done, I headed up to my room and open up the book to read. As I read, I picture Casey reading it also. I disliked the book, but I read it the way Casey would and pictured it through her eyes, which helped me to enjoy the story a lot more than when we read it in English. In class we are forced to read things we don't enjoy. But this time as I read it willingly, and it was the first book I had enjoyed in a long time.

Chapter 28
Casey

I sat in the waiting room, picking at my nails while I waited to hear from Mum. After returning from the party and finding her unresponsive on the lounge room floor, I called the ambulance. She was rushed to hospital with alcohol poisoning. I count my lucky stars that I returned home when I did. I don't want to think what could happen if I didn't.

I have no idea how long time has passed since I got there, or how long it will be until I'm able to see mum. In the meantime, I tried to call Corey, but his phone kept going to voice mail. My guess was he must have been in a loud place and couldn't hear the phone ring. I left him a text message to let him know Mum was at the hospital. I also left Dad a message, hoping he would care enough to know what had happened to Mum. Like Corey's phone, Dad's also went to voice mail.

I blinked back the tears, frustrated as I tried to get through to someone. On the television in the waiting room showed a band playing at a concert down at Sydney Harbour, entertaining everyone down there. There's an hour left until midnight. I was in no celebrating mood. I wanted the night to end already.

I stared at my phone like it will ring at any moment. I was tempted to call Tessa. In a situation like this she would be here at my side, making sure I was okay. But I couldn't help think about when she helped me off the ground after Amelia and her friends beaten me up. The concerned look she gave me was all I could think about. She had apologised, but I wonder if she really was sorry. I couldn't understand why she couldn't leave the party with me. She acted like she really wanted to help me, but was scared of what would others say. It shouldn't matter to them.

I put my phone away in my handbag. Even if I did call Tessa for help, she wouldn't drop everything to come be with me here. She has new friends now. I'm nothing to her.

Someone called my name, interrupting my thoughts. I looked up at the young Asian doctor, who was treating my mother, standing in front of me. His name tag on his blue scrubs reads Dr. Kim Mai.

I leaped off my seat when I see him, instantly regretting moving so quickly. I winced, clutching my rib. "How's my mother?"

He looked at my hand clutching my side with concern, but doesn't say anything. "She is alright. She is very lucky you found her when she did or she may not have made it. I will be keeping her in here for about a week unless I feel she is able to leave early. How much does your mother usually drink?"

I think for a moment. "She drinks almost every day. I don't know how much she drinks, but I often find her passed out the next morning. My brother and I have been trying to get her to seek help for her drinking, and some days she does fine, but others she will drink a whole bottle until she passes out."

Dr. Mai nodded, taking my information in. "While your mother is kept here, I will suggest to her some programs that can help with her drinking problem."

I smiled, hoping Mum will agree to a program that will help her. "Thank you, Dr. Mai. Could I please see her now?"

"Yes, you can. But before you go in and see her, I just want to see if you are alright? Did you get into a fight?"

The tears prickled my eyes, threatening to fall as my mind flash back to when I was in Amelia's backyard. I wanted to tell him what happened, but a voice in my head told me to keep quiet about what happened. If I say anything, I would probably be made to write a report to the police. If the police showed up to Amelia's house, questioning her on what happened, she would know I had reported her. Would she lie to get out of trouble or would she admit the truth? She would know I had told. Amelia and her friends might come after me then. I couldn't go through the whole thing again.

So I quickly come up with a lie. "No, I tripped down the stairs."

I had no idea if he believed me or not, but he nodded anyway. He then gestured to where my hand is on my rib. "Are you hurt?"

"I-I think so. I can't breathe without feeling agony. I haven't been able to check because I was too worried about my mother."

"Let's get an x-ray done and then you can go see your mother."

***

Two ribs are broken on my left side. As soon as Dr. Mai told me this, I wanted to curl up in a ball somewhere. All I could see was Amelia and her friends kicking me. What did I do for this to happen? The shame then switched to anger when I see Tessa in the flashback, watching me instead of doing something to stop the girls. Why didn't she stop them? She could have stopped them and I wouldn't be spending my time in hospital on New Year's Eve.

But I don't show Dr. Mai what I'm feeling. I didn't want to break down in front of him and especially not in front of my mother, who was finally been able to get some sleep after the doctor said it was safe enough for her to sleep after monitoring her closely.

It's not until a few hours after midnight when I felt like I couldn't hold my emotions back when Corey finally showed up.

"I'm so sorry I didn't get your message straight away, Casey," he said, walking in. "I didn't hear the phone ring."

"Of course you didn't hear it," I said, doing my best to not raise my voice. I didn't want to wake up Mum or have the nurses coming in to see why I'm yelling. The tears I have been holding finally let go. "While you were out having fun, I have been stuck here alone, hoping Mum wouldn't die."

"I didn't ignore your calls on pur –" He turned to me and cursed. "What the hell happen to you, Casey? Did you get into a fight?"

I touched the right cheek where I had scraped it on the concrete without knowing I did. There was also a bruise on my other cheek that I don't remember how I got it. Someone probably punched me, but it was something my brain wasn't allowing me to remember. There was also a cut on my lip from biting down on my lip so hard. I haven't realised how my face looked until a nurse had cleaned up the wounds on my palms and bandaged them. There were tons of black and blue bruises on my stomach and back. The biggest one was where my ribs were broken.

I should have told Corey right there and then what had happened. In the past if anyone did try and hurt me, he would stand up to me. When I first befriended Tessa, telling the bullies to back off her, they started on me the very next day, trying to take my lunch as well as Tessa's. Corey found out what these older kids in his grade were doing to us, and he made sure they wouldn't steal our lunches again. He was there whenever I needed him. So why couldn't I tell him what was going on between Tessa and I, or what happened to me tonight?

"No, I didn't get into a fight," I answered him. "I fell down the stairs."

Corey could see my lies straight away. "You don't get those kinds of injuries from falling down the stairs. You look like you scrapped your cheek on concrete, and it looks like someone has punched you. What did you do to your hands?"

My head felt like it was going to explode. I couldn't take the voices in my head any longer, as one told me to keep my mouth shut, and the other one told me to tell Corey everything. The flashbacks of the party and the image of Mum on the floor of our lounge room flooded my mind. I want the images and the voices to go away.

I leaped off the chair, groaning as I moved quickly, and wrapped my arms around my brother, crying into his chest. He isn't aware of my injury until I cried out in pain when he squeezed me too tightly. He pulled back, wanting to know what was wrong. But I don't tell him what I did to my ribs.

Instead, I pushed passed him and out the door, leaving him alone with our mother.

***

I found an empty bench in the courtyard of the hospital. It was almost three in the morning, and there was not one sound now that some people have settled down after the celebrations. Every now and again someone left off a fire cracker nearby, but other than that, it was peaceful.

I stared at my phone where my brother had texted me, asking where I was and if I was okay. His message is not what I wanted to see. I wanted to hear from Dad, wishing me a happy New Year and to ask me how Mum was, or at least tell me he was heading to the hospital. How could he treat our family like we don't exist?

But the number one person I was hoping to hear from was Tessa. She didn't need to text a happy New Year to me. I just wanted her to ask me if I was okay. Tell me she wanted to be friends with me again. There was nothing from her. Like my dad, I didn't exist in Tessa's world anymore. If I wasn't in their world, where was I? Did anyone really care about me?

I replied back to my brother's message, letting him know where I was and that I was okay. But I keep quiet about everything.

Chapter 29
Tessa

Writing speeches has never been my strong point, especially when we were made to write one for English. I never understood why I needed to know how to write one and stand up in front of the class reading from palm cards. I mean, the only speeches I will ever be making are the ones when I attend the Arias or any other music award show when my band wins an award.

Putting a speech together for Casey's funeral wasn't easy. It wasn't because I was terrible at writing something that wasn't song lyrics. No, it was about finding the right words to say. It took me a few days to write it all; terrified I would not get it finished in time by Friday. I would start writing something, only to rip the paper to a million pieces. I kept telling myself that I couldn't write the speech. I didn't deserve to get up on the platform of the chapel and give a speech about my formal best friend. I destroyed Casey's life. I could have stopped it all, but I didn't. I was busy punishing her for something stupid. Or maybe I was punishing myself over everything that was happening in my life. Rather than solving my problems, I took it all out on Casey. Why? Why did I do it? She didn't deserve any of this. She would have helped me get through everything.

There were a couple of times I wanted to message Corey and tell him I couldn't do the speech. But then I thought I should because no matter what I had done to Casey, I'm sure she would want me to write about her. She wouldn't want me to feel bad for what I did. She would want me to share our good memories with others.

I wrote as much as I could to tell everyone about our friendship, about the girl I loved so much that was and will always be my best friend, no matter how much I had put her through in the past six months.

As I write, I cried. I cried about the life I took away from someone who shouldn't even have thought of death. I could have helped her. But instead, I pushed her away when she needed me the most.

***

Kaiden and Jackson are playing their Nintendo. Uncle Harley was in the kitchen preparing dinner and had asked me to watch the twins. I wasn't thrilled with the idea, but I agreed to do it. At least it gave me a break from working on my speech for tomorrow.

I sat curled up on my dad's arm chair, lost in the book Corey had given me. I was half way through it. Some parts were a drag or maybe it was because I didn't fully understand some things, but I was enjoying it more than I ever have before. I imagine Casey hugging me excitedly knowing I was reading her favourite book. She would probably drag me into a bookstore and suggest what I should read next, which would end up being the entire store.

I was interrupted from my reading when I heard a car coming up the driveway, follow by doors opening and closing.

Jackson hits the pause button on the game and headed over the lounge room window, peeking through the window where I had closed the blinds now that the sun is setting. Kaiden follows him over.

"Dad and Hazel are home!" they shouted.

The twins race to the front door and ran outside. I place the bookmark in my book just as Uncle Harley walks into the lounge room, wiping his hands with a tea towel.

"What's going on?" he wanted to know.

I peek through the blinds to see Dad and Hazel getting the luggage out of the boot of the taxi, the driver helping them. Dad pays the driver just as the twins reached them, hugging both him and Hazel. I was surprised to see them returning home from their honeymoon on Thursday night when I'm sure they were supposed to return on Saturday, where later we would go out to dinner for my birthday.

I turn back to my uncle. "Dad and Hazel are home."

Uncle Harley looks as surprised as I am. "They are? They never mentioned to me they were returning home early."

Together we walk outside just as the taxi was pulling out of the driveway. Kaiden and Jackson were standing in front of our father and stepmother, excitedly telling them how much they missed them, and what they have been up to while they were gone.

"I didn't know you were returning tonight," Uncle Harley says, embracing his brother.

"I decided to come home early to attend Casey's funeral. We ditched the rest of our cruise, and decided to take the plane home. I thought to also surprise you guys with our homecoming."

I didn't stand near Dad or Hazel, but it did surprise me he wanted to attend my best friend's funeral. I honestly thought I would be attending it myself. A few teachers and students (who I still don't know why they are even bothering to come along) were attending the ceremony, including Mr Kelman. He also said in the assembly on Monday that any students going had a choice to come to school after the funeral or we could take the day off. I was planning to take the day off. There's no way I could go back to school after the funeral. Mark, Travis and Tim weren't planning to either.

Uncle Harley hugs Hazel next. He then tells everyone to come on inside where he was almost finished preparing for dinner.

But I don't move from my spot as I stare at my father. All I could think of was the conversation I had with my uncle the other day about how I should work things out with my father. I normally never missed my dad, and was always glad when he sometimes had to travel for his job. But since talking to my uncle, I wonder what would happen if we didn't see each other again after our argument on Saturday. After what I did with Casey, I didn't want the same thing happening with my dad. Seeing the endless sadness in Ms Emerson's eyes from the loss of her daughter, I wondered what Dad would do if it was me he had lost. He was devastated and lost when my mother passed away. Would he feel the same way with me? Would I feel the same way if he had died? How would any of us make peace with ourselves for never apologising and making up for the things we have said? I have still yet to figure out how to make peace with myself with Casey for never fixing our friendship.

Setting all of the reasons why I disliked my dad aside, I move forward and wrap my arms around his waist. My actions startle him, and he stops in his tracks, dropping his luggage on the driveway. He hesitates for a moment to return the hug. I don't remember the last time I ever hugged him. For years I have felt so much anger towards him, never wanting his affection. To have this moment with him felt good. Like it was something I have been needing and missing for the last few days when my world came crashing down when my best friend died.

Uncle Harley leads everyone inside, taking Dad's luggage so we could be alone.

"I miss you so much, Dad," I tell him, my arms still wrapped tightly around him. "I'm so sorry about everything."

Dad rubs a hand up and down my back. "I miss you too, Tessa."

I pull away from him. For the first time ever, Dad wasn't yelling and I wasn't screaming back at him. There's no way we could stand here and hug each other without saying something hurtful. Maybe the time apart has helped us to sort things out.

"I'm sorry for skipping out on the wedding on Saturday," I say. "I should have told you where I was going. I just needed to clear my head."

Dad nods. "I'm sorry for not listening to you. During some down time Hazel and I had, I called Harley to see how everything was going. We talked and he could see how the last few days had been stressful and emotional for you. It helped me to realise how important it was to listen to you rather than yelling all the time. When I'm under so much stress with you, your brothers and with everything else, I don't know how to deal with my anger except take it out on you. I apologise for how I have treated you, Tessa. Right now I just want to sit and relax now that I'm home. Why don't we talk on the weekend?"

"Talk about what?"

"About anything you want. If there's something we need to sort out, we can talk it over the weekend."

I smile at him. "I like that."

I give him another hug, thankful my uncle was able to talk through to him. If he hadn't, maybe this homecoming wouldn't end well.

"Let's get inside where it's warm," Dad says, swinging his arm around my shoulders, heading towards the front door. "By the way, you don't mind if I show up to Casey's funeral with you tomorrow? I thought it would be good to come support you."

"I like the idea of you being there."

"Are you going to school tomorrow?"

I shake my head. "No. I don't think I will feel up to it. Our principal said we didn't need to attend school if we don't need to. I'm probably going out to lunch with my friends."

"Tell me what's been happening with your band since you won the record deal last Friday."

***

I decided to get to bed early, but sleeping didn't seem like an option to me. I toss and turned for most of the night as the speech and the funeral will be tomorrow. I can't believe how tomorrow I will be saying goodbye to my best friend.

With it being a few minutes until midnight, I decided it was no used lying here if I couldn't get to sleep. I headed downstairs, thinking maybe I could watch a bit of television and see what night programs were on. Something could maybe help me sleep. I didn't want to get out my guitar because then I wouldn't get any rest once I start composing a song. I also didn't want to wake anyone.

But when I entered the lounge room, I found that watching television was out of the question. For the past few nights Uncle Harley had been sleeping in Dad's room. Now that he and Hazel were home, he was sleeping in the lounge room on a blow-up mattress.

When I saw him there, I thought of heading back to my room, until the kitchen light catches my attention. I head over there to see who was up. To my surprise Hazel was up, sitting at the kitchen table drinking something from a cup and a closed book beside her.

I thought of sneaking away, but she spots me, smiling. "Hey, Tessa. What are you doing up?"

"I can't sleep."

She pats the chair beside me. "Come sit down. I will make you a chamomile tea. It should help you get some sleep. I like to drink it before I go to bed."

I thank her and sat down beside her. Tea wasn't something I normally drink, but I accept her offer. Casey would have wanted me to be kind to her. Hazel gets up slowly so the chair wouldn't scrape on the tile floor and wake up Uncle Harley. She walks over to the jug that's still warm, taking a clean cup from the cabinet above. A yellow box labelled CHAMOMILE TEA was next to the jar of coffee. She takes a tea bag, puts it in the cup, and pours the water from the jug into it before walking over to me once she added the milk.

She sets it down in from of me with a smile. "Here you go, Tessa."

I thank her as she sat back down. I take a sip of the warm tea.

"How come you are up?" I ask.

"Oh, I was just doing some reading before I head off to bed. I'm guessing you're having trouble sleeping because of tomorrow?"

I nod as I take another sip of the tea. "I just... I just can't believe Casey is gone, and tomorrow I will be saying goodbye."

Hazel pats my shoulder. "You will be alright, Tessa. I haven't had the chance to know your friend, but I know she was a lovely person. I'm sorry for your loss, Tessa."

I smile a thank you at her. "Hazel, I'm sorry for always giving you a hard time for dating my dad. It's just I thought you was trying to replace my mother, and I despise Dad for ever dating you."

She doesn't get angry as I admitted what a horrible person I have been to her for the past year. Instead, she kept the smile on her face.

"I completely understand how you feel, Tessa. But I want you to know that I'm not planning to replace your mother. I couldn't do that. Don't think of me as your stepmother. Think of me as a friend. That way there is no reason for you to feel despiteful towards me or your father."

I agree to do that. I know Dad's happy, so maybe I can give Hazel a chance.

***

I lay on my side after hitting the snooze button of my phone. I dreaded the idea of getting out of bed, and if I could, I would probably spend the day in bed.

But I had to get up for Casey.

I didn't have a black dress. I chose to wear a black skirt and a crimson blouse. Casey's favourite colour was red.

My brothers complained they had to go to school when I didn't have to. Hazel decided to give my uncle a break and drove the twins to school.

Dad and I arrived at the cemetery just a few minutes after Corey and Ms Emerson did. Casey's father wasn't coming. For whatever reason he didn't want to come, it was like he didn't give a care in the world that his daughter was gone. Corey said it didn't matter how much he had tried to contact him, his father never called back. I never realised what a jerk Mr Rowland really was. How could he not show up to his daughter's funeral?

Mark soon arrived with Tim and Travis, the three of them giving me a warm hug. I was glad my bandmates were there to support me. I don't think I could attend here without them. And I'm thankful Mark had shown up, despite our fight the other day. I wasn't even sure if we had broken up.

Not many showed to the chapel for the funeral. Mr Kelman and two teachers from school were there, as well as a few of Casey's aunts, uncles, and cousins came, as well as her grandmother from her mother's side. It was no surprise that no other students besides my friends came along to the funeral. Maybe they weren't allowed to come or they just didn't care enough. Corey's friend Jett also came along.

Dad and I sat behind Corey and his Mum with my bandmates beside us.

The funeral director soon speaks, talking about Casey's life. A photo of her at sixteen sitting on her bike outside her house was displayed on a screen. I remember when the picture was taken. She had just gotten the bike for her sixteenth birthday. Seeing the photograph of her smiling face brought tears to my eyes, which I blink back. I couldn't cry right now. I needed to be strong for when I go up on the platform soon.

He talks about Casey for about ten minutes, about the seventeen and seven months of her life. I picture the memories in my head or if it was something I didn't know about her before I met her, I imagine it in my mind. He then calls Corey up onto the platform to give his speech, which he didn't even tell me he was doing. I don't make eye contact with him as he speaks, feeling Mark's eyes on me.

Right after Corey's speech I was called up next. Dad pats a hand on my back, whispering to me that I can do this. My bandmates also whisper it to me. I give them a small smile as to say thank you. I stood at the platform, taking a quick glance at the audience before taking a deep breath, exhaling it slowly and began reading from the palm cards.

"Casey and I have been best friends for the past eleven years. Anyone who knew us would know that we are inseparable. We befriended each other in kindergarten when she stood up to some bullies from another grade who wanted my lunch. Casey was shy, but she was always there when you needed her. We have been through a lot of things together. I remember when my mum passed away when I was ten, how she promised she would not leave my side. She slept over my house for a whole week after she had died, even when my house was pretty much chaotic where my dad had to juggle not only his job, but as well as me and my one-year-old twin brothers."

I glance over at Dad who was starting to get teary over the mentioned of Mum, but he remained strong so the tears wouldn't fall. I continued on.

"My favourite memory of Casey was when my family and I want to the beach together. We were six years old and Casey thought I would laugh at her because she didn't know how to swim. She had lessons, but she never felt comfortable in the water. So I took her hand and walked her to the water. We didn't go far in. We stand in the ocean to where the water was just up to our knees.

"What I would miss most about Casey is her cheery personality, and how she would always be there for you. She knew the best way to make you laugh. She has been the greatest friend I have ever had."

I leave the platform before I burst into tears in front of everyone. I sit back down just as the tears spilled out. Dad put his arm around my shoulders and lean me in closer to him so my head is resting on his shoulder.

The funeral director thanked both Corey and I for the speeches, and went on to read out a poem before allowing family members to walk up and place a flower on the coffin for one final goodbye. Later when we are gone, her body will be cremated.

Once the funeral is over, my bandmates hug me, telling me how I did a great job with the speech. Corey came up to me next, hugging me, follow by Ms Emerson. Mr Kelman also came up to me to say I did a good job.

We hang around talking to others before going our separate ways. Dad was talking to Ms Emerson. Mark leads me away from the others so he could talk to me.

"I'm still hurt with what happened between you and Corey the other day," he says. I went to open my mouth to speak, but Mark stops me. "I miss you, Tessa. I would hate to break up with you because if I do, our band will fall apart. It isn't going to be easy to trust you again, but I'm willing to."

I smile at his words and thank him for forgiving me, hugging him tightly.

Chapter 30
Casey

Some days were harder than others to even get out of bed. For a couple of days after the New Year's Eve incident, I found it difficult to get out of bed. It wasn't because my ribs were sore or even parts of my body where I was kicked, bruises visibly showing that I did everything to make sure they weren't showing underneath my clothing to avoid answering questions. No, I was ashamed to speak up with what was going on in my life, afraid of what others might think. I was happy when Freddy gave me four weeks off to recover from my injury.

Corey also helped out with Mum when she came home, making sure there was no alcohol lying around the house, and made sure she also attended group meetings for her drinking problem. Corey noticed I was also not being myself and wanted to know what was going on and if I was okay. He asked if everything was going okay with Tessa and me, especially when he hadn't seen her around here for so long. Right then I wanted to burst out everything to my brother. But the voice in the back of my head told me not to. It made me wonder if Corey was only asking for Tessa because they were once a couple. The anger inside of me built up like a volcano building up molten rock before erupting. The blood went straight to my head thinking about the night I saw them together, which made me light headed and I wasn't sure if my head would explode or if I would faint.

It may be school holidays, but I couldn't escape Amelia or her friends. They wrote nasty things about me online. I avoided them while online, but the things they would say stayed with me. I thought of it over and over in my head.

Mum was doing well with attending her Alcoholics Anonymous meetings, and I was almost afraid to tell her what was going on in my life. I was afraid of putting my burden on her in case she started drinking again. She had asked me how everything has been going, and there had been times when I was close to telling her, but I listened to that stupid voice in my head, telling me what could happen if I said a word. Mum had been so cheery since she had gotten help with drinking, and asked me to bring Tessa around for dinner. I haven't told her that we were no longer friends.

Once school started, there had been a couple of times I wanted to go to the principal and report what was going on in and outside of school. Katie-Lynn and Beth once followed me as I was making my way to the office. Amelia may not attend our school anymore, but it didn't mean she would make sure her friends stopped me from speaking up. I was terrified of what they would do if I walked into Mr Kelman's office. Besides, it's not like Mr Kelman will do anything to stop the bullying. I thought back to when Tessa and I fought, him ignoring me when I told him about what she had written on the bathroom walls about me. It's like he didn't even care what was going on or didn't want to deal with a quarrel between friends, and punishes me after Tessa physically attacked me. If I told him what happened on New Year's Eve, would he care? Or would he punish me again, like it was my fault I was attacked?

Either I report them for bullying and the reports will be ignored, or somehow the bullies will get away with it. They always do.

So what would be the point if I did tell anyone?

Tessa sometimes teased me, and there were other times when she would watch me from afar whether if it was in class or when it was lunch or in the school corridor. She wouldn't say anything. She often stared at me with this apologetic look on her face, or like she was unsure if she should approach me. I wanted to scream at her to stop looking at me if she was sorry. I wanted her to come up to me and actually apologise. If she was sorry, why did she allow these things to happen? Why doesn't she just stop it all?

But would I take her back as a friend, hoping we can mend our once strong relationship if she ever did apologise? I don't know. We probably couldn't be friends again, damage after everything that has been done.

By May, getting out of bed in the morning was getting worse. I didn't see the point in going to school. Not if I was getting bullied basically every day. Tessa stopped hanging around Amelia's friends, and was hanging mostly around her bandmates. But it never stopped Katie-Lynn, Beth or Parker to make fun of me whenever they had the chance.

When June finally came along, I had no idea how I was going to get through the month after what happened last year. After being sober for five months, Mum turned to drinking again as it fast approached the day Dad walked out of our lives. If Tessa and I were friends I would tell her how I felt about my dad. Corey and I have spoken a few times about him, but I like the idea of being able to discuss it with Tessa.

Some days I walk by Tessa's place when she had band practice. Her music was getting good, and I had overheard her talking her band into entering a contest to win a record deal that her dad and Hazel were going to be hosting during the morning news show. I hope that someday Tessa's band will make it big with their music, and I believe they will. Her dad's wedding was approaching fast, and Tessa had gotten her hair done two weeks before the wedding. She had cut her hair to a shoulder-length to where it used to be past her shoulders. There were so many times I wanted to compliment her, but was afraid of what she might say if I did.

As the days went on, I began to wonder who should I tell my problems to and who would listen to me. With everything that was going on, I most definitely felt like Mum or Corey couldn't help me. It wasn't a great time to tell them what was going through my mind, not when the day Dad walked out was fast approaching.

Even when I was at school, I thought of going to the school counsellor, but I was scared of what anyone would say if I went to the counsellor for something. They might think I'm crazy or something. I knew there was nothing wrong with going to the counsellor for help or if we just wanted to talk. Mr Carlton always encouraged us to come to see him when we needed someone to talk to. But I was scared of what would happen if I opened my mouth about being bullied. What happens if I mentioned everyone's names? Would I make it worse for myself?

I began to think what it would be like to disappear forever. Would anyone notice if I was gone? I'm already invisible, so it wouldn't be liked anyone would care. I do worry about Mum and Corey with how they will cope without me, especially with Mum's drinking problem.

I think about Tessa. Would she care if I disappear from this world? I mean, I know lately we have been fighting, but she often gave me mixed signals that maybe she does care about me.

But when I send her a message to see if we could really be friends again, she sent me a nasty reply back, saying our friendship has been over for a while now. I imagine her being annoyed with me for sending her this. I also imagine her laughing at what she wrote, anything to make me feel like I was worthless.

And that's what I am. Worthless.

Grabbing my shoes, I walked out of my room. I couldn't take this anymore. I don't want to go through my life feeling like I'm nothing.

Mum was passed out on the couch with an empty vodka bottle. If I walked out of here, she wouldn't notice I'm gone.

"Are you going out?" Corey asked me as he walked into the lounge room from the kitchen with a bowl of popcorn.

I give him a smile, hoping he won't notice what I'm planning to do. What am I planning to do exactly? I wasn't even sure if ending my life was something I wanted. I mean, I can speak up now and get the help I needed.

No. Why would anyone help me? I'm not worth helping. I would do the world a favour if I just disappear.

"I'm going over to Tessa's," I answered.

Corey returned the smile, popping a piece of popcorn in his mouth. "That's great. You haven't hung out for a long time."

There's a pinch in my heart as he said this. "No, we haven't."

"Okay, well you go have a good time. When Mum wakes up, I will let her know where you are."

I thank him, saying goodbye before walking out the door.

I walk around, not really sure where I was going or what I was doing. I thought of everything that has happened in the past six months. My mind felt lost as my head began to feel clouded about everything. Parker had once said I should kill myself, only because no one would want to be like me anyway. No one will care if I am gone.

Chapter 31
Tessa

Four weeks later

The nerves were trying to get a hold of me as the minutes passed by quickly before we were due on stage. It has been seven weeks since we last performed in front of an audience. It had been busy for us all once the funeral was over where we had been recording our first album that was due to come out at the end of September. Last week our manager announced to us that we will be one of the opening acts for a musician name Declan Page. One of the two bands in the opening act had to drop out so we were selected to replace them.

I took a couple of deep breaths to calm my breathing before we were due to go on stage in five minutes. I can do this. I have worked almost my life to fulfill this dream the moment I picked up the guitar when I was ten.

The nerves quickly disappear once we were on stage, playing the first note to *Forget It*, the audience breaking into a cheer. Our song that won our career had been playing on the radio stations across Australia for a week. After playing the Sydney show tonight, we will be playing again in Melbourne and then Brisbane. Once we get back from Brisbane, we were going to start filming a music video for *Forget It*. I couldn't wait to film it.

Our band was going to be on stage for half an hour, playing six songs. One of the songs we were going to perform was the one I wrote about Casey. It was the one song I was nervous about performing in front of everyone besides my bandmates.

"Casey would have loved the song," Mark had told me the other day.

I smile thinking of how she would have reacted. I imagine her smiling brightly and embracing me to say thank you.

And I wish she was here to hear it.

"How is everyone doing tonight?" I ask the audience when we finished the fifth song. The light dim and a spotlight focused on me.

The audience broke into a cheer. Someone shouts out and said they saw me on TV.

"That's great you saw us on television," I continue on. "I hope you enjoyed all the incredible musicians who performed during the contest. I also want to thank Declan Page for giving my friends and I the opportunity to perform in the opening act tonight."

The crowd burst into another around of cheers when I mentioned the singer's name.

"This next song I'm going to sing is the last one we're going to perform tonight. It's a song that means a lot to me. It's about my best friend Casey who recently committed suicide because of bullying. She felt like she had no one to turn to in the end. I don't like admitting this, and it's hard to admit it that I was one of the bullies after a stupid fight we had. Before you judge me, I want to say that we are all bullies. Whether if it's to someone else or to ourselves. We all do and say something we shouldn't. We all tell ourselves we aren't good enough. It's important to think of others before you say something, because you never know how your actions or words could affect someone. Even if you think it's something completely harmless, you don't know what is going through someone's head. You also don't know what they might be going through. Also, never say you aren't good enough, because you are. Never even let someone think you aren't. We are all good enough."

The audience is silent as I speak. "Depression can sometimes have no symptoms. I wasn't aware of what Casey was going through because she hid her feelings. If I had known the things I had done was having an effect on her, I would have never had bullied her in the first place. Bullying is never the answer to anything. It's important to treat someone with kindness, treat them the same way you would want to be treated. If you do know someone who is being bullied or maybe they have depression, remember to be there for that person. Let them know that they aren't alone. Let them know that there is help out there for them. If we work together, we can stop bullying because no one should have to go through what my friend Casey did."

I was almost terrified that the audience would judge me for what I had said, but they congratulated me with applause for what I said about putting bullying to an end. It wouldn't be easy to do, but it was something that could be accomplish if we all work together doing the right thing.

"In September, our first album is going to be released. I'm in the process of putting together a foundation in honour of Casey, helping to raise money for people who are struggling with bullying and depression. The foundation will be there for anyone who needs someone to listen to them. And when you buy our album, every dollar will go to the Casey Roland Foundation. And it will mean everything to me if you could support it. Do check out the Casey Roland Foundation on social media."

A stage hand walks onto the stage with an acoustic guitar, and hands it to me. I thank him.

"This song is dedicated to Casey and to anyone who lost someone to bullying."

I strum the chords on my guitar, the arena remaining silent as I was the only one who played.

"You befriended me when I had no one
You stood up to bullies when I couldn't defend myself
Friends forever is what we told each other we will be
I don't know what went wrong
Or why we drifted apart
But I wish I could take everything back to when we were young
and innocent.

I'm sorry for all of the things I have done
And I would do everything that I could
To make it all right again
To see the smile I once knew
To hear your voice and your laugh once again
This song is for you
To apologise for the person I have become
And to wish you were here with me once again
This song is for you."

Tim brings in the drums for the second verse. I bob to the music as Travis and Mark brought in the guitar next. I walk to the side of the stage to hand back the guitar to the stage hand.

"You were there for me when my mother passed away
I was there for you when your father walked away
We stuck together through the good and bad times
But nothing lasts forever
And I wish I could take it all back to when we were young and innocent."

The audience gets into the song as I sing the chorus, clapping their hands as they sway to the music.

"Whatever happened to the days when we would fight over stupid little things,
But then make up the very next day?
Like the dispute between us never happened
Why did we choose to let those stupid little things get in the way of our friendship?
I'm sorry for not being the friend I was supposed to be
I'm sorry for not being there for you when you needed me the most
And I wish I could do things all over again to see your smile,
To hear your voice,
To hear your laugh,
To make everything right between us again."

I belted out the chorus, and when the song ends, the audience broke into a deafening cheer. The excitement of the crowd has me in tears, but I'm not sure if it was from the crowd's reaction to the song or it was because it meant a lot to me. I thank the audience for everything, and I couldn't wait to see what will happen for our band.

Once we were off stage, Mark, Tim and Travis embrace me.

"You did great out there," Travis tells me.

"Casey would have been proud of you," Tim says. "She would be proud of all of us."

"Casey will also tell you not to cry over her, but to make her proud," Mark adds.

I hug the three of them lightly. "Thank you, guys, for being there for me."

And thank you, Casey, for being the best friend I could ever have. Thank you for helping me to realise the importance of friendship, to be kind to others and to think about your actions. Because you never know what is going through someone's mind. And maybe you could save someone's life if you think about your actions, what you say, and to always be with someone when they are going through a hard time.

If you or anyone you know are struggling, reach out for help.

Australia

Lifeline
  DIAL: 13 11 14
  http://lifeline.org.au

  Suicide Call Back Service
  DIAL: 1300 659 467
  http://suicidecallbackservice.org.au

  Headspace
  DIAL: 1800 650 890
  http://headspace.org.au

  Kids Helpline
  DIAL: 1800 55 1800
  http://kidshelpline.com.au/kids

  ReachOut
  http://au.reachout.com

  Dolly's Dream
  https://www.dollysdream.org.au

New Zealand

Youthline
DIAL: 0800 376 633 OR FREE TEXT 234
http://www.youthline.co.nz

Need to Talk?
DIAL OR FREE TEXT 1737
http://www.1737.org.nz

The Lowdown
FREE TEXT 5626
http://thelowdown.co.nz

United Kingdom

Samaritans
DIAL: 116123 (free)
http://www.samaritans.org

Childline
DIAL: 0800 1111 (free)
http://www/childline.org.uk

United States

Crisis Text Line
> If you are in crisis, reach out for help. Text HOME to 741741
> http://www.crisistextline.org
> Free, 24/7, confidential

National Suicide Prevention Lifeline
> DIAL: 1-800-273-8255
> http://www.suicidepreventionlifeline.org

Canada

Kids Help Phone
> DIAL: 1-800-668-6868 (Kids Help Phone)
> http://www.kidshelpphone.ca

Thursday's Child
> DIAL: (818) 831-1234
> http://www.thursdayschild.org
> For bullying, eating disorders, self-injury, suicidal ideation, sexual assault, etc.
> 24/7 and confidential for children, teens and young adults

Acknowledgements

This story is finally published! For quite some time, I struggle in trying to figure out if I should publish this. This story was half inspired by a teenage girl who was only fourteen years old when she took her life in January 2018 because of bullying. When I heard about her story on the news, it inspired me to write a story about bullying. I have written a few stories in the past on the topic, but I wanted to write something different. The TV show *13 Reasons Why* was also a huge inspiration with this story. I started working on *This Song Is for You* shortly after season 2 was released. Though I only watched the first two seasons, I told myself that if I ever publish this book that I will thank the cast and crew for the excellent work they did on the show, as well as the author Jay Asher. The TV show and book helped me to look at everything in a different way with mental health, and how your actions can affect someone, especially when you don't know what the other person could be going through.

Thank you to Nikki Chartier for the encouragement and helping me to decide to publish this story. You understood the fear I had about publishing something that meant everything to me, and the impact it could have on others.

Thank you to Sarah Swartz, who has been with this story since it was on Wattpad. I enjoy the conversations we would have when we would talk and share quotes about *13 Reasons Why* online, and how the show inspired our own stories. Thank you also for listening to the suggestions I had with this book during the editing process, unsure about some of the things I could add into the book. Though, I'm sure the ideas could have worked, but in the end I didn't add them into the book. I felt like they suited a different story than this one.

Another person I would like to thank is Matthew Perry. For some quite some time I was terrified of publishing this book, afraid of backlash if people knew this story was half inspired by *13 Reasons Why*, especially for those who criticised the show. After Matthew's death, I watched a tribute to him. At the end if the tribute, a clip was shown from an interview of his book. He said "Secrets are what kills us." His words really hit me, and immediately made me think of Casey. Matthew's words are what finally helped me to decide that this book was worth publishing. While I edited the book, I read his book, which felt like an encouragement to why I was publishing this story in the first place. Because somewhere out there is someone who may be struggling with their mental health, maybe they are going through bullying, or dealing with alcoholism. Or maybe they are dealing with something that nobody knows about. If you are struggling with something, I hope this book finds you and helps you in some way.

Thank you to my editor Emily for working on this book with me, and believing in this story and how much it meant to me.

Lastly, thank you to all of my readers who picked up this book. It means a lot to me.

285

About the Author

Jessica Madden was born and raised in Sydney, Australia. She began writing stories since the age of eight. When she was nine, she realised that she wanted to be a writer more than anything in the world. At twenty-three years old, Jessica published her first book *Right Here Waiting for You*. Writing about characters falling in love has always been her favourite thing to write about.

When she is not writing, Jessica is often daydreaming up new storylines, and can be found lost in reading a good book.

You can follow her on Instagram and X @JessicaCMadden

Also by Jessica Madden

Right Here Waiting for You
The Jet Lag Diaries
Silent Love
Chasing The Storm
If You Had Stayed
Hating Jamie Jackson
Chasing Tornadoes

I Wasn't Supposed to Fall for You series
I Wasn't Supposed to Fall for You
It's All Because Of You

With You series
One Whole Night with You
Every Moment with You